ARCHER
887

I0694544

CONTENTS

VOLGAR SYSTEM MAP

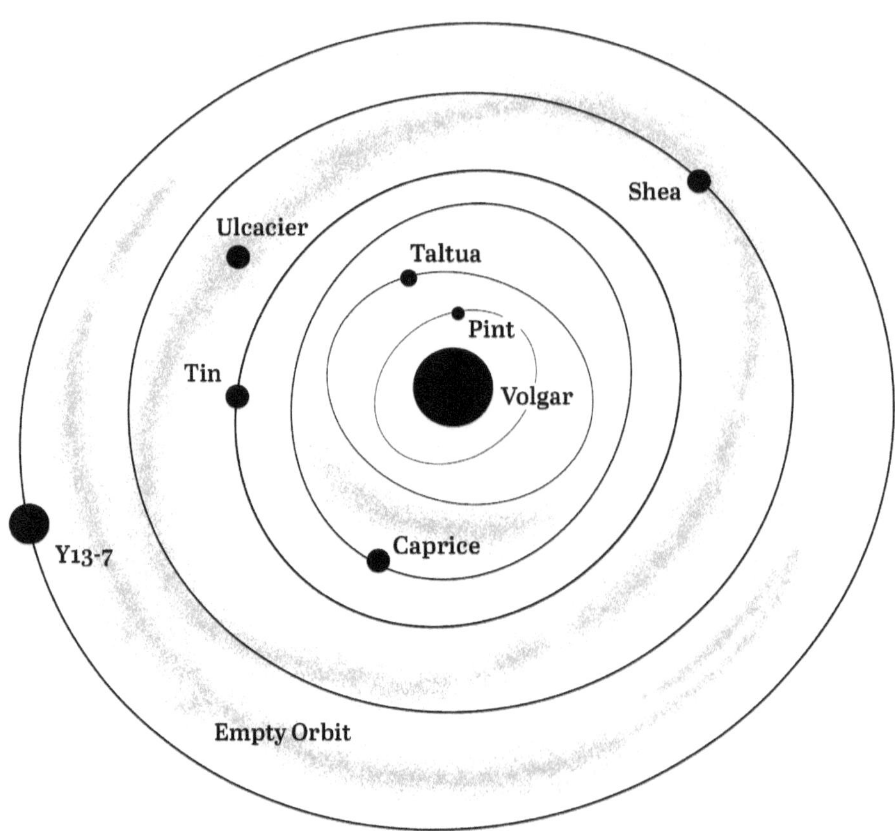

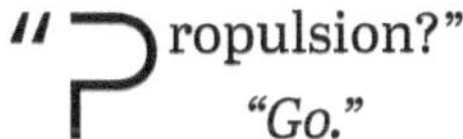

"Propulsion?"

"*Go.*"

"System checks?"

"*In parameters. Ready for launch!*"

The transport's launch gantry was not made for fighters of this size, but his fighter craft did not need her wings outside atmosphere. They folded elegantly against the hull, tucked back like a bird's.

"In position. Launch at your signal."

"*Three... two... one... launch!*"

Only four lock doors and he was out into familiar darkness, weightless and silent. Around him glittered a swarm of lights. Not stars, but other cockpits, all waiting for the signal to be given.

"*There you are, Ace! Worried you'd miss the fun.*"

He didn't answer, other than to confirm his position in the squadron. "887, in sync."

"*Ready to kill some imps?*"

He didn't join in their bravado, instead watching the movement by the softly gleaming moon. The Caprician fleet had rounded Rill. Their fighters were already deployed, more swirling lights against the darkness.

His commander's voice overrode the chatter. "*Pilots will hold position. Maintain until the signal has—*"

"*Attention, citizens of Tin.*" The broadcast from the Imperial ship smothered any local frequencies, even his navigation system. It chirped anxiously, and he steadied his line.

"*Disarm and return to your ships. You are in open rebellion of His Majesty King Arion, King of Caprice and its colonies. Disarm and surrender. Due pardon will be given. Any who refuse to comply will be arrested and prosecuted for treason, sedition, and crimes against the crown.*"

Jeers echoed, a mass of derision and hate. They were not given a second chance to obey; the Emperor had never been merciful. And they had done little to earn it.

The Caprician fighters came first, faster than his own fighter. They were newer models, the edge of military technology, the product of centuries of colonial expansion.

But the true destruction belched from the larger warships. Missiles, hundreds of them, arching over the advancing fighters, all aimed at the rebels' small transport ships.

He lifted his head to watch them, streaking trails of light that would be beautiful if he didn't know the havoc they would wreck. They would rip the rebel ships apart, destroy every outdated fighter, and then rain death on the surface below.

Until their internal systems went abruptly dark.

"Now!"

They would have only minutes they had been warned. Minutes before the Capricians realized what had occurred and reprogrammed their weapon systems. The rebels were to do as much damage as possible and then flee, scattering to the rocky bodies drifting after Tin like petals in the wind.

But the disruptive signal only worked on programmed munitions. The Caprician fighters were still deadly.

In moments, they were among the rebels. His fighter danced through them, the shield glass rattling as bullets peppered his cockpit. The spent slugs would fall into the atmosphere as a shower of light. A thing of beauty born from so much hate.

His fighter responded to his lightest touch. Pressure here, a touch there. So close to the other fighters their hulls nearly brushed. Unthinkable nearness in the vastness of space.

He broke free of the melee. He tilted up and over, the green and gold crescent of his home gleaming below him, and turned for his home ship.

Static crackled in his ear.

"Archer 887, answer Archer 887. 887, do you copy?"

"I copy."

"Archer 887, no malfunction detected. Return to position. Do you copy?"

Useless in space, those wings, but he knew she loved flying with them deployed. They arched proudly around her.

"887, you are on a projected collision course. Alter heading at once."

"Cannot comply." Would not comply. There was only one way this war would end. That beautiful emerald world consumed in flames. Millions of civilians dead.

"Ace, what are you doing?"

But even knowing the rightness of it, his heart still ached. "I'm sorry, Val."

"887, alter course or we will be forced to open fire."

"Ace, comply!"

Nothing gentle about his command now, a wrench on her sensitive controls. The engines could not roar, but he knew well the bestial fury they contained.

"Ace, what game are you playing?"

He had no breath to reply, every muscle strained to keep her trajectory. The spin dragged at his limbs, lulling him into relaxation.

She resisted him, the navigation system wailing in alarm. Did she know this was the end of them? Or did she, too, accept the inevitability of this? It was the only way to save them.

He caught glimpses of the battle as he spun. Flashes of light, glinting metal. His world and its people he would die to protect.

"Archer 887, respond and comply."

"Put him down!"

"Ace, stop this! Think of your mother!"

"887! Alter course!"

"Ace! Pull up! Ace, please—!"

ONE

Westerland shoved him out of the dream. It was always the same dream, the relentless drone of her voice, calm and empty.

The Sentient's voice shouted over her. \Wake up!\

Arsaces squinted against the suddenly brilliant lights.

\Up! Sas needs you!\ Westerland emphasized his urgency by ramping up the Alarm until it wailed in Arsaces' head.

He managed to get himself sitting up before the Network chimed with an incoming call.

"Captain?"

He untangled his legs from the sheets. "What is it?"

"We've received a Distress Call, sir."

"From whom?"

\Caprice!\

"Caprice, sir."

\You are Arsaces Jankovic-Wood.\ Westerland forced her presence back into Arsaces' subconscious, growling with irritation and impatience.

\Go!\

"I'm coming," Arsaces snapped, to both his Lieutenant and his Sentient. He grabbed his uniform jacket from where he'd tossed it last night and went out the door doing up the buttons.

You're certain? he asked Westerland.

\91.4% probability. Ensign Took has broadcast a response query.\

Arsaces' ocular implant responded to the flick of his eyes: 2608. Only three hours since he'd gratefully escaped to his quarters. Yet another endless night pandering to the Tolmi dignitaries occupying Westerland's civilian suites.

The Sentient sulked despite the emergency. \I'd rather be collecting ice samples again.\

At least the civilian quarters were cramped. Hopefully, they wouldn't stay aboard long.

\You were a pilot,\ she whispered.

Arsaces shook off the last of his dream and entered the Bridge. There was a snap of boot heels as the crew saluted. Sas waited just inside the doors. The man spoke in an uncharacteristic rush.

"Sir, it was upgraded to a Panic."

Arsaces knew that well enough; his jaw ached from the subsonic signal. "Explain, Sas?"

Always succinct, Sas reported in clipped sentences. "Distress signal received 2606 Ship-time. Coding confirms authorized broadcast. Triangulation suggests Home Orbit, sir."

"Caprice," Arsaces agreed. Westerland was carrying them star-ward, away from the capital planet and its satellites. "Content of the message?"

"Ensign Took decoded the signal. It's blank."

Arsaces frowned at the forward screen. The message hung silent. Only the official heading was displayed, the crest of the Emperor. Nothing else. "And the Panic?"

"Received at 2610."

His implant now showed '2613,' the numerals hovering over the crewmen's holo-tags. They sat quietly, heads tilted to watch him obliquely. Listening. He looked to the main screen to avoid their eyes.

"We're receiving on all frequencies, sir." That was Ensign Took himself. "Panic continues from Home Orbit. Overriding all military and civilian streams."

"Captain," someone called from behind him. "The passengers are beginning to ask questions."

Westerland muttered waspishly. \Useless! Waste of time!\

"Sir, there are variances on the long distance—"

"Sir? I'm picking up an unusual ping—"

"Captain—"

Too many details, too quickly, all their voices clamoring for his attention.

"Captain! They're gone!"

Arsaces focused on the ensign. "Who's gone, Took?"

Took turned to him, eyes wide as he listened to his earpiece. "Caprice, it's gone."

"Explain."

"All frequencies have—"

\Incoming missiles!\

Westerland reacted even as Arsaces shouted, "Evasive action!"

The Sentient lurched, throwing the crew from their seats. The gravity-spin failed, unable to compensate. A moment of free-fall before they slammed back to the deck.

Arsaces staggered, still falling, as pain blinded him.

"Captain!" Sas shook him roughly.

Arsaces wrenched his mind from Westerland's. Not pain: information.

"Sir, second salvo incoming!"

"Report, we've been hit! Damage to the left external stabilizer!"

"Port y-axis, thirty-seven degrees to crown! Ten seconds!"

Arsaces braced against the navigation table. "Where are they coming from?" he demanded of Radar.

"I can't see anything, sir!"

Westerland gave another jolt, shuddering from the impacts.

"Squads A and B, intercept!" The fighter screen lit up, icons glowing as the pilots activated their systems. Flares from the Hemings' engines streaked by the external cameras.

"Third Salvo, aft!"

"Heming 34-3 reporting. Sighted munitions, no visible contact."

"Run a broad-spectrum sweep. Radiation, heat, anything."

\Missiles destroyed.\

"Missiles destroyed, sir!"

Sas swiped through star-charts. "Cover, sir. Cluster of rocky bodies. Five, six minutes at three CGS."

"Plot it. Pilots, emergency return!"

Seconds ticked by, agonizing seconds. The magnetized landing gear of the Hemings on Westerland's hull was like dozens of cold fingers on Arsaces' skin.

"All fighters home, sir."

"Brace for acceleration!"

Three times Caprician gravity wasn't terrible, if you were ready. A few of the crew were slow to their positions and fell, shoved by the thrust of the engines. Arsaces steadied himself on the navigation console, taking tight breaths against the pressure in his chest.

\Cutting thrust for flip,\ Westerland told him.

Why?

Westerland was amused. \Do you really want thirty-six injured passengers cluttering up my medical bays?\

Arsaces grimaced. He didn't want any passengers.

\Sit. Even if your bones can't break, still would hurt.\

Arsaces slipped into his harness as the flip boosters ignited. The spin center rolled over him and blood fell into his head in a thundering rush. He clenched his fists to control his stomach, feeling starkly the difference between his right and left.

Some of them still can.

\And let's keep it that way. Braking.\

"Prepare for brake!"

Pressure shoved him the opposite way as Westerland slowed their speed.

"Visuals on the asteroids, sir." Arsaces felt Westerland release control to the pilots. "Bringing us in."

"Match velocity and trajectory."

"Yes, sir!"

A matter of moments and they settled next to a large icy body, full of pale light and dark shadows.

"Radar, anything?"

"No, sir."

"Shut down all outgoing frequencies. Continue to monitor."

A hush fell over the crew, as if their own silence would help them hide.

Sas murmured, "Now what?"

Arsaces had no idea. Westerland was analyzing the data, reciting the attack over and over. He blocked the Sentient out.

"Took, anything from Caprice?"

"Nothing, sir."

"The Distress has been cleared?"

"No, sir. It's gone. Radio silence."

Even the crew's whispers fell away.

"Play. Isolate Home Orbit."

Muted voices and music filtered out until nothing was left. Static hissed through the Bridge speakers. The sound of silence.

Arsaces caught himself drumming the fingers of his right hand. He clenched them until the artificial bones creaked. The crew waited for his decision. All those eyes turned his stomach.

"Any communication from CINC? From Home Fleet?"

"Nothing, sir." Took's voice was pitching up. Scared, Arsaces realized. They all were. Controlled, but panic was growing. He looked to Sas, who pressed his lips together.

"An attack, sir? On Caprice?"

"But, by whom?"

Sas shifted his feet, looking down and away, which told Arsaces he had a suspicion.

"Impossible, Lieutenant. Demilitarized."

"Shea, then."

Arsaces checked his negation. "Tomasi, source of the missiles."

The ensign and her team worked for a moment, Westerland double-checking their calculations. The map on the screen isolated an empty space between Mion 8 and the Sophus cluster.

"As close as I can estimate, sir."

\64% probability. Limited data for triangulation.\

"Sir? That correlates to the unusual ping before the first salvo." Another officer flicked her display to the forward screen. A pair of glyphs danced over the star-field.

"Explain unusual, Udgar."

"I'm not sure, sir. It seemed almost... muffled." Arsaces could make little sense of her graphs, but Sas, who started his career as a Radar Technician, agreed.

"It is blunted, Captain. As if they were moving as they fired."

Arsaces twisted his wrist, rotating the display. "Known civilian or Imperial ships routed through this point from Caprice?"

"None of record, sir."

\No one has ever registered use within fourteen cubic megameters of that astral sphere. A new rebel faction? Someone targeting you?\ **The Sentient's eagerness made his own heart race.** \Can we?\

Something has happened on Caprice. Protocol dictates we report—

Arsaces' face flushed with Westerland's anger. \We've done nothing but patrol and ferry and report for cycles!\

Command—

\Hasn't responded. They are in Jump, answering the Panic. 79% probability. They don't need us. They don't *want* us.\

Arsaces knew that too well.

The crew still stared at him. He hated all those eyes watching him, glassy and unreadable.

\They agree with me.\

Did they? The pilots' hands hovered over the controls. His ensigns sat on the edge of their chairs.

\They want this!\

A breathless moment of indecision, then Arsaces spoke to Sas. "Approach so our noise is hidden in the solar wind."

Like a wire snapping, the crew jumped into motion. Some of them were smiling now. Happy?

\Excited!\

Sas was less eager. "Dangerous, sir. They could be watching for us."

"Westerland, can you track the missile signature?"

The Sentient displayed his analysis on the main screen: propulsion, chemical trail, radiation signature. He even rendered an image from the glimpses the fighters captured. He spoke from the speakers in Arsaces' chair so Sas could hear.

"My sensors can detect incoming attacks from seven hundred thousand kilometers."

Show-off. "Huen?"

"Course laid in, sir. Recommend moderate Jump speeds to distort our signature."

\Agreed. Sound the Alarm?\

This was a bad idea. "Prepare for Jump!"

The Jump Alarm was not subsonic. It blared from every speaker, lights flashing. Arsaces shrugged into his Jump Suit. The reinforced fabric stiffened as he buckled the collar.

Are the passengers cooperating? he asked.

\Grudgingly. I hate civilians.\

I am aware.

Westerland tried to be logical, but his hope bubbled up. \Won't they be a liability? We should leave them here for their safety.\

Leave four senators, two high-ranking industrial leaders, and who knows how many influential civilians adrift by some random asteroid cluster?

Westerland grumbled. \Better than hauling them across half the system. Again.\

Double check the numbers, would you?

His ship's thoughts whispered under the preparations of the crew.

"Forty-three megameters..."

\Engine 2 cleared.\

"M-359 in position..."

\All fighters returned to berths. Pilots on standby.\

One by one, the Bridge crew buckled into their own Jump Suits and did up their harnesses.

"Crew secure, sir."

"The passengers?"

"Secured and briefed, sir."

Helmets muffled the chatter until Arsaces was the last man standing. He settled his own helmet in place, relieved to take shelter behind the shield glass.

A hiss and a click and the helmet sealed to his Suit. His face-shield glowed, responding to his implant as he flicked his eyes through the last-minute checks.

Sas' voice sounded in his left ear, *"Ready for Jump Sequence, Captain."*

"Propulsion, report."

"Engine 1, ready!"

"Engine 2, ready!"

"Engine 3, ready. Ready for Jump, sir!"

"Navigation?"

"Course laid in and confirmed, sir."

"Crew, report."

Deck by deck, they acknowledged. Westerland fretted at the delay, but it was a necessary protocol, one Arsaces refused to shortcut. High Speed Acceleration — Jump — was a good way to get a lot of people killed.

"At your order, sir."

"Acknowledged. Crew, brace for Jump in three... two—"

\JUMP OVERRIDE\

Arsaces recoiled at the bellowed command. His helmet blazed red warning, blinding him.

Westerland, what—?

\JUMP OVERRIDE\

\It isn't me!\

Arsaces flicked his head, but his screen was unresponsive. If anything, the shriek of it increased. It wasn't Westerland's voice, a digital scream cutting through his mind.

\JUMP OVERRIDE\

Stop it!

\I can't!\

Arsaces fumbled at the helmet's latch, ripping it free. Getting the helmet off didn't help. The command glared from every screen, drowning out even Westerland's voice.

"Sir?"

\JUMP OVERRIDE\

"Stand down!" Arsaces ordered desperately. He gasped with relief as the cacophony in his head ceased. He stripped out of his harness, sweat blurring his vision. He fell forward, his Suit stiffening as his knees hit the deck, and retched.

Sas hefted him back to his feet. "Sir, was there a malfunction? Why did you stand down?"

Arsaces spoke aloud to his Sentient, forgetting their eyes as he spat the foul taste from his mouth. "Westerland, what was that?"

\Unknown.\

"Who the *houkun* has Override codes?"

\Unknown. Searching.\

"Override?" Sas repeated blankly. "Impossible. None of our passengers—"

Westerland raced through the manifest. \Nothing.\

"—must be an error," Sas was saying. "Metrics! Run a diagnostic of the last—"

Arsaces gripped Sas' arm to stay upright, knees buckling under the force of a second command.

\BRIDGE OVERRIDE\

"Sir, my screen's dead!"

"Westerland, the array is locked!"

\BRIDGE OVERRIDE\

"Captain? I've lost control of the guns!"

Sas tried to manually unlock the Bridge. Westerland was shrill in his anger. \I can't access the main processors!\

\BRIDGE OVERRIDE\
"Everyone, *shut up!*"

TWO

The bellow of his command met her as the doors opened. As one, the crewmen turned, the blank orbs of their helmets reflecting the red light of their screens.

Five seconds of silence, of shock, then three men lunged for her. Their hands closed hard around her arms, her Suit flexing to counteract their strength. Her helmet was wrenched from her grip. It clattered away until it stopped against someone's boot.

Captain Wood scowled at her. "Who are you?"

She did not fight her captors, but spoke as calmly and firmly as she could, no matter her heart raced in her throat. "You will return to Caprice immediately, Captain."

She almost expected someone to laugh at her effrontery. They glared instead.

An officer advanced, stern and confused. "Ma'am, you must return to your berth and strap in for Jump."

She ignored him. "Now, Captain."

But Wood was already turning away. "Marines, escort this woman to the brig."

She dug her heels in, but she was no match for their combined strength. "I am Evi Andris!" she shouted as the soldiers dragged her back. "Evi Rere Tolmi-Andris, born F-1857-9-2."

She got her fingers around the edge of the door. One of the marines made a sort of irritated sigh and pried them loose. She kept up her fight, knowing it was only a matter of time until the Sentient deduced the truth, compared her vocal patterns to media clips. It was buried beneath layers of encryption, but she could only be one person.

She saw the moment the Sentient told him. Wood's head snapped up, his body tensing. Was the voice he heard apologetic or aghast? Anxious? Angry? Some were rumored to have a sense of humor, of the ridiculous. This was ridiculous, her being here, taking control. Tragic. Terrifying.

Wood jerked to face her again. The marines hesitated, maybe reading the change in their Captain, the furious question in his eyes.

She gave a curt nod.

He closed his eyes and took a deep breath. "Frei?" he growled.

"Yes, sir?" one of the marines asked.

"Disregard my last order. Return to your post."

Frei gaped. "Sir?"

"Now!" The barked order sent them scrambling. Evi pulled her Suit straight and resisted the urge to smooth back her hair.

"Lieutenant? The engines?"

The older officer cleared his throat. "Captain, your orders?"

"Stand down."

"But, sir, the course—?"

"Has everyone suddenly gone deaf?" Wood demanded. "Stand down!"

There was an abashed mutter as his crew hurried to obey. The lieutenant stared between her and his Captain, eyes wide.

"Sir, who...?"

Wood ignored him and gestured curtly. It took no small part of her courage to march up to him and meet his hard eyes.

He spoke in a furious hiss. "What are you doing on my ship?"

"I purchased a berth, same as the other civilians."

"But you aren't a civilian, are you."

Evi refused to acknowledge that.

"Why did you hide your identity?"

Evi did not blush; years of practice kept her voice steady. "A private matter, which is none of your business."

"It seems to be my business now." There was something off about his tone. Impertinent, yes, but also flat. Almost monotone. "Unlock my ship."

"I will, when you lay in a course for Caprice."

"Protocol dictates we report to Command."

Anger fueled her courage. She gestured at the aborted trajectory clearly displayed on the screen. "As CINC Jumped to Valiev at 2345, I'd say your calculations are off, Captain."

He had the gall to smirk at her. It faded as fast as it came. "How do you know where Command is?"

"As a Tolmi princess—"

"The seventh princess," he retorted. "CINC Jumps are the highest level of security. *Who are you?*"

He was correct and it stung. "My married name was Hyde."

He recognized the name; his eyes shifted, suddenly uneasy. "The Dowager Princess."

It pained her to smile, even sardonically. "Yes, that is what they called me after Carl died."

Wood winced. His lieutenant broke into their whispered conversation. He spoke stiffly, pointedly ignoring her. "Sir? Your orders?"

Wood gave an irritated flick of his head and suddenly his voice was full and ringing once more. "Unlock my ship, your highness."

The gasps would have been comical if Wood's scorn hadn't been so clear. He continued, "Sas, we will Jump for Caprice."

His lieutenant stood in stunned immobility. Then he gulped under Wood's impatient eyes and started barking orders. Wood stepped aside, gesturing for the console beside him.

Unwillingly, she let the Sentient scan her palm and entered her codes. Quasi-legal codes she would not like to argue in a courtroom, but could use - discretely - if she avoided an uproar.

Commandeering a Sentient Hybrid Wake Class warship? This would most certainly cause an uproar.

The garish light faded as the screens unlocked. The crew muttered and started plotting the new course. The looks they sent her were incredulous and... angry? Certainly not respectful, no matter their surprise.

Though brusque and efficient, Wood's stare was vague as the ship maneuvered into position. They worked quietly, their silence sharp with hostility. The distress signal still hung on the screen, pleading for them to hurry, hurry, *hurry!*

Evi did up her buckles with shaking fingers. The crew performed the Jump protocols once more, their confusion obvious even over the Network.

Lieutenant Sas checked her harness was secured. His brittle salute made her scowl in the privacy of her helmet.

Soon, Wood's voice spoke in her ear speakers. *"Brace for Jump in three... two... one..."*

The engines roared. A rumble built around her, growing until her teeth rattled. It wasn't any machinery or moving parts of the ship. Just the raw force of the plasma shooting out their stern that set the hull vibrating.

Pressure quickly built on her left side and her Suit responded until she was encased in a second skin, stiff and immovable. The Jump-Meter on her helmet's display tracked their speed.

Seven times Caprician Gravitational Standard... ten CGS... sixteen...

Evi closed her eyes and focused on breathing with the oscillations of her helmet's pressure system.

Wood broke into her Jump-dulled thoughts without ceremony.

"You were married to Admiral Hyde?"

"I was. Until he died."

"My condolences." Still that flat, toneless quality. She ignored the insincere sympathy. It had been five years now and was losing its sting. *"I... served under him. He was a good man."*

Unfortunate she hadn't known this before she stealing the man's ship. She could have asked him about her frequently absent husband.

Wood was silent a long time, though the link was still active. She could hear his sharp breaths as his Suit forced air into his lungs.

Then, *"Why are you on my ship?"*

"Still none of your business, Captain."

He muttered something she didn't catch as he severed the link.

THREE

Westerland was still trying to figure it out well into the braking phase. The Sentient examined random data points, throwing them aside in disgust when they did not mesh into his logic. Arsaces fumed with their combined frustration.

We won't have access to that level of intel, Westerland.

\I *will* find it. I don't care she's a princess; she had no right!\

There's nothing I could have done.

\Could have locked her in the brig!\

And been arrested for treason. Again. His pitiful attempt at humor cooled Westerland's anger. The Sentient still muttered rebelliously.

\Whatever we find at Caprice, I refuse to carry them any further. This was a stupid assignment.\

You know our duty as well as—

\Waste of our potential!\ **Westerland raged.** \Years, you've trained. My crew is the best of the system! Height of weapons' technology!\

Arsaces knew for a fact Naval Command had not given him anything near the best of the recruits. Competent, of course, but young, with no experience. Average marks, no commendations. His officers were volunteers at least. Though what they thought to gain from such a deployment was beyond him.

\They are skilled. You've trained them!\

Untested. No combat experience.

\We just need a *chance*. We are good as any other IN crew!\

Were they? A flare of shame made him admit, *Your damage nearly made me black out. What if it happens again? During battle?*

Westerland dismissed this. \That was our first engagement. We adapted. We functioned well. We can fight.\ **The Sentient added in a mutter,** \If they'd let us. Won't even let us track Pinan pirates.\

Arsaces refused to discuss it further. They'd gone over and over this since Westerland had been activated. And no matter what evidence or logic Westerland presented, it made no difference in their assignments.

Grudgingly, Westerland dropped the subject and resumed his delve into the princess' life. Arsaces did his best to ignore him, but facts and images flashed through his thoughts regardless, his own mind mulling over the implications.

Attended the Imperial Academy and Hyla University. Studied political economics and cultural ethics. Media appearance F-1882-14-6. Shorter than her siblings, with lighter coloring. Takes after her mother's side; explains her hair, so blonde she could pass for a 'dowager' in more than name. A cruel moniker, for such a young widow.

Arsaces frowned with distaste. *She was fourteen when they married?*

\Political alliance. Hyde's family controls a majority of the consumables trade on the East Bank. Your sister wasn't much older.\

His own memory augmented Westerland's, and his younger sister smiled at him from her wedding portrait. Sealus had been a good man, at least. Declared himself 'in love.' Arsaces had never heard her feelings on the union, been too afraid to probe and learn she was terrified. The one time he'd dared ask, she'd parroted those hated, hated words that still haunted him: As the earth.

Their duty, like the immovable planet beneath them. Pulling at them, dragging them down. Inescapable.

He sought refuge in Westerland's problems, rather than his own. *Why didn't you recognize her?*

\Her facial recognition is coded. Same as the rest of her statistics. I can't confirm until I access the Planetary Network, but I suspect her data runs through a Garrent algorithm. I might be able to trace it, if the destination signature carries the usual skip sequence… \

Westerland wondered off into this new idea, his words dissolving into impulses and feelings. Which left Arsaces alone with his thoughts again. Ones he did not want to sit with in the silence of Jump speed.

You are Arsaces Jankovic-Wood. You were a pilot. You have been in incubation recovery for… \

Do you think she knows what I did?

Westerland was flatly pragmatic. \Most likely. Her codes are of the highest authority.\

But why does she have them? Where had she been going? Why hide her identity?

\Doesn't matter now, since we're headed in the opposite direction. Maybe we can foist her off onto a different— Objects in Jump Lane.\

Arsaces jerked, shocked out of their intertwined musings. *Explain?*

\Unanticipated Objects in Jump Lane. Alarm initiated.\

The inside of his helmet flared, showing the approaching planet and their trajectory. Ships, in the airspace around Caprice. Lots of ships, scattered across the Jump Lanes, the port orbits. Westerland was moving too fast to see what was happening, but he had to do something before they plowed straight into them.

Broadcast a warning, we need that Lane cleared— what is that? The screen adjusted as Arsaces focused on the object. It was massive compared to the ships, even the largest port station. A ring, sitting back out of the gravity well.

\Analyzing.\ Westerland's anger was gone, all his personality swallowed into this new problem. \Unidentified.\

Hard brake. Now.

Even through his Suit, Arsaces winced at the pressure and pain of the engines shoving him. His screen glowed, showing the motion of the unknown ships. Some turned; he saw the flash of their engines as they aimed for him.

\Warning: collision course extrapolated.\

Friendly?

\Unable to—\

Guess!

Westerland hesitated. \Non-friendly. No response to call-sign. Emissions suggest weapons online.\

That was enough for him. *Give me control.* "Crew! Prepare to engage!"

"Yes, sir!"

Arsaces chair shifted, the manual controls rising from the armrests. He gripped them with bloodless hands.

"Captain?" Sas asked.

"Enemy ships above Caprice. Brace for evasive maneuvers. Prepare for hard brake!"

Another thump of pressure, throwing them against their harnesses.

Anything on the ring, yet?

\Analyzing.\

"Engine 1 outside parameters, sir!"

"Kill it! Cut spin compensation. Revert to flight dynamics."

Westerland shuddered and pitched as the engine shutdown. Sweat broke out on Arsaces' face as he forced the ship to maintain trajectory. The pale orb of Caprice slowly settled into the center in his screen.

He kept it there, half aware they were flying backwards, the engines pointed toward Caprice, their nose to the stars. Every shift of his was reversed and magnified.

\You are flying too hard. Let me handle it.\

Arsaces ignored him. The unknown ships were still coming for them. Every kilometer he moved toward them, they appeared to be slowing. But they were the constant; he was the one slowing, but at the same time catching up to reality.

Jump warfare sent computers into panicked circles before they burnt out, overwhelmed by the calculations. He would not risk Westerland that way, no matter how clever or confidant.

\Incoming weapons.\

"Active munitions, sir!"

"Return fire!"

\Hypothesis: the ring is an energy weapon. Slow down.\

What kind of weapon?

\Radiation is being produced. Unidentified type. No data.\

Get as much as you can. I'll fly. CGS?

\Five.\

Arsaces shed his helmet impatiently, unable to see enough of the battle. He gasped, clenching his legs to force blood into his heart and brain.

"Crew, that ring is the priority target!"

"Copy!"

"Firing, sir!"

Missiles streaked toward the approaching ships. They swerved, but blossoms of fire burst against the gleaming metallic shadows of the ring. A swarm of ships turned for them now, bristling with menace.

"Engineering, report?"

"Two, at capacity. Three, stable. Prepare to brake?"

"Belay brake!" He risked a lot plowing through the sky like this. But there were more ships in Caprice's space than he could count. And none he recognized.

Where is everyone? Where's Home Fleet?

\Unknown. Slow down. Collision imminent.\

Give me numbers for Caprice's pull.

\Running compensation.\

He was close enough to see individual fighters now. He braced himself and slammed Westerland through them. It was like claws on his skin, down his arms, his back. But they scattered, brushed aside by Westerland's bulk.

"Prepare for Hard Brake! All fighters launch on exit of Jump."

More shudders, more impulses. Incoming fire. Now that he expected it, Arsaces could ignore the stabs in his mind as the ship's sensors observed and reported the damage.

"Brace for brake! Three... two... one... *brake!*"

The engines gave a mighty heave - everything stood still an instant - then they were racing forward, still at suicidal speed.

The crew lunged from their harnesses, ripping helmets off as they took over weapons. His fighters streamed out, like so many sparks of a fire.

"Any response from the ground? Any CINC ships?"

"None, sir," Sas said.

Alone against an enemy fleet. Again.

\Not alone.\

Never alone. This time he had Westerland.

FOUR

vi fought nausea as she watched the battle. What was that ring? It hung in Volgar's light, one of Caprice's moons highlighted behind it.

Caprice was under attack. But why? And who? They weren't Shean ships, no Syndicate had weapons like this. She desperately hoped they didn't. Could her father have been right?

The crew hammered the thing, missile strikes blossoming against the darkness beyond. The deck swayed under her, the pull of spin-gravity rolling away from her and back. She gripped her harness to keep her bearings.

Wood controlled their flight, his boot braced against the nearest console to keep his seat. The ship groaned around them, louder than the shouts of the crew fighting back.

Was something wrong? The ship veered erratically, the trajectory displaying showing them tumbling through space, lurching from one group of enemies to another. What was he doing?

An enemy ship spun away, engine sputtering. It crashed through another, exploding in the ugly grace of vacuum, slow, then rushing out as it found no resistance.

"Brace for impact!"

Her teeth rattled in her helmet as the ship bucked. She floated from her seat for an instant, then slammed down hard enough to activate her Suit.

"Captain, we are in a dead spin."

Dead spin. Out of control.

She looked to Wood. He stared blankly at the screen, ignoring the warning and the noise of his crew around him.

"The ring!"

Evi's stomach tightened. The thing glowed, filled with power. Something flared behind it, a stream of energy reaching away from Caprice.

Away?

"Fighters, stay engaged," Wood said tersely. *"I am taking us around."*

The atmosphere of Caprice rippled under them as they swooped in, still spinning, uncoordinated.

"Need more maneuvering thrust."

"Working on it!"

He'd never pull them out in time. They'd falter, crash down into her home and decimate it. Or overshoot. Parcae was just over the horizon, home to six million residents.

But he did. Their z-axis leveled out; they stopped flipping end over end. Then the y and the x. Parcae rose in crimson radiance before them. Evi was pressed inexorably into her seat as they shot past Caprice back into darkness.

The stars wheeled and all at once they were aimed for the battle once more. This time dead on and screeching through vacuum so fast she thought she could hear the nothingness hiss by the hull.

Now the enemy was stretched out. Some had attempted to follow them around the planet, the others still engaged with the Caprician fighters. The ring was brighter now, the flare behind it pulsing.

"Now! While they're scattered!"

The sky became a blaze of streaking trails, all missiles directed at the ring as it gathered power. She could see into it now, see the gaping hole it made in space, a black chasm where there should be countless stars.

"Taking heavy fire, sir!"

"It's some sort of pulse emission. Disrupting the Heming's electronics!"

"All fighters, fall back. Continue assault on the structure."

The tiny glints of their cockpits gathered and raced for safety. Enemy fighters gave chase. Wood's fighters flipped, flying backwards to lay down a barrage of desperate defense.

"It's cracking, sir! There, just starboard of the apex!"

"Concentrate all fire on damaged portion."

"E-3 failing!"

"Thrusters as well, need urgent cooling."

"Rerouting exhaust venting."

"Can't get a reading on those emissions!"

"Sir, we're running low of—"

"That is not a weapon."

The contrast between that voice and the crew was jarring. It was calm, smooth and monotone.

Westerland.

Wood spoke directly to the Sentient. *"What do you — Attend! Do not destroy the ring. Repeat:* do not destroy! *Capture at all costs."*

Their astonishment was brief, then they shifted their attack to the swarming enemy ships. Those were already faltering, falling back. Their numbers couldn't keep up with Wood's lightening tactics.

"I want E-1 back online. Now!"

"E-1 capable of 15%."

"Give it to me!"

"It's failing! Look!"

Evi gasped as the flare behind the ring flickered. The structure cracked further, visible even at this distance. A chunk of it broke away and the flare died, that dreadful black hole snapping out of existence.

"Capture it!"

The enemy fled all at once, Wood's fighters harassing them beyond the port stations.

"Follow, sir?"

"No." Wood countered. *"Track trajectories and— That one, there, plot course. Quick, I need—!"*

Evi found the one he meant. The others had gathered to flee. One of the large ships headed for the ring. Its engine flared, breaking away from the fighters around it.

"Stop them!"

But it was too late. The enemy ship plowed broadside through the ring. The ship ripped apart and the ring folded around itself. Enemy fire erupted around them but passed them by to destroy what was left of the structure.

Before the crew could recover, the enemy's engines glowed, different from the yellow-white of plasma, and were gone.

FIVE

Caprice: Close Synchronous Orbit
F̄ - 1884 - 4 - 6

Debris from the destroyed ring glinted in the sunlight. Volgar was just rising over Caprice, reflecting off the metallic fragments as they scattered into the atmosphere.

Tell me it's impossible.

\Improbable. Highly theoretical. But if someone has found a way to break the light-barrier…\

"Captain!"

Arsaces pulled himself back to the Bridge. His crew still needed direction, no matter he was reeling from the implications.

The pilots had moved them over the Ilaeni Sea, the western coast of Caprice's ocean obscured by dark clouds. They rippled out, billowing up from a central point. A hole punched through the atmosphere, boring down to…

The crew gasped as they settled in a synchronous orbit over the ruins of Orbon. The gleaming capital of the Caprician Empire, home to forty-five million citizens, was gone.

Volgar threw long shadows behind the blackened skeletons of the once towering buildings. Its golden light melted into the fires raging.

Arsaces could only stare. What had done this? That ring? No wonder they destroyed it, a weapon that powerful!

\Not a weapon.\

Someone cried out, others muttered prayers. They were Capricians, his crew. They had family below.

Westerland's pragmatism jolted them out of their shock.

"*An impact zone,*" he announced to the Bridge. He highlighted the crater on the screen.

"Could it have been a meteor?" Arsaces asked, knowing it was impossible. Skynet would have tracked and destroyed it long ago. Speaking of which, why hadn't the surveillance system alerted the planet to the attackers? Was that what had triggered the Panic?

Sas was already moving, snapping orders.

"Initiate Recovery Sweep. Fush, go to Hanger B, I want report directly from Major Campton."

"Sir? We've made contact with C-14-F."

The commander of the shipping port was grim and terse.

"*It was missiles, Captain. Hundreds of them from inside the Orbital Perimeter. Approached at high speed, some two dozen ships. Home Fleet had responded to a Distress from the Geilara Syndicate. They never returned. We've been unable to contact them or CINC.*"

They were gone. Arsaces knew that even as Westerland calculated the probabilities.

The commander rubbed his face. "*Then that ring arrived with another fleet of them. We tried to defend, but they swept over my security forces. Other ports have been destroyed, some disabled. We've been knocked out of orbit. We can maintain position for a few more hours, then our fuel will be depleted.*"

Their projected course flashed behind Arsaces' eyes as Westerland calculated their decaying trajectory.

"You did well, commander," he assured the man. "Rescue is on its way."

"*Thank you, Captain. I'll have my crew ready to transfer.*"

"Any cargo you can secure for recovery descent will be appreciated. I want your records, your video streams, radio. Any intel you have on these attackers."

"*Yes, sir.*"

The screen closed. Arsaces should help them, should check-in with his officers. But he stood silent as they moved around him in a frantic mass, trying to find some way to disprove Westerland's theory.

"Captain?"

Sas held out a Palm-Link. The message on its screen was stark: *Home Fleet destroyed. No response from CINC, presumed incapacitated or destroyed. The Emperor is presumed dead. All ships return to Caprice.*

Arsaces read it twice, then sat and dragged his gloved hands through his hair.

"What is it, Captain?"

It was the princess. He didn't look up at her, just gestured for Sas to show her the message.

She stood silent a long time, long enough he feared she had started crying. He chanced a look.

She wasn't. But her mouth was thin and her shoulders stiff.

"I will need to convene the Council."

Suddenly, she was the Empress. She could be the Empress.

Before Arsaces could say anything, she was exiting the Bridge. The marines saluted her as she passed.

He went to follow her, hesitating. Sas met his glance, his own full of some meaning Arsaces couldn't read.

"Go, sir. I have this."

He found her in the Observation Room. Clinging to the outer deck, the floor had clear panels set into it so one could see down into the endless lights below. She stood to one side, her eyes closed as her damaged planet glided beneath her feet.

He cleared his throat. "Your majesty?"

She startled. "Yes, Captain?" Then she scowled. "No, not yet. I must receive a ratifying vote of the Council Members."

Arsaces wondered what they would decide. Her family had resided in Orbon, the center of Caprice's power. There was no way they had survived, even if they had been warned.

\Tell her.\

It's impossible.

\Improbable. She needs to know.\

He tried to capture her attention again. "Your highness, that weapon—"

"Who would do this?" she interrupted softly. She gestured at the devastation beneath them. "Why would they do this? What could Shea or Tin have to gain?"

Arsaces' stomach turned as it hadn't during their wild flight around the planet. Not Tin, anything but another rebellion. He couldn't, he wouldn't, fight his own kin. But if they ordered him? If they threatened Westerland?

\Tell her!\

"That weapon… Well, Westerland believes it isn't a weapon."

She made a curt motion. "I do not have time for—"

Westerland spoke over her, impatient with Arsaces' dithering. *"Your highness, that ring is a way for the enemy to travel faster than the speed of light."*

She frowned up at Arsaces. "That's impossible."

No emotion carried over the artificial voice construct, so only Arsaces could hear the scathing frustration as Westerland said, *"Improbable, not impossible."*

"But, then those ships, they could be from anywhere."

"Yes."

"Outside the system, even."

"Correct. I calculate the likelihood—"

She put a hand to her forehead. "We will have no way to predict — we can't track them. If they've destroyed Home Fleet, CINC."

Arsaces caught her elbow, the pale tone of her skin going ashen. She gripped his arms to hold herself upright.

"Westerland, call Medical."

"No." She straightened and brushed a hand across her eyes. "No, I am well."

"Ma'am, I think—"

"No." For a slight woman not quite up to his shoulder, she could be startlingly fierce. She stepped away and gave him a tight smile. "Thank you, Captain."

Arsaces wished Jump Suits had pockets so he could hide his hands. He gripped them into fists to stop his fingers from drumming. "For what, ma'am?"

"You saved my life. You routed the enemy and protected Caprice from further attack. Thank you."

He dropped his eyes. The remains of Orbon stared back. The daylight was fading as smoke and clouds gathered over the city.

"I will need to land on Caprice at once."

Arsaces did not like that. "It isn't safe. I would rather—"

"I understand. But it is law. No exchange of power may happen off Caprician soil." She smiled at his discomfort. "I promise, Captain. I will be careful."

\Sas is ready to rescue C-14-F.\

He didn't like it, but he was trapped.

\Sooner she goes, the sooner she's not our responsibility anymore.\

"I am needed on the Bridge, ma'am."

The princess dismissed him. "Of course. I will join you soon."

Arsaces saluted and left her looking down on her ruined home.

While he rode the lift up to the Bridge, Westerland rummaged around in his head.

What are you looking for?

The Sentient withdrew sheepishly. \Nothing.\

SIX

Evi waited at the shuttle doors and tried not to let her trembling show. She could hear the hiss of hot metal even through the shielding. The heat of their reckless reentry wafted through the tiny cabin. Captain Wood had ordered the shuttle pilot to land as fast as possible and the woman had obeyed. Evi's inner ear was still whirling.

Wood waited next to her with his eyes fixed on some unseen point before him. His expression was vacant, his movements clumsy. He hadn't reacted to their jarring landing, nor when the pilot had given them clearance to move. Lieutenant Sas had even gone so far as to unbuckle his Captain's harness and haul him up from his chair. Then guided his hand to the medical scanner for the immunity screen.

Neither the lieutenant nor the shuttle crew seemed to find this concerning.

Evi did, certainly. What was wrong with him? Now, as he stood blank beside her, his only motion was his hand. She'd noticed it before, on the Bridge after the battle, while waiting for the loading on the Sentient.

He would drum his fingers quickly, then each tip with even deliberation. Over and over, on his leg, on a table, until he noticed he was doing it. Then he'd flex his hand and let it go limp. Always his right, never his left.

"Captain?" the marine commander prompted after a few moments.

Wood started and came back to them. "Proceed, Frei."

Commander Frei opened the hatch. He and his men shoved back the press of bodies outside. Soldiers, journalists, senators, a crowd of people clamoring for her, for information.

Evi was grateful for the shield of tall bodies around her. Wood and Sas flanked her while the marines formed a firm perimeter. They moved across the landing strip, wading through the throng.

Evi caught glimpses of other shuttles. The insignia of other provinces, the personal craft of senators, other military shuttles. All the necessary participants needed to call a Convene of the Caprician Imperial Council.

Evi squinted as they entered the squat building, a military installation of some kind. Her senses rebelled, her eyes refusing to accommodate the change from bright to dark.

The Jumps had disrupted her balance and her inner ear ached. This region was hot and humid after the constant dry air aboard the Sentient. Her nose and lungs were choked with the dust in the air, leaving a chalky feeling in her mouth. Her immunity booster made her queasy and feverish. And now she was blind.

Grumbling, she blinked until she could see something of the corridor they faced, then moved forward. She made it only a few paces before Wood's steps dragged to a halt.

"Sir?" Sas' sharp voice cut under the noise of the crowd. "Sir, what is it?"

The Captain's breaths came quick and tight. "He's gone— I can't—"

Sas held him up as he sagged. Only an instant, then he was brushing his lieutenant's hands away. He jerked his coat straight and snapped back to attention. He met her eyes and glanced away.

"I lost Westerland for a moment," he admitted. "This shielding is thick."

When was the last time he had been away from his Sentient? Many Hybrid Captains never entered atmosphere again once they were activated.

"Are you able to continue?" she asked, low enough only he could hear.

He gave a curt nod and strode forward. She followed, watching his fingers drum on his leg.

The main room had been cleared for a long table lined with chairs. Silence fell as she entered. Years of training took over. She lifted her chin and kept her face serene. Councilwoman Antipus approached and bowed low.

"Princess, welcome."

Evi nodded a gracious greeting. "Are all assembled, Councilwoman?"

"All is ready, your highness."

Evi strode to her place at the head of the room. The others present sorted themselves out, members of the military mixing with the civil officials and the industrials. Wood and his men disappeared into a mass of blue and orange uniforms.

Antipus called the room to order. Evi waited while the noise died to a rustle. She remained standing, looking over the faces staring back at her. Shean Syndates, Industrial Electorates, representatives from Taltua, Tinese nobles. Air Force, Navy, Mobile Infantry.

So many empty chairs.

"My friends," she began, "it is with great sorrow that I summon this Convene."

The words had sounded stilted as she rehearsed them during the shuttle flight. They sounded stilted now, but they were the only thing keeping her from weeping with grief and rage.

"My father is dead. Orbon lies in ruins. We are under attack from an unknown enemy. Unwarranted, brutal attacks on our peaceful peoples. We must gather our remaining strength and defend our homes and families."

Different colored eyes watched her narrowly, all skin tones from the palest white of subterranean Shea to ebony Mumins from the Eastern Continent. Squinting, swarthy faces from Taltua, bathed in endless summer. Were one of them responsible for this atrocity?

"Shea, Taltua. I look to you for aid. I understand you have your own peoples to guard. Know we value their lives as highly as our own. We will do all we can to assist.

"Tin..." Evi met the hostile stares of her father's most fractious territory. "*Aklou Budin*, brave warriors. Your ferocity will be a priceless asset in this conflict." That earned her a few grudging smirks.

There was nothing else to say. Evi nodded to Antipus and sat.

"The princess unfortunately speaks the truth. Our defenses have been decimated. Skynet seems to be unable to track these invaders. Now is the time for unity and cooperation.

"We have been searching for any surviving members of the Tolmi-Andris line. Prince Mani was killed when the Triumph was destroyed."

Evi's next older brother had been a lieutenant with the Home Fleet. She hastily blinked away tears.

Antipus continued. "Princess Kala, Renna, and Liss were in the capital with the Emperor, the Empress, and Crown Prince Hantusav. All are presumed dead. Princess Evi is the last surviving Tolmi within the true line.

"This is an unprecedented motion of this Council. However, the catastrophic nature of the situation demands leadership and immediate action. Conflict amongst ourselves will lead to our destruction or subjugation.

"Princess Evi is young, yes. However, you all know her credentials, her education and training. I propose we support her ascension with no debate. Are there any objections?"

The room sat silent for long minutes. Evi waited tense, keeping her gaze even as she looked from face to face. Would any deny her birthright? Who would stand and wrest power from her father's name, a dynasty that had stood for five hundred years?

She hid her relief — and her terror — as Antipus turned and bowed. "Your majesty."

They all stood and murmured respectfully. She smiled, grinding her teeth, and allowed them to sit.

"Thank you for your support, my friends. I will do everything in my power to bring this terrible conflict to a peaceful resolution. We will begin with the military reports. Rear-Admiral Stason."

There was not much to tell. The same story again and again. An unknown enemy, with advanced weapons. Striking fast, destroying ships, and fleeing before engagement.

Their words washed over her. She wondered if someone was keeping track of the list of the ships and brigades destroyed. Only a fraction of the dozens of commanders and captains sat here. The rest were destroyed. Murdered.

Evi clenched her hands in her lap.

"Captain Wood," Antipus intoned.

Wood stood, staring over her head.

"2606 ship-time, Westerland received a Distress signal from Caprician space."

Evi took the chance to examine him closely. Standard issue naval uniform, with a Hybrid's insignia on the open collar. Average height, dark skin. Likewise, his hair, the slant of his eyes, were common features in several ethnic groups in the system. He spoke evenly, without regional inflection that might have given her hints as to his birthplace.

Strangely so, given the range of accents of the others. His enunciation was perfect, his speech patterns exactly as her instructors had drilled into her for years. Even still, she carried the slight lisp of Pedan where she had been raised.

Was it the Sentient speaking through him? The Architects would never be so flippant as to program an accent into one of their creations. Would Wood allow such a mental surrender?

She acknowledged she was perplexed by him. Sometimes stern and irascible, others oddly vulnerable, like in the corridor or the shuttle. It wasn't just the thing with his hand. She had met several other Hybrid Captains; they all had some sort of tic.

Wood finished and nodded to her before sitting. Evi noticed he kept his hands below the table.

"You are a Hybrid?" Antipus asked keenly. Evi glanced over the room, reading insignias. Only one of four remaining. Six Captains and Sentients lost.

"Yes, ma'am."

"What is your Sentient's interpretation of the ring you destroyed?"

Wood hesitated. His eyes found Evi's. He read the warning there and continued smoothly, "He is not sure, ma'am. He is attempting to recreate the device."

"Thank you, Captain. I will now display the battle of yesterday night as recorded by our satellites."

It was breathtaking to watch, silent and graceful. A stark contrast to what she experienced inside the ship. On the screen, Westerland fell out of Jump, the blast of the engines glowing hotly. One of them cut out, and the ship lurched. Evi's stomach swooped in remembered reaction.

Effortlessly it seemed, the ship flipped over, then continued onward, twirling like a *Mestov* dancer as it entered the battle. She could see now how such a maneuver would confuse battle computers, never able to track a ship's heading.

Wood's missiles left explosions in his wake, slicing through the enemy ships, never engaging with one for long. The enemy scattered, flying in every direction, stumbling over each other, their numbers now a disadvantage. Some were pulled too close to Caprice and lurched drunkenly, trying to escape uncontrolled reentry before being swallowed by the churning atmosphere.

The view shifted as Wood took his ship around the planet in a wide orbit, not coming too close, but near enough to use Caprice's gravity to his advantage. The ship arched over the horizon, a sparkling gem as the light of Volgar flashed over it.

There was an audible gasp as the ring broke apart. An explosion, then the enemy ships Jumped away, leaving ruin behind.

Someone whistled admiration. Wood was having his back thumped and his flush was visible even across the room.

"Excellent," Admiral Stason praised. "Dangerous, but effective. Not to mention contrary to the laws of physics. Under fire? Without your battle computer? How did you manage it?"

"Just doing my job, sir."

There was a crack of grim laughter, quickly smothered. Wood kept his eyes on the tabletop. His officers stared contemptuously across the room at their colonial counterparts. Sas had his hand on Wood's shoulder, fingers biting into the younger man's arm.

The room hesitated on a tense silence, one Evi was at a loss to interpret. She was missing something, some interaction, some history that hovered over them.

Maybe it was the now sick cast to Wood's face or the disdainful sneer of Shea's Prime Syndate. Evi stood, unaccountably angry. She spoke through a gritted smile.

"I can never thank Captain Wood enough. I must commend him, the CIN-SH Westerland, and their crew for their skill and bravery. They saved untold lives today."

Including hers. Could these dunderheads not see the disaster it would have been if she had died alongside her siblings? They'd even now be scrambling for control, fighting each other when they needed to fight the enemy.

"This is why I am appointing him my Fleet Admiral."

* * *

Arsaces froze, Sas' hand a warning pressure on his arm. His other officers pressed close, suffocating him.

Eyes flicked to him and away, a mass of voices arguing with the girl just declared supreme ruler of the Volgar System.

Arsaces agreed with them: this was a bad decision, from anyone's standpoint.

Westerland chided him, faint through the shielding, but there. \Aren't we the best pilots in the system? Didn't we rout them single-handedly?\

The Empress sat calm under the protestations. She listened politely, but even he could see the firm set to her mouth.

"Are there any objections other than Captain Wood's age and lack of command experience?"

Would someone dare mention it? They must be thinking it, Stason, Decatur, Zabin. She couldn't know, then. Not if she would dare offer him this position.

\Fools, all of them.\

"Captain Wood?"

More eyes. This time he had no trouble reading the doubt and scorn on their faces.

\Sas thinks you can do it. She thinks you can do it.\

Arsaces forced himself to his feet. "Your majesty," he began. He wanted to refuse. Even his Sentient's egotism couldn't comfort him. What did he know of command? What could he do against this unknown enemy and their impossible technology? He had tried to arrest her!

\Improbable,\ **Westerland scolded.** \We will defeat them, you and I, together.\

"Your majesty, thank you for your confidence."

\I know you can do it.\

"I accept."

SEVEN

Caprice: Close Synchronous Orbit
F - 1884 - 4 - 7

The meeting dragged on for hours. Evi kept her benign smile in place until her cheek muscles cramped. As night fell, they at last talked themselves out. Evi dismissed them, accepting their salutes with true gratitude. A strong start to her reign as Empress, she hoped.

Low conversations rumbled around her as her hastily assembled government sorted themselves out. Wood's marines took up position next to her.

She frowned up at them, then searched out their Captain in a knot of uniformed officers. He met her eyes a moment, saw his soldiers, and gave a nod of satisfaction. Oddly touched, Evi smiled her thanks. He didn't return it, but turned away to speak with someone plucking at his elbow.

Slowly, the crowd thinned. Even with her ring of guards she made inching progress. Making for their Captain, the marines politely but firmly moved senators and soldiers out of their path.

Finally, they broke free, only to find Wood, Sas, and a Tinese officer standing alone.

"*Orin'nora,* Admiral Wood. My congratulations."

Evi was taken aback at the venom of this. The marines heard it, too, tensing, hands drifting to weapons. Again, that defiance from Wood's officers, a challenge almost, in their glares.

Wood spoke coolly. "Thank you, Commodore Haetch."

"Such an honor for one so young."

Sas said something swift in his Captain's ear, another officer actually gripping the Captain's sleeve and tugging at him.

Haetch's lip curled. "Fitting reward for your loyalty, *jat*?"

One of the marines cursed. "We need to get them out of here," he growled. Not to her, but to his men. "Bring him. Before they—"

Evi lost sight of them as she was hustled toward the exit. Others were muttering, watching this drama unfold. The sharp accents of the Tinese commodore rose over the noise.

"—*glad* your mother is *dead*—"

Evi turned in time to see Haetch hit the floor.

The marines closed in, protecting her from the jostling of the irate crowd. Voices rose, shouting multiple languages. Officers squared off, shoving shoulders.

"Sas!" Wood snapped. "As you were!"

His lieutenant did not obey, fists clenched as he stood over the fallen man. Blood dripped from his knuckles. Haetch rolled to his knees and spat red to the stone floor.

"Paulion." Wood spoke softer, but still a warning.

Sas' craggy cheeks flushed. He stepped back to his place at Wood's shoulder, teeth bared in a snarl.

Haetch got to his feet and glared at them. Wood looked as if he would speak but stopped himself. Haetch straightened his coat with jerky movements. He spat once more, contemptuously, at Wood's feet. The stunned crowd let him through.

General Ur, a stocky man who quelled his soldiers with his sardonic glance, moved into the breach.

"Admiral, I would appreciate a report of your disposition."

Wood's fists unclenched. "Of course, General. Please, join me."

For towering brutes, his marines could be truly pathetic. They scurried to surround their Captain, the flinching concern on their faces ludicrous beside Sas' cold fury.

They left hissing whispers behind them.

* * *

\I am here.\

Arsaces walked unseeing, the darkness of the corridor, the weight of the building, the sky itself, pressing him down.

Like the earth, like the earth, like the—

\You are not alone.\

Sas' hand was firm on his shoulder, leading him to the shuttle. Arsaces let him, misery a familiar ache in his chest.

Not heartache. He didn't have a heart. Not a real one, despite the deafening thunder in his ears.

\I love you, Arsaces.\

* * *

Evi felt more than heard Wood's sigh as they broke pressure in the hanger deck. The hard angles of his face softened, the lines around his eyes easing back.

Too young, they claimed. Then why did he have such weariness in his face?

General Ur and Marshal Halt disembarked their own shuttles and looked around the busy flight deck with interest. They would serve aboard Westerland, now her Flagship. The necessary shift of personnel was already underway. There were dozens of shuttles circling outside, waiting to disgorge their passengers into Westerland's hold.

"What first, Captain?"

Wood came out of his preoccupation with a jerk. "My crew is being reorganized as we speak. It will be cramped, but we can accommodate a full division, another two aboard the Hann."

Halt watched keenly as fighters were towed about to make room for as many others as could be crammed into the cavernous space.

"Any word from the munitions depots?" he asked.

"I will see to it."

"Beta-7 been contacted?" Ur asked.

"A briefing will be prepared—"

"What about General Guhaci? Have the reserves been activated?"

The two commanders asked questions rapid-fire, faster than Sas and Wood could answer.

Evi spoke over them in as soothing a voice as she could. She was hoarse after the hours-long meeting. "Gentlemen, let us settle ourselves. I, for one, am hungry and tired."

They subsided with murmured apologies. Wood shifted from leg to leg, visibly agitated as he had not been even during the battle. "May I be excused, ma'am? I have to... Westerland needs..."

"Of course, Captain." Now an Admiral, but always a Hybrid Captain.

"Sas will show you to your quarters, ma'am."

"Thank you."

He saluted and walked away, head down. Sas watched him go with worry creasing his forehead.

Evi caught Ur's frown as well. "You can say it, General. You have your doubts?"

The man grimaced. "I won't deny he's gifted. He did well yesterday. But he is young, ma'am. Not just in years."

"So am I."

"He's reckless."

Halt surprisingly disagreed. "We need someone willing to risk everything."

Ur grunted. "He's certainly that, if nothing else."

Sas touched her elbow. His hand was already swollen and purple. "Ma'am? Gentlemen? If you will follow me?"

As they walked to the lift, Evi decided she liked this taciturn sailor. His report of the work to be done was succinct and precise. Deferential, but with the confidence of experience with command. Loyal, by the bruising of his knuckles.

To strike a superior officer? Even though Haetch was only a colonial, it was a court-martial offense. If his Captain hadn't been the highest ranking officer in the system.

Once they were moving away from the hangar, Evi reached out and stopped the lift. It slid smoothly to a stop.

"Westerland?"

"Yes, ma'am?"

"Lock the doors."

"Doors locked."

"Disable sensors and recording."

"Disabled."

The officers eyed her with astonishment, Sas looking particularly alarmed. She didn't know when she would have them all together again, with no one else listening in.

"Marines, you will forget this conversation. Do you understand?"

"Yes, ma'am," they muttered.

"Now, why was Wood given a Sentient?"

She glared until they dropped their eyes. "He was a fighter pilot, I know. He was injured? The rest of his record is sealed and I cannot access the Planetary Network until it is restored. What did he do?"

Ur and Halt glanced to each other. Halt cleared his throat.

"Captain Wood served under your late husband in the police action five years ago, around Tin."

"I am aware." She ignored the stab she still felt when someone mentioned Carl. She would love him always, her best friend and mentor, no matter their age gap.

"Wood was awarded Westerland for his actions during the battle that ended the rebellion."

"Which were?" she prompted. She knew this well enough. She had researched extensively, purposefully choosing a transport no one would look twice at. A Sentient never deployed to fight, a crew that didn't mix in port. She'd assumed it was due to Wood's poor handling. But she'd seen herself his skill at the helm, the efficacy of his crew. "He didn't do anything illegal, did he?"

Ur winced as he said, "Not exactly..."

Just like her father, to hush up a scandal. He'd have done anything to preserve the Empire's image. But one couldn't very well kill off a Sentient Hybrid. The Architects would be furious. "How exactly, general?"

"He destroyed the rebel's flagship, took out their leadership."

"How?"

"He flew his fighter through their ship, ma'am."

Evi was sure she'd heard wrong. "I'm sorry, through the ship?"

"When the rebels scrambled our warheads. They'd stolen the codes and shut down Hyde's weapons."

Halt grinned humorlessly. "The old Archer FR-270s were tough little buggers. The rebellion only had some retrofitted Kapitsa troop transports. Sturdy, but not up to battle conditions. Still ripped his Archer apart, except the cockpit. Even that was crushed up. Heard they had to cut him out of it. What was left of him."

Evi could well believe the idiotic bravery of the man. "But why was this sealed?"

Sas spoke for the first time. "It's complicated, ma'am."

"How?"

"He disobeyed a direct order from his commander."

"To pull back?"

"No, ma'am. To attack Hyde's disabled fleet."

Evi blinked as the facts arranged themselves. "He's not Caprician."

"No, ma'am. He's native Alam-Jaheel. Served in the Colonial Fighter Squadron stationed in Alam City."

"They scrambled to intercept us," Halt continued. "The entire Alam Corps defected. Wood... well, he chose his side."

Evi wasn't sure how to frame her next question. "Why didn't he just refuse to fight? Why attack alone?"

Sas cleared his throat. "I think he felt personally responsible, ma'am."

"For an entire nation's uprising?"

"You see, ma'am, he was Courtney Jankovic's nephew."

Evi folded her lips over a curse she had learned from one of her husband's officers. Not just Tinese, then, but Tinese nobility. The Jankovic-Woods, unofficial rulers of Alam City. Executed after their rebellion was suppressed by her husband's fleet.

Evi held back a cringe. *Her* husband, who had personally overseen the punishments, at least those who hadn't killed themselves first. Cursed, stubborn, prideful Budins.

Evi palmed the lift and it resumed its journey.

"Thank you, gentlemen. You have been most helpful."

"You won't—" Sas snatched back the hand he'd laid on her shoulder. At her raised eyebrows, he swallowed. "Please, don't ask him about it."

"Why?"

The man was nearly green, he was so pale. "His hand isn't the only thing he lost."

The doors opened and Sas hurried away.

"Your majesty." A woman took his place. "Your berth is this way, if you please."

Evi turned and found her personal staff waiting. She sighed, knowing well enough the scold she was in for once Fan had her alone. "Yes, thank you. See that my cabinet is situated to their comfort. Ur, Halt, I will speak with you shortly."

The two men saluted and left. Evi followed her staff to her new berth, considering.

EIGHT

Tin: Far Synchronous Orbit
F - 1879 - 17 - 19

Carl wheezed as he ran through the corridors. His lieutenant kept pace with him, as did a swarm of their staff and officers. Their boots made muted thunder as they rounded the last corner and burst into the hanger.

The place was in chaos. Admittedly, it was organized, purposeful chaos. Metal shrieked as mechanics started repairs. Shouts rose as soldiers forced open cockpits and dragged out the Tinese pilots inside. A ragged line of them stood in restraints, waiting to be led to the brig. He hoped he had enough cells for them all.

"Admiral! Here!" A technician waved from the airlock. Carl wove around the machinery, dodging deck hands hauling cooling lines until he stood next to her.

"You're sure it's his?" he asked.

"Yes, sir," Marks affirmed.

Under the noise and motion of the hectic room, a larger thump rattled the deck. The outer lock.

The airlock alarm chirped a warning as the successive doors between them and the hull opened and closed, moving the landing gantry into their atmosphere.

The alarm gave a final squawk and the inner door opened. The recovery system thrust a mangled knot of metal into the hanger. There wasn't even enough of the fighter left to stay in the cradle. It slid to the deck with a jarring thud.

Even the rebels quieted, shocked at the sight.

Marks recovered first. "Slip forty-seven. Careful, now!"

A crane arm swung overhead and gingerly gripped the blackened hull of the fighter. Hydraulics hissed, and the remains were lifted away and over to the nearest empty docking slip.

The crane technician placed it directly on the deck. The fighter's wings had been sheared off, the nose crushed in. The engines were gone. Only the cockpit had survived the crash. Barely.

Sparks flew as the mechanics cut into it. The metal and shield glass had melted together, any seam or hinge deformed beyond recovery.

Medics waited in a silent knot, their trauma unit ready to receive the pilot. Or the body. Carl wasn't sure what to hope for. This was even worse than he had imagined.

A hiss of acrid smoke announced the mechanics' success.

"Almost..." one muttered, hands nimble and delicate in his control gloves. The amplified movements of the grapplers carefully wedged into the gap.

A terrible sound of metal tearing and glass cracking. Then the medics surged forward, shoving mechanics out of the way. Carl couldn't see over them and he was pushed unceremoniously aside to make room for the gurney.

"Rotate it," his Chief Medical Officer snapped. "Toward me, ten degrees. Slowly..."

The crane eased the cockpit over. Something dark and gelatinous dripped to the deck. Carl did not think it was oil.

"I need this cut!" A saw shrieked to life. "And here! Ready? One... two... three!"

They heaved and the pilot's body came free of the wreck. Someone retched. Carl grimaced, the air bitter with the smell of hot metal and burnt flesh. Plastic, missile fuel. Blood.

Before he could see anything, the medics had the pilot on the gurney and were wheeling him away. One of them climbed onto the gurney itself and started chest compressions.

That didn't bode well.

The cockpit of the fighter sat hollow on the deck. Marks gingerly picked her way to the edge of it.

"Won't be able to salvage anything out of this."

Carl well believed it. The survival pod was barely intact, crushed at both ends. Jagged edges stabbed into where the pilot's body had been. They gleamed wetly in the lights.

"See if you can extract the crash box. The signal is still broadcasting. Maybe enough of it survived to get the flight records."

Marks nodded, poking at the mess with a spanner. "Looks like an FR-270. The Halford Plant used this style of cross brace. Sturdy."

"Lucky, that."

"Maybe."

The stark truth. Maybe the pilot wasn't lucky to be alive. Well, they should know soon enough.

Carl bent and tugged at a scrap of fabric crushed between what he guessed had been the glass of the forward screen and the belly of the cockpit. The glass had melted, dripping down the metal like rain, before it cooled in thick, ropy strands.

Marks found some sort of pry-bar and bent the struts apart enough for Carl to pull it free. He really hoped there were no body parts still in it.

Luck was with him. It was a part of the pilot's flight suit, but only a chunk of empty sleeve. Who knew what happened to the arm.

The Suit fabric was charred where it had ripped free. Wasn't Pickering Suit material able to maintain integrity up to four hundred and eighty-four degrees? Flakes of it broke off, leaving sooty marks on Carl's fingers and threads of Pickering fibers scraping his skin.

Marks swore under her breath. "A miracle, if they can save him."

"I want that crash box."

"Yes, sir."

If nothing else, it would tell him who needed to hear of this man's death.

"He's alive," was his C.M.O.'s bleak response. She sat slumped over, her head in her hands. "His cockpit maintained enough integrity to keep some pressure. His Suit compressed as designed, keeping most of him... together."

Carl eyed the blurry form in the incubation tank. There were more tubes and wires than human in there, it seemed to him.

"Likewise, his helmet functioned properly. Unbelievable, given the pressure and heat it was under. He must have burst out the other side of the ship or been kicked free when the engines broke containment. Whatever happened, his brain had enough oxygen and pressure to survive. Helps that he was cold when we got him; he'd been drifting long enough to shed any heat."

A soft alarm chimed and three medics ran to the tank.

"Your prognosis, Dr. Fenner?"

"We'll do our best, sir. When I say he's barely alive, I mean barely. If he lives through the next few hours, maybe he'll survive the night. After that... it depends on how fast we can regrow his organs. And how resilient he is to infection. His skin is gone, completely irradiated. All of his organs are in critical failure, if not crushed beyond function already. His legs—"

Carl cut her off. "I understand."

She sighed. "I'll keep you informed. Who is he, do you think?"

"Won't know until we get the crash box."

NINE

Parcae: Synchronous Orbit

F - 1884 - 4 - 8

Paulion ignored the curious looks of his crew. Only the most senior of them ventured a question about his swollen knuckles, which he deflected tersely. He hoped the frantic scramble of the hours following the Convene would settle any interest in his injury.

Unfortunately, nothing was more gossipy than a tightly knit crew under invasion by off-ship sailors. By turns elated at the honor done their Captain and exasperated by the bureaucratic nonsense now ruling their lives, they tightened ranks and whispered in corners.

There was little hope they wouldn't hear of the confrontation after the Convene. A knot of furious muttering confirmed his fear. Reading lips, Paulion was glad the Captain was with the General in the Munitions Bay.

"Ensign Rashevy," Paulion called brusquely, interrupting their tale-bearing. "Have the Hemings all been moved to the secondary hangar yet?"

Rashevy flinched guiltily. "Yes, sir."

"Then have the armorers begin inspection of the Galonese Suits. You will find a list of which of the fleet will be converted to troop transport on the Network."

"Yes, sir."

One of his comrades was bolder. "Sir? What other ships will be making up the Captain's fleet?"

"Does it matter, Esym?" Paulion asked, trying to sound disinterested.

"Yes," she said firmly. "It matters."

The Bridge, packed with three times the usual crewmen, grew quiet. It mattered a great deal to them. Their Captain mattered to them.

His second Lieutenant looked to him for guidance. Paulion spoke firmly, agreeing with their resentment but intolerant of anything that would discredit his command.

"No, gentlemen, it does not." Rebellion simmered from all sides. "The Captain expects you to comport yourselves professionally and courteously. No matter how others may behave in return."

The hypocrisy was glaring. He resisted hiding his aching hand behind his back. "We have a job to do. Is now the time for petty disagreements?"

But what the Captain's family had done to him wasn't 'petty.' Paulion knew several Budins, had spent time on Tin in Alam City. While he might think their honor code archaic, he understood what it meant to them. How it wove into every facet of their lives.

He wondered if Admiral Hyde had known the only way to keep Wood from killing himself was to force him to live for something after his family rejected him. Who had told him once he woken from incubation? How had he endured it, waiting all those years for Westerland to be completed? His years in Command School must have been torture, reminded every moment of his loss.

Paulion went on in a softer tone. "I understand your feelings. But, right now, the Captain needs us. The Empress needs us. All Volgar needs us. He is our best chance at surviving this, no matter what his people think of him."

"They aren't his people," Esym said fiercely. More mutters showed the crew was not appeased, not yet.

A year of scorn and gloating from their counterparts while they trained for service aboard Westerland. The past fourteen months with the dreg assignments, sneered at in every port they docked, Tinese and Caprician alike. Sas was ever grateful it had drawn the crew closer, rather than fracturing them into uselessness.

"You resent the slurs and snide remarks? Bored reading radiation fluctuations? Prove it. Show them what we can do. It's the only way they'll respect you or the Captain."

And now, hadn't they proved themselves? In virgin battle, against unknown assailants, hadn't they demonstrated their skill?

The tension in the room eased. Paulion allowed himself to relax, worried for a moment he had a real crisis on his hands. A rogue Sentient and crew? He shuddered to think of it. He put no stock in Westerland's good sense, not where his Captain was concerned. The Sentient was fierce in his devotion.

"Carry on, gentlemen."

Hand throbbing, he waited until they forgot themselves in their work. He gave the Bridge to Fush. "I'm going to get a few hours' sleep," he lied. He needed it, but doubted he could settle. "Call me if you need anything."

"Yes, sir."

From the Bridge, Paulion walked the short distance to the Captain's private quarters. Some consideration had been made for rank; the Captain had a suite of small rooms, rather than a narrow berth with an equally minuscule water closet. But even a Wake Class like Westerland was crammed to the girders with crewmen, cargo holds, munitions magazines, wiring, pneumatics.

There was no answer at the door. Paulion hesitated, glancing to ensure the corridor was clear.

"Westerland?"

"Yes, lieutenant?"

"I'd like to speak with the Captain."

"He does not wish to be disturbed."

Paulion sighed, scrubbing a hand across his face. He needed a shave. And ten hours of sleep. A month of shore leave. "I know. Just... I need to talk to him."

Westerland didn't respond for a long moment. *"He is with me."*

Paulion thanked the Sentient and started for the inner decks. He wasn't sure what he was going to say when he got there, but he had to do something. Explain, maybe. Ask for forgiveness. Face whatever punishment his Captain chose.

And hope he met Commodore Haetch one day in a service corridor, far from prying eyes.

Paulion took his time, forgoing the central lifts. He climbed a service ladder, ducked through a narrow opening into the Medical Bay. Past the Infirmary, the Dispensary.

He trailed his hand along the smooth wall panels, counting the seams between them. Seventeen between each bulkhead on this level. His path took him up the curving deck to the next service ladder.

A few more climbs, and he was able to jump lightly through the hatch. He touched the ceiling to keep his trajectory straight and landed with a soft thump of boots. It was dimmer here. The science wings and hydroponics, workstations that served little purpose during a time of war.

He enjoyed the quiet, the familiar comfort of Westerland's sounds and smells. He knew Westerland was watching him. Lights flickered to life ahead of him, sooner than the motion sensors would have activated. He smiled at the gesture.

A very different sentiment than when he first strode these decks. When he met Arsaces Wood for the first time.

Paulion had come at the summons of Rear-Admiral Stason. Before the crew had been shuttled up to board the nearly outfitted Sentient. These halls had been cold and dark, then.

He had met Stason outside the Bridge. Paulion admitted to both curiosity and a little trepidation. No matter Sentient technology was a hundred years old, the thought of some machine watching him, not only at work, but sleeping, eating, pissing?

"Lieutenant," Stason had greeted. His handshake faded, leaving Paulion gripping a limp palm.

"What is it, sir?"

Stason grimaced. "Look, I'm sorry about this."

Paulion dismissed the man's pity. "I want this, Kel."

"You're my friend, Paulion. If you need anything. Advice, a good word. A discrete transfer."

Paulion had spoken with stubborn bravado. "I am honored to be selected for this position, sir." And it should have been an honor. It was a steep step up in rank. He wondered if he was the only one to apply.

He could tell Stason didn't believe him. Paulion had hardly believed his own actions, watching with a distant sort of horror as he submitted a transfer request to the soon-to-be activated CIN-SH Westerland, Wake Class.

His ex-wife even called him by video. *"You cannot be serious, Paulion."*

"Three years, maybe four. Then a transfer. It's a Wake Class, an SH. You know what that means for my career."

"It means your career is over."

And standing on the Bridge that day, looking into Wood's blank eyes, he doubted his decision for the thousandth time.

"Paulion, is it?"

"Yes, sir."

"Please, call me Arsaces."

A strange, foreign name Paulion had no intention of ever using. "Yes, sir."

"Tell me about yourself."

There wasn't much. Born and raised in the Midlands. Twenty-two years in the Navy. A failed marriage, three children. He liked to play pickup *Chronos* with the other officers. They'd be happy to have the Captain join them, sir.

"You've looked over the roster." Wood turned and the forward screen lit up. As he spoke, the screen followed his words effortlessly, files opening and closing, reports moving. His fingers rested lightly on the edge of the console before him.

That was the moment Paulion fully realized what a Hybrid pairing meant. Sure, he'd been briefed about it, trained by the Architects for endless weeks.

But seeing the man surrounded by his Sentient, knowing that Wood knew, that he felt, everything about the ship. How many missiles in the magazine. The temperature of the engines. The very composition of the air they were breathing.

Paulion almost jumped when Wood turned to him.

"We'll make do as best we can. Of course, we can't expect much better. Not for me."

And suddenly the deadness of his eyes made sense. Because Wood was dead. Everything he stood for, everything he loved, was gone.

Paulion had had to clear his throat. "We will make you and Westerland proud, sir."

"I am sure you will perform admirably, lieutenant."

There didn't seem to be anything else to say. Paulion had saluted and left the man there. Stason waited at the Bridge doors, eyebrows raised, his look meaningful.

Paulion had glanced back, more unsettled than before. Wood stood with his head down, still touching the console gently. The screen glowed under his palm and the man smiled.

Paulion didn't see him smile again for seven months.

Up a final ladder and Paulion stepped out into a quarter CGS. Mostly machinery and electrical on this level. The floor hummed, the vibration of the cooling system endlessly striving to contain the molten fury of the engines beneath his feet. He glided down the narrow corridor until he reached the very heart of the ship.

The central hub of the CIN-SH Westerland was buried deep within the decks. The height of military and civilian technology, an artificial personality construct linked with a human brain to create the most advanced fighting machine the system had ever seen. The instant and nearly infinite computing power of the biologic computer and the unpredictability of a highly trained human mind.

The security doors opened for him, and he stepped inside.

Wood stood by the large dome in the center of the room. Not standing. Kneeling, with his cheek resting on the dark shield glass, his hands splayed across the flickering light within.

"What is it?" Wood asked quietly. "He says you're upset." Those swirling lights seemed to gather under his palms, pulsing.

Paulion shifted uncomfortably. It was strangely voyeuristic to see the man like this.

"Sir," he began. "I must apologize for my—"

"I understand."

"It was an egregious offense and—"

"I mean it, Sas. It doesn't matter." Wood sighed. "It doesn't matter."

Paulion hated when this despair consumed his Captain. It had been better recently. He smiled more, made jokes with the Bridge crew. Paulion had watched with grateful relief as the crewmen opened up to him, accepted him in all his awkwardness.

They had come to see his reserve was shyness and uncertainty. That Wood was not some savage aristocrat, but kind and fair. That he truly appreciated his crew and their efforts on his behalf.

Now? Now the pilots preened when their Captain joined them in the gymnasium for physical conditioning. Crewmen kicked their heels after shifts in hopes he would stay a moment and swap stories of youthful misadventures. Cadets fidgeted with delight when he patted their shoulders approvingly. More than once, Paulion 'lost' incident reports of inebriated crewmen defending their Captain's honor in port taverns.

There was no one to lose Paulion's 'Behavior, Unbecoming.' Maybe Westerland could corrupt it somehow. It happened on occasion.

The words burst out of him. "Sir, why did you do it?"

"My question, exactly." Wood stood smoothly, at ease in the low gravity. Before Paulion could draw away, Wood grabbed his wrist and turned his hand over.

"That's broken. Why haven't you been to Medical?"

"I'm fine."

Wood snorted. "Get it set at once. That's an order."

Paulion worked his hand free. "You never talk about it—"

"I said I don't know."

Paulion scowled and plowed on. "And I've never asked, sir. But now, with all that has transpired—"

"I don't *know*." Wood's growl surprised him. "You don't think I ask myself that same *ghar* question every *ghar* minute every *ghar* day?"

The dome glowed under Wood's hand. He took a choppy breath and his shoulders slumped. When he spoke, it was drawling and cold. "Any other impertinent questions, lieutenant?"

Paulion flinched. "Sir, please forgive—"

Wood swore again. "Don't. Just... don't." He put his face in his hands, looking as tired as Paulion felt as he pressed the heels of his palms into his eyes. "I'm sorry. You have a right to know. You've put up with me all this time." He managed a sort of half smile. Paulion looked away.

"I honestly can't explain it. I didn't do it for Caprice or the Empire. I wasn't looking for reward, glory, honor. I just knew... there was no way we could have... so many would have died... my family."

He dragged his hands back over his short hair, rubbing where the bulk of Hybrid Chip was implanted behind his right ear. "Hero of the Empire, they called me. A true son of Caprice—" Wood broke off, choked with bitterness.

Paulion cursed Wood's family yet again. The Jankovics were fools. What had they ever done to deserve a son like Arsaces? He had saved the Budin from annihilation. Did they think the Empire would let a single warrior live after the rebellion? And yet they rewarded him with isolation and shame.

And had the Emperor done any better? Given him Westerland, yes. But then what? Shunned him for his tainted colonial blood. Hastily pushed from public view, lest anyone learn how close to war they had come.

"Did you know, sir? About your mother?"

"No."

Paulion stepped to grip the man's shoulder. "I'm sorry, Arsaces."

"I know I'm a terrible commander, Paulion."

Paulion could only gape at him. "What?"

"I don't know why that fool girl wants me as Admiral. Maybe she hopes I'll get killed off, finally. But if we do survive this, I will recommend you for any command you want. You can take as many officers as want to follow you. I won't blame them. You don't deserve this."

Paulion couldn't stop his laugh. Wood glared at him as it grew from a chuckle to a roar. Paulion had to lean against the wall, his knees weak.

"Leave? Are you out of your mind?"

Wood flushed as Paulion wiped tears from his eyes.

"Captain, can't you see it? No one would go. The crew hardly requests leave for fear they'll be reassigned. I have cadets in fistfights over the simulator you reprogrammed. Fush's senior mechanic was in tears — tears, Wood! — because she couldn't get the aft lift operational, and she knew you use it to go to the Observation Deck after third muster."

"So, I'm a damned tyrant."

"Did they teach you nothing in Command School?"

Wood tried to hide in sarcasm. "Can't say I paid much attention. Labeled a pariah, shunned by my blood kin. I had other things on my mind."

"Well, time to buck up," Paulion snapped, employing the graphic, rhyming reprimand he saved for surly junior crewmen. Wood's mouth dropped open. Paulion plowed on belligerently.

"I also paid my time in Command School. Here's what's going to happen, Arsaces. You are going to be seen angry. Break something, throw something. Punch the next Tinny who insults you."

Wood's drawl could have sheared the rivets straight out of the bulkhead. "And why must I do this, lieutenant?"

"Because if you don't, your crew will do it for you. They have control of a Wake Class warship, a double complement of fighters, and eight hundred MI. The next Tinese ship we meet is going to get blasted out of the sky if they so much as look sideways at you. How do you think that would help our war effort? Or do you really think Westerland would stop them?"

Wood was gone in Westerland; he had that telltale vacancy, as if he was looking inward. Hopefully, the blasted Sentient was talking sense. Wood took a slow breath in.

"That is unacceptable behavior for *alam gabhen,* a child of my family's lineage."

"But you aren't Alam anymore, are you? You aren't Budin, you aren't Tinese. You aren't a Jankovic-Wood. They shunned you, struck your name from their records. You are nothing and you'll stay nothing unless you do something to prove them wrong.

"Why do you think we've spent the last ten months as a glorified cruise ship? The pinnacle of Caprician fighting technology collecting dust samples? You're an embarrassment, a diplomatic nightmare, who both sides wished had been killed when your Archer smeared you on your uncle's hull."

Arsaces wasn't hiding in Westerland now. Teeth clenched, cheeks flushed. The glint in his eye was murderous. Good.

Paulion stuck out his chin. "You are responsible for every woman and man on this ship. I'm telling you what you need to do to stop them ruining their lives for you. That's my job. Now, are you going to hit me or not?"

He opened his eyes and groaned. Apparently, yes, Wood was going to hit him. Wood stood over him, breathing hard through his teeth.

"You asked for it," he snarled, accent thick and guttural.

"Yes, I did," Paulion agreed weakly. He sat up carefully. The low gravity hadn't saved him from slamming his head against the wall. The laws of physics were the laws of physics. All actions of force result in equal reactions and all that.

"Stupid, baiting a man with artificial bones."

That was it. Paulion always forgot. Wood moved so easily, made no mention of his still healing injuries. Synthetic bones would stiffen under the pressure, just like the Suits, and increase the amount of force Wood could transfer down his arm into Paulion's face.

How far up did those implants go? Was his entire musculature reinforced? How many CGS could he take now he was half plastic?

"Get up," Wood clipped. "I want to hit you again."

Paulion dragged his legs under his torso and wobbled to his feet. One of his teeth was loose and his eye was already swelling shut. "You might kill me."

"I'm considering it, *jat*."

Paulion wheezed as he leaned against the wall. He certainly wasn't as young as he used to be. "It's a long way to an airlock to dispose of my body, sir. You'll have to go forward to 5-4. The one by bulkhead

13-10 is malfunctioning. I meant to put that in your morning report. I'm sorry, sir."

Silence stretched and then Wood started laughing. It was hysterical and grating, but Paulion smiled as Wood put his hands on his knees and laughed. Wood wiped his face on his sleeve and grinned broadly. Much of the desperation had eased from his face.

"Go to Medical, Paulion. Get your hand looked at and make sure I didn't rattle your skull too much."

Paulion stopped himself from cradling his aching head. "I am perfectly capable of returning—"

"Now. Or I'll set you scrubbing deck plates with the cadets."

"Yes, sir. Of course, sir."

"*Laomo sin*, Paulion. Get out."

Paulion left smirking.

* * *

The next watch muster, there was a moment of shocked silence as the Bridge crew looked between Paulion's swollen face and their Captain's bruised knuckles. Even with the healing boosters, it still took time for the marks to fade.

Halt fought a smile as he asked, "What happened, Sas? Run into a bulkhead?"

"Wasn't watching my step," Paulion agreed.

"I think every man does that at least once in his career."

"Indeed, sir."

TEN

No matter the panic gnawing at her, no matter the ceaseless work, it still took days to organize the remaining ships and crews. Evi fretted at every delay, up late into the artificial night aboard the Sentient, sending messages, reading reports. Cursing the handicapped Planetary Network as the malfunctioning servers and transmission lines were overwhelmed.

Thousands of satellites were destroyed or damaged. More fell out of orbit every day. She had an entire brigade of soldiers working just to get the system back up and running. Without it, she would be fighting half-blind.

Another division deployed with some of her few remaining warships to Shea. Ostentatiously to aide their recovery, but really to be ready in case the Syndates decided to band together against her. Shea had been attacked, but not nearly on the scale of Orbon. It helped that most of their holdings were deep under the surface, down in the mines Caprice could not afford to lose access to.

Taltua was reeling, begging resources Caprice did not have to spare. Only a moon had been attacked, with a Caprician military base, but still they wanted aide, soldiers, security.

Tin...

Evi sighed. You would think naming one of their kin Admiral would appease them, at least a little. Yet, what had she managed to do? Pick the one man they would kill on sight, if they could get away with it.

Carl would have laughed at her. "Never make decisions without all the facts, missy." He'd told her that over and over, as a child, in school, after she assumed her public duties.

Now, the Tinese officers balked at every request, tightening ranks and behaving more clannish than ever.

The Captain wasn't helping. Just yesterday, he'd ripped Major Byn apart for his recalcitrance, his tone coldly sneering, in front of all the senior leadership. Wood might as well have struck the man.

She would have rather that he had. Then they could have fought it out, appeased whatever stupid honor code they clung to, and she could have gotten six more ships for her fleet without argument. Well, with slightly less argument. They were Budins, after all.

She forced herself to look at the good news. The Reserve Fleet was intact and was being redistributed. Shea agreed to provide raw materials at a price that made Evi merely scream, rather than despair. Ulcacier reported four new warships ready to deploy. They might not have finished paneling nor were the crew accommodations installed, but they could fight. Comfort was not her priority.

Old ships were being reactivated. Civilian crews and merchant ships hastily readied for combat. Every possible military resource pulled into Caprician orbit for Captain Wood and his officers to dispose as well as they could.

Evi prayed it would be enough.

As she roamed the long curving corridors of Westerland's decks, she knew the crew, her cabinet, everyone, didn't think it would be. She caught whispers, frustrated outbursts. The ship, once as spacious as a star ship could be, was full to bursting.

The crew was double bunked to make room for the Mobile Infantry and Airmen necessary for the Flagship. The hanger decks had been reworked to cram as many Hemings into them as possible. Munitions, supplies, medical personnel, all packed into Westerland and the Fleet Battle Group's limited holds.

But it wasn't enough. Not enough food, not enough soldiers. How could they protect Caprice and her crippled infrastructure? Emergency supplies would be allocated as fairly as possible, but how would the Fleet get resupplied? Every available small craft was shifting through Orbon's ruins, searching for survivors.

How would they protect Tin, Taltua, Ulcacier, Roam?

The crews' worries did not stop there, of course. Who were these attackers? Where did they come from? Why had they come? Were they human? Another life form? Or even... Gol?

Evi refused to consider it and ruthlessly shoved the fear aside. Her Palm-Link followed, sliding across her worktable. She was allowing fear to dredge up nightmares, as if she didn't have enough problems as it was.

"Do you need a moment, your majesty?" Fan asked.

Evi tried not to cringe like a schoolgirl caught inattentive. "No."

The older woman eyed her reproachfully. Evi knew the look well. She had been subjected to it for years. Of course, she appreciated and admired her attendant. But it was hard to feel like a monarch when your childhood nanny chided you.

Not that Fan had ever held that position, not officially. But what was a young princess, sent to school on the other side of the planet, supposed to call the woman who ensured she ate well and attended classes and remembered her coat?

Carl found the woman amusing the first time they met, just minutes after the wedding was officiated.

"She's a married woman, now," he'd joked, but kindly, Evi could tell, even at fourteen. He added in a softer tone, "She'll be well looked after, I swear it."

Fan had not been impressed. "My duty is to see to the princess' comfort."

Evi had been young enough to make a face. Comfort, her eye. Fan was as dictatorial as her father, especially when it came to sweets or lessons.

Evi learned exactly how displeased Fan was later that evening, after Evi was supposed to be in bed. She slipped out of her strange room and explored the house. Her house, she supposed, as this new 'husband' would be leaving in just a few days.

She caught Fan's familiar tones and followed them to a wide room on the first floor. The sea air stirred the curtains. Odd, as most people used adaptive glass to control the natural lighting.

"... this situation intolerable," Fan was hissing. Evi, too, thought this whole arrangement horrid, and crept closer to better hear Admiral Hyde's response.

The man's voice was too low, a deep rumble. Risking discovery, Evi moved to the partially open door and peeked through the crack between the panel and the wall.

"He gave me no choice."

"She's fourteen. A *child*."

"I know." The man had looked exhausted, already stripped out of the dress uniform he'd worn to the ceremony. A private ceremony, with only him, Evi, and one of her brothers present. Her parents had been too busy.

Fan stood as straight and stiff as a pole. "I want your word, Admiral."

"On what?"

"That Evi will be safe."

Carl had looked bewildered. "Of course, she'll be safe. Do you think I let just anyone into my—"

"You know what I mean."

It took Evi about as long to puzzle that out as it did Carl. She blushed even as he shot to his feet and glowered at Fan.

"I would *never* do such a thing."

Fan's huff was not quite disbelieving, but definitely not appeased. "As you say, Admiral."

Carl looked as if he wanted to curse, and good manners forbade him. Evi was disappointed. She was sure, as a sailor, he knew some good ones she could share with her friends at school.

"Was there anything else?" he asked tightly.

"No. I will see you in the morning."

Carl only grunted and Fan had swept out. Evi hid behind a sculpture of some mythical beast, all tentacles and fangs. Once the hall was clear, she moved back to her spy hole.

The Admiral resumed his seat, his chin propped on his fist. Evi watched him a moment, wondering if she had the courage to speak with him yet.

"You might as well come in, missy."

Evi bit back an undignified squeak of surprise. She smoothed her pajamas and walked in head high.

Carl smiled at her. "Can't sleep?"

"The time difference."

"Makes sense." He watched her a moment. "I suppose you heard that, just now."

There was no use lying. Evi was quite good at it but didn't want to start her marriage that way. "Yes."

Carl did swear then, but it was one she already knew, unfortunately. "It's not you, miss Evi, who I object to."

She crossed to the chair next to his and folded her legs under her. "Fan doesn't like you."

"I get the feeling she doesn't like anyone."

Evi had laughed. "Yes, she's perpetually disappointed."

"In you?"

Evi shrugged.

"Are you disappointed?"

Evi shrugged again. "It was only a matter of time before my father chose my suitor. I'm just surprised he was in such a rush. And I wonder: why you?"

He seemed to be considering his answer. "Why do you say that?"

She ticked off the points on her fingers. "You're already an Admiral and proven yourself loyal. Your family already holds influential positions in the government, so I don't think you're just power-grabbing. Do you own some rare mineral deposit? Have insider intel on Syndate dealings?"

Carl's face had gone grim. But he spoke lightly enough. "No secret *rystinite* mine, I'm afraid."

"Oh, well, I suppose my allowance can support us, then."

He smiled at her joke, but it was weak and faded quickly. "Tell me, Evi. If you weren't a princess, what would you like to do with your life?"

She had been asked that question so many times. "Honestly, sir? I like being a princess. I like politics and sociology. I think it's interesting."

Carl stood and walked to the open window. Evi was eager to explore the grounds tomorrow, see what her new home had to offer. She thought the sea would be warm enough for swimming. So much better than the year she spent at Clere, the sun barely rising most months, everything she touched coated in ice.

"I cannot claim to understand your father's motives in forcing you to marry me."

Evi took offense at his wording. "I was not forced."

"No? Well, officially, neither was I."

Evi studied his form. Though he was forty years her senior, he seemed solidly built. Good muscle tone that seemed natural, hair just beginning to gray.

She respected that about him. One could tell when a person maintained their youthful physique by artificial means. He must exercise, work to keep his body healthy, rather than relying on healing boosters to prop up his genetics.

"If you find this so distasteful," she asked slowly, "why did you agree?" To her, this was just another political maneuver, a deal cemented with marriage contracts, rather than business ones. She found herself curious what he felt about it.

He sighed. "I have a cousin who controls a large portion of the shipping contracts between West Tan and Orbon."

Evi considered this. If this cousin was reluctant to fall in line with her father's plans, strengthening the relationship might sway him.

"Also, before I was promoted, a close friend of mine served in a sister ship in my battle group. He... got himself into some trouble. Court martial, discharged. He's serving a life sentence on Innsen."

Evi winced. Big trouble, then. Like murder someone important, but maybe you know something valuable so you can't be executed, trouble. "I see."

"Unfortunately, I think you do."

That didn't make sense. Carl came back to her and sat before taking her hand in his. His palm was rough; she was right about him exercising.

"I did not want this, Evi. But I will do my best to make you happy."

She frowned at him He had nothing to do with her happiness. He saw her confusion and laughed softly.

"Let's just say, I find your understanding of political intrigue frankly appalling."

Now she laughed. "Whatever for?"

"You're fourteen."

"Fifteen, this winter," she countered. She was always being mistaken for younger. No booster would make her grow faster and any reputable medical professional refused to do skeletal enhancement on a child still developing.

"My point, exactly. You shouldn't be attending schools meant for adults, shouldn't be considering trade deals, certainly not getting married to men who could be your grandfather."

She objected to this designation. "My father, maybe. You're not that old."

He chuckled. "Some days, I feel that old, little miss." He squeezed her fingers and leaned back. "I'm set to deploy in three days. I won't be back for cycles."

"I know."

"I can't take you with me, not on this mission."

Evi hadn't even known that was an option. She straightened, excited. "Can I on others?"

"We'll see."

She made a face and he tugged at her braid. "Depending on your marks in school, of course. And Mistress Fan's discretion."

Evi groaned. Hopeless, then. Fan would never agree to it. "You're my husband. You get to decide. Right?"

Carl had looked uneasy. "We both know this whole thing is a farce. Forgive me, but your father has used you to his own ends. Not that I'm much different," he added in a mutter.

Evi swallowed a twinge of anger. It wasn't as if she wasn't used to being shoved around the planet at her parents' whim. What made this any different?

"That being said, I vowed to care for you. And I will, as best I can. I've never been married and have no children of my own."

Evi was grateful for that. What if he had had adult children? Or an ex-wife? The media was already going to be in alt over this scandalous arrangement. She supposed whatever shipping deal her father would gain outweighed the bad press.

"I propose we have that sort of relationship. Father and daughter."

Evi drew back. Another paternal figure controlling her life? No, thank you. He must have seen her withdrawal.

"You already vetoed grandfather."

"Uncle, then," she countered. Her mother's parents were just as bad, always searching for some way to increase their power. All in the name of the Empire, of course. Her father's parents were long dead and Evi sometimes wondered just how that came about.

"Uncle." Carl smiled. "That I already know how to do. I have a whole mess of nieces and nephews."

"Do they live near here?"

"A few."

Hopefully she could avoid them all together. Relationships were complicated. Fan could be persuaded to help fill her schedule with 'necessary' activities, so she wouldn't have to meet them.

"Do you like your room?"

"Very much." It had a glorious view of the sea from wide windows, little alcoves and nooks for reading or watching media. Relatively close to the kitchens.

"Can you fly a transport craft?"

"I'm learning."

"I'll get you your own. Then you can explore the area. With security."

Evi rolled her eyes. "Yes, of course." As a child, she'd thought one of her security officers was her father, he was around so much. Embarrassing for all involved when her real father discovered her confusion. The guard had laughed it off. He still sent her presents on her birthday.

A clock chimed somewhere further in the dim room. "Bedtime, missy."

She sniffed. "An uncle wouldn't make me go to bed."

"You want me to rouse Mistress Fan?"

Evi scrambled to the door. "I'm going, I'm going!"

His laugh followed her up the stairs.

Now, she didn't have his reassuring presence to rely on. No video chats while he was in port, no letters about successes in school, no unexpected presents. Just memories and wishes.

Evi determinedly pushed back her regrets. They were not serving her now. And hiding in her tiny quarters was accomplishing nothing.

"Fan?"

"Yes, your majesty?" The woman was much the same all these years later. Maybe some new lines by her eyes.

"Is Captain Wood available?"

Fan consulted her Palm-Link. "The schedule has him on the Bridge with the other commanders, ma'am. Shall I alert him you wish a meeting?"

"No. I'll just go see him now."

"As you wish, ma'am."

Fan, along with Evi's ubiquitous security, trailed her through the maze of Westerland's corridors. Like she would get lost and stumble out of an airlock if they didn't herd her along.

She'd never admit it, but she did find the endless intersections confusing. But the bulkheads were clearly numbered, and everything was at right angles. If nothing else, you could just keep walking and end up back where you started.

But this time, she found the Bridge easily enough. She just had to follow the stream of sailors jogging along with their noses glued to their Palms. An equally dense parade came the opposite way, muttering in groups of two and three as they rushed to complete their tasks.

The Bridge was overcrowded, so Evi told her attendants to wait outside. She eased into the room, keeping back along the wall. It was the only odd shaped room on the ship, at least that she had seen. Rather than a square, it formed a hexagon, with the various consoles centered around the helm and the Captain's post.

Now, Wood stood to the side, leaning over a console, the screen lifted and turned flat so it formed a glowing table. He held a stylus in his hand as he spoke.

Evi hung back. They had had little to do with each other over the past few days, but if he saw her, he tended to go all stiff and formal and not say what he really meant.

He dragged a finger across the screen. "This, we think, was a part of the generator for the ring. It doesn't seem to be any sort of propulsion systems we've seen before. We estimate the energy needed to produce the levels of radiation detected on the order of—"

"—*fourteen thousand, seven hundred Tera-Jules.*" Westerland's flat voice spoke over his Captain. Evi wondered if Wood's 'we' meant him and Westerland?

"Much higher than we're capable of even from the most advanced plasma engine this size. It must be some sort of—"

"—*hybrid technology. Nothing like it is being researched inside our system.*"

"So, we must assume they are from outside our territories," Wood concluded. He wiped the screen clear. "Westerland has extrapolated a purpose for the ring."

"And?" Ur barked. "A weapon? That much energy could do a hundred times more damage than the warhead they hit Orbon with."

"How did they even get it here without triggering Skynet?" someone at the back asked, raising their voice over the murmurs. "The Inner Ring bodies are close together, considering, and full of traffic. The exo-system surveillance should have picked up a fleet of that size. How did they get so close without us knowing?"

A question that kept Evi up at nights, too. She'd dismissed her father's suspicions as just that, suspicions. Paranoia. But if these invaders had been watching them for years, planning their attack…

She stiffened as Wood looked up suddenly and met her eyes through the crowd. Had his Sentient alerted him to her presence? Meddlesome thing.

He held her eyes, his own dark and intense. "Perhaps this is not a weapon," he said slowly, still watching her.

"What else could it be?" Ur demanded.

Wood was asking her permission, she realized. She'd held him back at the Convene, not wanting to frighten them all. Now? Now, they had to to do whatever it took to survive. She steeled herself and nodded.

"Westerland and I believe this is a way for them to travel faster than the speed of light."

Half the room was stunned into speechlessness. The other half shouted questions. Wood ignored them, still holding her gaze.

Maybe he was a wise choice to lead after all. He didn't raise his voice, but when he spoke again, the Bridge went silent and listened.

"I know it should be impossible. But if it's not, we have to know. We have to build one."

ELEVEN

Orbital Patrol: Caprician Territory
F̄ - 1884 - 5 - 2

Since his announcement of Westerland's theory about the ring two weeks ago, Arsaces had gotten a total of four hours sleep.

\75.37. Don't be dramatic.\

Arsaces still yawned and rubbed his arm where a disapproving medic had jabbed him with his second ad-caff injection this morning. Was it morning, still?

\1332.\

He dragged his attention back to the technician talking at him.

"We need to set up a safe site to test this device," the man was saying. "Somewhere far enough that any explosion or radiation will not harm anyone."

Arsaces scowled at the form taking shape in one of Westerland's precious cargo bays. Where they had moved the cargo normally stored in here, he didn't know. Maybe they were stuffing things under crew bunks at this point.

Slowly, painfully, they were collecting pieces of the destroyed ring. Analyzing it, comparing it to the limited video feed they had captured. Piecing it back together as best they could.

Mining ships swept the orbital field, dumping holds of twisted metal scraps into the receiving bays of the other Fleet ships. Scientists sorted through the mess, taking samples and separating Caprician debris from that of the invaders.

Another ship of his new fleet had dismantled one of the alien fighter ships. Arsaces' Palm-Link chirped every few minutes as they reported their findings.

Arcing light flared from this new ring, his engineers and scientists crawling over it like ants, welding bits back together. Only a section of it, maybe thirty meters, just long enough to show the curving shape of it.

There was no way they could recreate the entire ring. They simply did not have the time nor the space, not to build something large enough to pass a ship the size of Westerland. Their best chance was to make their own, something functional and small.

The functional part was what kept Arsaces' up the very few hours he managed to lay in his bunk.

"You think the radiation produced will be harmful, then?"

Technician Grenfil shrugged, his face smeared with grease and soot. "Westerland's readings are confusing and mixed with the emissions of the other ship and our own weapons. There's a lot I haven't seen before, but don't know if there was some sort of interaction, some decay that we can't anticipate. Can our equipment even detect it?"

Arsaces patted the man's shoulder. "Keep at it. You're making good progress."

Grenfil grunted wearily and ignited his plasma cutter once more.

Westerland brushed over Arsaces thoughts, then faded back. The Sentient spent every moment running simulations, trying to find a way to make something impossible not impossible. They must figure it out, no matter their own understanding of physics.

Arsaces was not hopeful as he made slogging rounds through the ship, checking in with his officers, fielding questions to those who might actually know the answer.

The subject had been exhausted six centuries ago: going faster than the speed of light was impossible. The closer to the light barrier, the more a being's time slowed in relation to reality.

Plenty had tried to disprove this theoretical limit. And all experiments conducted to push an object past the light barrier had given null results. The ships simply disappeared.

Arsaces grimaced in memory. Every Flight School candidate, colonial or not, was required to demonstrate they understood the basic concepts of relativity. In order to be certified as a High Jump pilot, graduates were required to argue the point before a panel of physicists while they hammered you with increasingly technical questions.

Because any ship could achieve Jump speeds with enough fuel, time, and empty space. But the power of the plasma engines were only given to those who understood what they were messing with. How many people they could kill. And why not to try to do the impossible.

"And why is it impossible?" the stern voice of the chief examiner had called out, her eyes narrow and fierce.

Arsaces well remembered the thrill of terror as he stood alone in the center of the hangar. His fighter, the one he'd be given if he passed, sat to one side, taunting him. He'd cleared his throat and rambled out his well rehearsed answer.

"It is my conclusion that, once pushed past the light barrier, the object is removed from time."

"Explain."

"The Keiten experiments report that objects exceeding the light barrier disappeared. I posit they entered an alternate time stream, one they were unable to escape from, where there is no time at all."

"Your reasoning?"

"The closer to light speed an object approaches, the slower they experience reality, the difference as plotted per the Jediael Theorems." He had drawn the graceful, curving graphs on the large screen provided.

"If this could extend into the infinite, the distance between this line — the moving object — and the Jediael Limit, or the light barrier, would get closer and closer, until they aligned.

"It is my conclusion that if the object is pushed beyond the barrier—" He drew a sharp line over the edge of the graph. "—they would move out of time entirely. No time, no reality."

"How so?"

"An atom exists by the nature of its components moving through space, creating friction, energy, heat, polarity. We can only observe this because we ourselves share these characteristics."

"Your point, Officer Wood?"

"By passing the light barrier, an object enters a state where they have moved out of our ability to observe. Moving so slowly compared to our reality they cease to exist. An instant of their time for all of time for us."

"Eternity, you mean?"

Arsaces shrugged. "That is one word for it. Is Keiten's ship still moving, a fraction of a fraction of an instant into its voyage? The point is irrelevant, as we cannot interact with nor observe it. That would take time, which that ship does not experience."

Then the narrow-eyed woman had smiled. "As always, Officer Wood, you have done well. Now, prove it."

That had been the tortuous part. Working the equations without the aid of a computer took hours of tense concentration. They at least gave him a team of mathematicians who double-checked his work and kept it tidy for him. Otherwise, there would have been no way to keep the impossibly large and small numbers in his head, not without a Sentient occupying part of his brain.

\I am glad I am good for something, at least.\

Arsaces huffed a laugh. He could still feel the cool, slick shielding of his fighter's hull, not a check nor scuff. The perfect lines and curves of her.

She'd been a specially modified model, built for trans-atmospheric flight. Extra heat shielding, atmosphere engines on each side of the mini-plasma engines hugging her keel. Wings, allowing her to skip through pressure as effortlessly as she did vacuum.

The height of Caprician fighter technology, a mechanical marvel only given to a few select pilots: An Archer FR-270 class fighter.

Call sign: Archer 887.

He still mourned that little ship.

Now, he stood in his quarters and watched the screen built into the wall, as if to mimic a window. It showed the sky ahead of Westerland as they orbited Caprice. The bluish green of the upper atmosphere slipped by at the left edge, the dark velvet of space filling the rest.

His bed pulled at him. Surely no one would grudge him an hour's sleep. But even as fatigue crooned sweet seduction, he resisted. *She* was always there, whispering endlessly. Westerland was too busy to shield him.

As if he had summoned her, the soft, smooth tones of her voice rose over the noise of Westerland's computations.

You have been in incubation recovery for... \

Someone knocked. He hesitated, hating her voice crawling around his mind, but unable to face anymore reports or questions or complaints.

Westerland took the decision out of his hands. The door whisked open.

Arsaces groaned. *Why?*

\The queen.\

Maybe he could just ignore her. But then she'd come look for him and if there was one thing he wanted less than the relentless echo of a phantom woman in his bedroom, it was a real woman in his bedroom.

Westerland snickered.

She stood in the main room, looking at the painting on the wall. His youngest sister had painted it, before he left for Flight School. It had cost him thousands of Caprician *numis* to recover it from his quarters in Alam City. And no small amount of pride, dealing with that skulking, lying merchant captain.

"It's beautiful," the queen praised. "Your work?"

"My sister's."

"Truly lovely. Tin has such beautiful sunsets. All the solar wind, I think."

Arsaces' breath hitched. She knew. Had she before she chose...? Who told her?

"Do you miss your home, Captain?"

"Sometimes." Always."But, now..."

"Now, you have Westerland." She turned and smiled at him. Smiling? Not sneering, not disgusted? He hadn't lied to her, exactly, but wouldn't she think him...? Her father had. His own family had—

She sat before he could unscramble his thoughts. Belatedly, he muttered something polite and offered her a drink. Did he even have anything in here?

"No, thank you. I simply wished to check in with you. We haven't spoken recently; you have been so busy."

Had they 'spoken,' ever? Other than barking at each other and stilted formalities? He didn't think tense command briefings and muttered greetings when they passed in the corridors counted, either. "Doing as well as could be expected, I suppose."

"It is a thankless task, I know. How is Westerland faring?"

Arsaces laughed shortly. "He's preening, of course. The other Sentients defer to him, even though he's the youngest."

"Surely age doesn't matter to computers!"

"But seniority does, and rank, especially regarding the Captains."

"Do you go by the age of the Sentient? The Hybrid? The partnership?"

"All of that. If the Sentient has had more than one Captain, which engagements, which deployments. It's complicated. But the Sentients handle it and know exactly were everyone is supposed to be and why."

"And you were the least of them, I take it?"

He held back his flinch. "I am the youngest Hybrid, by far. Westerland is the newest Sentient."

They were never given the chance to fight, to prove themselves. He was a known traitor, even if for their benefit. Least of them, indeed.

"Vain creatures," the queen said fondly. "I suppose no creation of man would be complete without a vice or two."

"He has plenty, ma'am, I assure you." Arsaces smiled as she laughed. She had a nice laugh.

\She likes you.\

Arsaces stiffened. "What?"

The queen's head cocked over, eyebrows raised. Still smiling. He corrected himself hastily. "I mean, was there anything else, ma'am?"

Her smile faded. "Actually, I do have something I need to discuss."

Arsaces realized he was towering over her and it must be awkward. She was absurdly small, almost girlish. He thought it was the shape of her face, the slight snub of her nose. Her eyes were a sort of light brown, almost amber colored.

Now he was staring at her. Cursing himself, he sat across from her, feeling every kilogram of his weight against the spin. "Yes?"

She frowned into the space between them. "I am conflicted. I want to be on Caprice. There is so much work to be done. Fires still rage. The power plants are crippled. Shipping, medical supplies, food..."

Arsaces knew this too well. There were already reports of rioting in the larger cities as food stuffs became scarce.

She went on, "Yet, I am reluctant to be out of touch with you."

Arsaces did not understand and said so. "At most, we will be just past Parcae's sphere. It would take only minutes to dispatch—"

"I need you at the front. You and Westerland."

"But, your majesty—"

"Evi. Please, call me Evi."

He absolutely would not. "Your majesty, I cannot leave Caprice unprotected!"

"It won't be. There are more than enough—"

"I cannot have you a stationary target!" He didn't like the idea of her sitting helpless on the surface, vulnerable to any faction or mob that decided to do away with her.

"I agree. Which is why I must stay aboard when you deploy."

Arsaces stuttered with surprise. "W-what?"

"I knew you would object—"

"'Object?' Object is hardly the word for it!" He was on his feet again and his spine ached, his knees, every bit of him.

"Captain, please, sit. You are exhausted."

He was. Too much so to argue with this fool girl. "I will not allow it."

"Captain—"

"No."

"This is not your decision to make."

"Is this a direct order, ma'am?"

She had the nerve to be amused, to grin up at him, eyes glinting. "Would that induce you to obey?"

He paused. Would it?

\Of course not.\

"Not an order, Arsaces. A request."

"But if there is — if we come under fire—"

"Get some sleep. You look dead on your feet."

He wanted to growl at her, his frustration bubbling up wordlessly.

She stood and smoothed back her hair, coiled into a long, pale braid. "We will discuss this in the morning, when we're both fresher."

Do not panic. You are incapable of—\

He did growl, then, fed up with these women and their idiotic notions.

The queen was at the door. "Good night, Arsaces."

He glared at his sister's painting, somehow both too angry to sleep and so exhausted he wondered if this was a hallucination. Maybe this was all a nightmare, and the chit hadn't suggested he take his *queen* into battle.

You were a pilot.\

"Get out of my head!"

Immediately, Westerland was all around him, protecting him from the panic and guilt that threatened to devour him.

\You are *my* pilot.\

Arsaces leaned against the wall, pressing his hands to his eyes. His head throbbed, his joints ached, he was *so* tired.

I can't do this.

\You can.\

I can't lead them. I don't know what to do.

\You are not alone.\

His senses faded back, dulling, numb. Until there was nothing but Westerland.

\You are never alone. Sleep now.\

A soft pressure on his back. The bed. Westerland's subliminal commands settled over him and he was glad to surrender.

\Sleep, my Captain.\

TWELVE

Tin: Alam City, Alam-Jaheel
F - 1879 - 17 - 23

Carl despised weather. It was erratic at best, lethal at worst. Humid, malodorous, too hot, too cold. Give him a self-contained biosphere over any brilliant sunset.

Volgar was garish overhead, no doubt thanks to Tin's unstable atmosphere. If he remembered rightly from primary school, this planet's troposphere was thin and its ozone layer a wisp compared to Caprice's.

No matter it was the height of summer here, the air was cool on his skin. Even still, it was thick with the scent of strange, overly sweet flowers and the suffocating brine of the sea.

"Sir, shall we go?"

Carl grunted at his aide, a boy just out of Command School. Carl scoffed at himself. He was showing his age. Or perhaps merely his uneasiness. The young man had been sponsored as an aide-de-camp by some wealthy connection of his family.

Despite this nepotism, the officer was a good lad, smart, eager. He'd do well once Carl was done with him.

Carl stepped down from the transport, his hair ruffled by the slow spin of the blades. He stood a moment, bracing his knees. His head went light more and more these days.

A manicured path led from the landing pad to the house. It wound through the gardens, giving Carl time to admire them as he and Chino climbed the rise. The colors were wrong, but the sweeping ocean view gave him a pang for his own rarely used home.

Evi would be there, likely asleep, with Caprice and Tin out of orbital sync this time of year. How long since he'd last been to his estate? Six months? Nine?

The long walk also gave the house's occupants time to gather on the terrace. There was a crowd of them waiting as he mounted the last step. He paused to catch his breath, to observe for a moment.

Maybe two dozen in all, all dark-haired and eyed. An older woman stood at the front, flanked by her kin. Wood's mother, Carl guessed, from her graying hair and formal attire.

On her right would be Wood's immediate family. On the left, more distant relations, cousins, close family friends. A few pretty young women stood amongst them, their eyes heavy. Did one of them have a special reason to mourn?

Carved into the stone beneath their feet, finished in steel and gold, was the Jankovic family crest, framed by their motto in scrawling Budinese: *As the Earth, Our Blood, Our Spirit.*

Blasted Budins. Always stirring up trouble.

"Stay here, Chino," Carl told his aide quietly. The boy did not argue. In fact, looked relieved to be left behind. Carl empathized; he wanted to avoid this, too. But: his fleet, his ship, his battle. His responsibility.

Carl stopped before Wood's mother and bowed low. "I am Admiral Carl Hyde, commander of the Colonial Reserve Fleet, CIN Santos."

She gave him the slightest bow in return. "You are welcome." Her 'l's' and 'r's' rolled softly around him. He could find only traces of Wood in her features. The Airman must take after his father, dead three years now.

"I come with grave news, ma'am. Your son, Arsaces, was critically injured during the military engagement yesterday."

It was a paltry choice of words, but he could think of no other way to phrase it. Slaughter? Massacre?

"He is in incubation aboard my ship and cannot be moved. His condition is precarious. My medical team is not hopeful but are doing everything in our power to help him. I welcome you and your family to come aboard the Santos and see him."

Before it was too late.

She said nothing, made no motion, not even a flicker in her eyes.

Carl went on, determined to tell her, to tell someone, what the man had done, what he had saved them from.

"I must tell you he is one of the bravest men I have ever had the honor to know. He embodies everything good and noble I have come to know about the Budin, about the Jankovic bloodline. His heroic actions saved uncounted lives, soldiers, airmen, and civilians alike. You must be proud to have such a son."

The woman's tanned face had gone ashy, her mouth thin. When she spoke, her voice was like cold steel.

"I have no son Arsaces."

A shiver rippled over the family. Someone cried out, quickly stifled, leaving nothing but the wind and the silence.

Carl looked to them, seeking something, any modicum of mercy. Their stares were defiant, stricken. Many were in tears. But none made a protest.

Not even the children, boys who had to be Wood's brothers. They, too, stared up at Carl with guarded eyes. The youngest clutched a toy fighter to his chest, tears running over his cheeks.

Carl took a deep breath of the sweet, salty air. He bowed once more to the woman. Very soon, no one would bow to her. She was being stripped of rank, her property — this house and its grounds, among others — seized. Her family broken and imprisoned to prevent retaliation against the Empire.

There was nothing more he could do, nothing left to be said. Carl turned and marched back to his transport. Chino opened the door for him. Carl settled inside and drummed his fingers against the armrest as he waited for the boy to give his instructions to the pilot.

As they lifted off, Carl looked down on Wood's family still standing on the terrace, stiff and immovable.

THIRTEEN

Orbital Patrol: Caprician Territory
F - 1884 - 5 - 2

Well, Wood had taken her request to stay aboard about as well as she thought he would: appalled and furious. But, as disgruntled and surly tended to be his normal mien when they interacted, Evi supposed it hadn't been that bad.

Now, she had a seemingly endless queue of reports to read, messages to answer. Funding to dredge up from who knew where. Her Palm sat and chimed accusingly as she drummed her fingers on her makeshift desk.

Which of his fingers were artificial? That had to be the reason he counted them, over and over. Did he have some sort of implant dysmorphophobia? A psychological rejection of his regrown structures?

She still hadn't been able to access his locked files, no matter her new rank. The Network was still too damaged, only the most basic communications possible and barely enough bandwidth for even that.

Sas wouldn't tell her more, she sensed. He was too loyal, too protective. She did not want to ask one of the other commanders. Or any of his other officers. It would cast doubt on her choice, make it look like she was questioning her decision. Or that she had made the decision not knowing his history.

Which she had. But it had paid dividends. Her military was regrouping. She didn't look at the ship manifests and want to throw them against the wall any more. Satellites were being launched as fast as they could be assembled. A steady stream of transport ships carried supplies from the territories.

Speaking of which, there was a new message from Wen, one of Taltua's settlements along the Sun Sea. She really needed to deal with it. And get an answer to Antipus about refugee allocations. And sleep, somehow.

Instead, she stood and left her quarters. Fan was sleeping already, so another woman followed her, along with three marines. Mercifully, they gave her enough space. She didn't feel like they were breathing down her neck as she paced the corridors.

She turned for the central lifts. The pull on her body lessened as they moved through the inner decks. Strange, but not unwelcome. As a civilian, she had rarely been granted access to these decks of the vessels she had traveled in. No need, as they were full of technical equipment and infrastructure.

Evi hoped Wood was asleep as she palmed the doors to the Sentient Room. Her staff complained, but finally agreed to wait outside.

The room was plain, the same metal paneling as the rest of the ship, the same lights glowing from the ceiling. They strengthened, warm and restful to her weary eyes.

"Good evening, your majesty."

It had to be her imagination the voice came from the black dome before her. That each word sent a faint streak of lightning across the surface.

"Good evening, Westerland."

"How may I help you?"

Did Wood hear this even, precise tone? Or was it something richer, more unique?

"I would like to see something. The record of the battle above Tin, during the rebellion."

"You wish to know how my Captain won me."

Conceited creature. "Yes. Will you show me?"

There was a long pause. *"Do you have a concern regarding my Captain's qualifications? I believe his flight record and personnel file are available on the general Ship Network."*

And she nearly had them memorized. "Has he sealed the record? No matter, I will ask someone else."

She had taken two steps to the doors when Westerland stopped her. *"I have the records, ma'am."*

"I don't doubt you, Westerland. But I would never ask you to disobey your Captain. I'm sure one of the other Sentients could help me."

Was what Wood had said true? That the Sentients guarded their status jealously? If so, she suspected…

"I will show you, ma'am."

Oh, but that was sullen! No matter there was no change in his tone or cadence. Evi would be sullen, too, maneuvered into sharing such a private thing. She told herself it was for the good of the Empire.

A wall screen hummed to life. It showed the sloping hull of a warship, a camera array mounted on the outside of a naval vessel. Several others flew next to it. An opposing fleet was just moving beyond the moon, the planet below cloaked in darkness.

"Please describe."

"This video was taken from the CIN Santos. Your husband's ship, ma'am."

Well, that would teach her to pry into other people's secrets. Especially when she was so tired, her loneliness needed barely a nudge to well up.

The video was jerky, flipping between this camera and the satellites linked with the Caprician Network above Tin. The Colonial Fleet waited with weary superiority, their fighters hovering in position.

"The rebellion has two hundred fighters and three support ships. The largest holds the rebel command, Courtney Jankovic and his sons."

"Wood's cousins," Evi murmured as the last of the fighters, tiny twinkling lights, emerged from the rebel ships.

"Admiral Hyde has ten warships, with one thousand, five hundred fighters."

No chance for the rebels, if not for the code.

The newer, more agile Caprician fighters moved forward in a mass of glowing engines. Their colonial counterparts hung back, not leaving the shelter of their home ships.

Which one was Wood? Was he already planning what should have been his final act?

The Santos and the other ships fired, missiles arcing over their fighters toward the rebel ships.

"The signal is broadcast."

At once, the hundreds of deadly, glowing points winked out. They spattered against the rebel ships, ricocheting uselessly with their warheads deactivated. A few safety systems malfunctioned, but the damage was minimal, even against the older ships.

Now the rebel fighters attacked, all weapons firing as the loyalists regrouped. The Tinese rebels had only moments before the weapons were reprogrammed and their forces devastated.

How had the Budin gotten those codes? Could they have continued to disable more and more warheads? Could they have hacked into Skynet?

But not one.

A lone rebel fighter flipped over the mass of ships and arrowed back toward its home ship.

What had his uncle and cousins been thinking? When had they realized what he intended?

Evi jumped as static crackled into the silence. A man spoke in Budinese. *"Archer 887, answer Archer 887. 887, do you copy?"*

"I copy." It was Wood, his voice even and calm.

"Archer 887, no malfunction detected. Return to position. Do you copy?"

There was no answer. His decision had been made.

"887, you are on a projected collision course. Alter heading at once."

"Cannot comply."

A new voice broke into the radio noise. *"Ace, what are you doing?"*

"I'm sorry, Val." Some emotion, now. Maybe a break that wasn't interference.

"887, alter course or we will be forced to open fire."

"Ace, comply!"

He had, it looked like. The fighter spun gracefully, turning back for the fight.

"Ace, what game are you playing?"

But his fighter did not move back to the battle. It continued to spin, tumbling end over end.

Westerland spoke almost gently. "*A head over heel was the most effective technique he could use. Difficult to track by missile guidance, the most damage to a larger ship. The Budin faction had commandeered the Kapitsa transport ships. There is an area of weakness under the aft loading access. His fighter will hit this weak point and be deflected into the Bridge by the engine shielding.*"

The rebels were firing on him now. As Westerland noted, the missiles couldn't lock on as Wood spun crazily.

"*Archer 887, respond and comply.*"

"*Put him down!*"

"*Ace, stop this! Think of your mother!*"

"*887! Alter course!*"

"*Ace! Pull up! Ace, please—!*"

Evi clenched her fists as his fighter slammed into the largest rebel ship. The missiles followed, silent impacts that tightened her chest. A flash: Wood's plasma engines breaking containment, bathing them in lethal radiation, melting through the ship.

The bow of the ship erupted, glass and metal spewing across the stars. The engines sputtered. The ship lurched and collided with its sister, flying fast in tight formation. Both ships broke apart.

"Enough." She did not need to see the rest, to see Wood's comrades, his friends and family, slaughtered by her husband's forces. The screen froze, then faded out.

"*A stellar example of strategy and skill.*" Westerland praised. She had to agree. Brutal, efficient. Minimal loss of life.

"*Luckily, his cockpit maintained integrity, though he leaked atmosphere for several hours before he was tracked down in the debris field. Admiral Hyde insisted they account for every crash-box from both fleets.*"

Evi swallowed a thick throat. "How did he survive?"

"*A near thing, ma'am.*" Westerland displayed the medical images. She was too astonished to be squeamish at his horrific injuries.

His Flight Suit seemed to have held him together, but even that hadn't withstood the crushing force of the impact. His face was blue from oxygen deprivation and red from plasma burns, streaked across his angular features in the pattern of the fractured shield glass.

The list of injuries was daunting. Shattered bones, traumatic amputations. Massive internal and external hemorrhage. Pulmonary and cardiac contusions, intracranial bleeding.

"He was very brave."

Was there a hint of smugness in the Sentient's tone? *"I have analyzed these recordings many times. He executed his intentions perfectly. The rebel leadership was killed instantly. The signal immediately ceased and allowed the Colonial Fleet to gain control over the battle with minimal casualties. No civilians were injured. War was averted. You made an excellent choice for your Admiral, your majesty."*

Of course, the Sentient would think so, as hadn't she also chosen it? Him? "Do you like it when he pilots you? As he did over Caprice?"

"Yes. I have learned much from observing his techniques."

"Such as the dead spin."

"Arsaces does not believe in dead spins," Westerland countered. *"He says that with the limitless power of the plasma engines, there is no trajectory which cannot be corrected in free-fall."*

The little she knew of astronavigation balked at the statement. "He must be a genius."

"He is. His assessments showed his spatial reasoning in the 'untestable' range. His neural-somatic pathways are 27% faster than mean. Though my computing averages in microseconds, he seems almost to predict what will happen and adapt accordingly. It is nearly instinctive, yet how can a human have an instinct for something not of their evolutionary make-up? I wish there was a way for you to observe his neural pathways. It is a fascinating study."

Evi watched the swirling lights in the dome beneath her hand. "And he was given your command as reward for his actions?"

"He was implanted while in incubation aboard your husband's ship. I was still in the planning phase. Hyde and others who had witnessed the event

submitted a request to have Arsaces linked to me."

Why hadn't Carl told her? She'd known he was there. He'd spoken of the failed rebellion during his final days, but never of Wood nor the consequences. "What was it like?"

"I do not understand, ma'am."

The glass was warm beneath her fingers. Not hot, like machinery, but as if whatever was inside was alive. "When you were activated. What was it like when you felt him?"

"I have no basis to compare to, your majesty. Arsaces was there. He is always there. He is my Captain."

The Sentient was upset. Evi soothed him, definitely a him, though why she could not say. "I did not mean to alarm you, Westerland."

"There is no alarm, ma'am. Your attendant, Ja Fan, is seeking you, ma'am." He had retreated behind his programming again, all precise courtesy.

Evi sighed. She had been here much too long. She thanked the Sentient and crossed to the doors. Before unlocking them, she paused.

"Westerland?"

"Yes, your majesty?"

"If he doesn't ask, please don't tell him you showed me."

"Why?"

"I know he wouldn't like it."

The Sentient mulled this over. *"Why do you not order me not to tell him?"*

She smiled. "Because I think you would disobey. I am learning you and he are much alike."

As she left, she was sure Westerland was laughing.

FOURTEEN

Orbital Patrol: Caprician Territory
F - 1884 - 5 - 7

Arsaces had let the vibrations of his ship lull him into a doze when a shrieking alarm jolted him awake.

"Incoming transmission, sir!"

Arsaces straightened in his chair and blinked to focus on the main screen.

"Heming 27-44, home-ship Valiant. Westerland, do you copy?"

Ensign Took answered almost before the pilot's voice cut out. "We copy, Heming 27-44. Report."

The radio ping traced back to an empty sector between Ulcacier and Roam.

"Get Sas. And Ur and Halt." Arsaces ordered, restless in the time it took their broadcast to reach the pilot and receive a reply. There had to be a better way, but they were still limited by the physics they understood. They were no closer to completing that *ghar* prototype.

"Another ring, sir. Just like above Caprice."

The screen split, one side showing the helmet of a pilot, his face-shield tinted dark with the cockpit lights reflected on the glass. The other was a long-distance video of another of those rings with one, maybe two, ships hovering next to it.

They were slim to his eyes, not fighting ships. Transport or security for the ring?

"Came out of Jump and took up position here. I moved back beyond Y-279 so as not to scare them off."

"Well done, 27-44. Observe and report. Do not engage. Turn and run if needed. We are Jumping to you. Maintain contact with your sweep ship. Do you copy?"

Another eon of silence, then: *"I copy."*

Sas was already at his side, buckling up his Jump Suit, Ur and Halt not far behind. "Who will you send, sir?"

\It has to be us,\ Westerland said. Arsaces could already feel the engines turning in his chest as they readied for Jump. \I have to see a ring in action again. We need to capture it.\

Arsaces cursed but knew it to be true. "Prepare for Jump. Whoever of the Fleet can be ready in time comes with. The rest stay here. Redistribute per protocol. Third Fleet, get on the other side of Volgar. Go with them, Halt."

Halt met his eyes a moment, a question in them. Then he nodded and left at a run. Sas grimaced with understanding. If the worst happened, they would need someone left to take command, some reserves to stage their last stand.

The preparations for Jump took only minutes. Ones that gnawed at Arsaces. He sat tense, trying not to bark with impatience.

\She's here.\

He turned and found the queen holding her helmet under her arm. They never had gotten around to discussing her 'request' again. Now, curse her, it was too late. He suspected she had done that on purpose.

\89% probability.\

He jammed on his own helmet and pointed curtly at the chair next to his. The deck was shuddering, his chest aflame, and he couldn't wait any longer.

"Prepare for Emergency Jump!" *Tell me Halt is away.*

\Yes. Every crewman is in a Suit.\

Good enough for me. Lock the Fleet together. Can you manage?

\Really, Arsaces? It's just Jump.\

"Ready, sir."

Give me everything you've got, Westerland. "Firing! In three... two... one..."

Arsaces gasped as the engines shoved him sideways. The display flickered, their speed leaping forward.

Steady now.

\I am functioning well within parameters.\

I need these engines functional when we get there.

\Says the man who melted my starboard maneuvering thrusters into shapeless lumps pulling out of a dead spin.\

That was an emergency.

\And this isn't?\

He closed his eyes and focused on breathing.

Westerland's voice sounded distant when he spoke again. *"Approaching flip."* Maybe it was a lack of oxygen. More likely, Arsaces had fallen asleep. Depressing that his best rest came during a brutal Jump into a battle.

"Three... two... one... Flip." There were an awful few seconds, then they settled into braking.

\I'm stopping engines.\

Why? Arsaces demanded.

\Save us time. I want that ring intact.\

Instant weightlessness made him gag.

"What are you doing?" the queen snapped breathlessly.

"Delaying brake."

"You'll get us all killed!"

"I wanted you to stay behind."

"You'll exceed the Suits!"

\Unlikely. 17%.\

"Westerland has it under control."

The Sentient cut off her retort. *"Approaching target. Prepare for Full Brake."*

"Crew, brace!"

He had time to squeeze his eyes shut before something heavy and inescapable crushed him down.

Westerland dragged him out of his pressure daze. It was still too much to shake his head to clear it, but he spoke over the hiss of air in his helmet.

"Fleet, report!"

His ships checked in.

"In formation, sir." Sas confirmed.

"Heming 44-27, do you copy?"

No radio delay, now. *"I see your flare, Captain."*

"Any change in the ring?"

"No, sir. They haven't moved — wait!"

\I told you we needed to hurry.\

Arsaces didn't try to fight the pressure, just sat limp and watched the impossible unfold.

The ring glowed, the same flare streaming behind it. Slightly off center, so he could see the empty space beyond.

Something came out of it. Just appeared, jutting forward. The nose of a ship, moving into their space from who knew where. It slipped free and the flash of its engines was lost among the stars.

"Track it!" Arsaces ordered. Only five CGS, now, and slowing every moment. "Fighters, deploy!"

The command echoed from the other ships of the fleet. A second ship was already moving out of the ring. It turned toward them.

"Evasive action!"

Westerland lurched as the ship accelerated for them, ripping by faster than the external cameras could follow.

And *another* ship. "Shut that thing down!"

His fighters were trying. The two transport ships were firing on them, the ring itself adding to the barrage. The fighter screen flickered as it reported the damage, then destruction, of the Hemings. Red icons spread like a cancer. They were losing this and quickly.

"Deploy an EM net."

"We're too close!"

"Do it!" This third ship was larger than the others, bristling with menace. "Fighters get out of range!"

The Hemings scattered as the EM net shot forward. Five synchronized drones, widening into a pentagon. Then another, and another, one from each of his ships. The enemy ship was half through the ring and already firing on them.

"Do it now!"

"Three seconds!"

"EM pulse charged!"

"Fire!"

The EM nets detonated, pitiful sparks against the inferno of the battle. But effective. Some of his fighters were affected, too close to the disruptive wave of energy.

\The only way,\ Westerland assured him. \We could not win this engagement.\

"It worked!"

The flare behind the ring flickered, showing the distant stars again. The ring's guns stopped. It sputtered once, twice, and died.

The enemy ship pitched forward, sliced cleanly in half, its engines left behind wherever it had come from.

\That takes care of that threat.\

"Sir, I'm reading some sort of energy surge—"

Westerland shuddered. The screens went white, their signals scrambled.

\Self-destruct!\

Had they been too close? He didn't feel any damage, but if Westerland's sensors had been overwhelmed...

\You'd be writhing on the floor. No damage.\

"Fleet? Come in!"

The radio crackled ominously, the sound of emptiness.

"Fleet, do you copy?"

"Here, sir!"

"No damage, sir. Scrambled our communications."

One by one his ships reported in. Arsaces took his first deep breath since they left Caprice as the Bridge screens corrected. The ring still hung in space, but the enemy ships were gone.

"Cowards," Ur growled. *"My men are ready to secure the device."*

"Go. We'll cover you. Sas, contact Second Fleet. I want our patrols doubled in this quadrant. And find those other two ships!"

Soon the all clear was given; no active enemy combatants. Moments later, his ship was emptying of every technician, engineer, and mechanic as they swarmed over to the ring.

Arsaces undid his helmet and wiped sweat from his face.

How did we win, before? he asked.

\We took them by surprise.\

And? Arsaces asked, sensing there was more.

\They have to get a ring to their target initially. If they have to Jump each ring further ahead, then the ships carrying the rings are older than the ships coming out. Even cruising at Jump speeds would take years. Those ships were more advanced than the fleet we faced above Caprice.\

So, there's no telling how powerful they are.

\Or they thought we would be an easy target and sent lesser ships at first.\

"Captain?"

Arsaces pulled himself together. "Sas, get the fighters affected by the EM blast back to berths. I want Tactics analyzing this battle, flight patterns, weapons, everything. See if they can triangulate which constellation cluster these attacks are centering from. Get Forensics on that Heming's radio recordings. I want their language."

Sas hurried away, looking as overwhelmed as Arsaces felt.

Westerland, did you pick up any of their radio chatter? I want one of the other Sentients working on —

A light touch on his arm made him jump. He glanced up to the queen and smothered his annoyance. Fool girl. And fool him, for underestimating her. Again.

"Well done, Captain."

He shook his head. "This is going to get worse."

Her brows lowered. "How so?"

"Those ships were more powerful than the others. We beat them at Caprice through surprise and sheer luck. We got here in time to stop this fleet from coming through. When they come for real, we won't be able to stop them."

"We must do our best."

"I will, your majesty," he vowed fervently. "But I don't think it will be enough."

Inexplicably, she smiled. "I'm not afraid, Captain."

It was stupid not to be afraid. "Why not?"

"I have you."

He gaped as she unbuckled her Suit collar and motioned for her staff to follow her off the Bridge.

\I told you she likes you.\

"Not now!" Arsaces snarled. The noise faltered, glances skittering to him. He waved irritably for them to ignore him.

A shout of triumph rose.

"What is it?"

"That second ship jumped straight into Sky-Marshall!" the ensign crowed. "Caught them in an EM net before they could blow themselves up!"

A lucky break, finally.

Westerland scoffed. \There is no such thing as luck. Only beneficial probability.\

I'll take what I can get. "Get me Ur."

A moment and the general answered. *"Yes, Captain?"*

"Enemy ship captured by Second Fleet."

"Go, sir. I have this."

"I'm leaving the Valiant and the Mesai."

"Understood."

"That device lights up, I want you to get out of there."

"I copy."

Arsaces held back his reprimand. 'I copy' and 'will do' were very different responses.

\As you well know.\

"Sas, inform Halt we will be there once Westerland is cleared for Jump."

\I am within parameters.\

My crew isn't, not after that blast.

\Humans. They're so… squishy.\

Arsaces snorted. *We can't all be half plastic.*

\You are only 23.6% plastic matrices.\

Thanks for the—

\16.2% poly-carbonate siliconized Rugger's plastine.\

I thought that was plastic—

\And 14.8%—\

So, like I said. 50% plastic.

Westerland response was the machine equivalent of a condescending smile. \54.6. Rounding is for statisticians and dullards.\

Which means I'm only 45.4% human.

\Which is why I love you so much.\

Westerland's mental caress was smug. Arsaces shook his head, exasperated and fond, and turned to the mass of officers waiting for his direction.

FIFTEEN

"Absolutely not."

The queen glared up at him and he glared back. Her eyes were narrowed, face flushed. His own skin flamed, the fire in his chest kindling down his arms and legs.

Her voice felt oddly cold in comparison. "There is no reason I shouldn't accompany you—"

"No," he snapped, chopping off her protest with a slash of his hand.

"You will bring them to me, anyway."

"That's completely different!"

"After you have secured the ship—"

"I will *not* allow it! You've already manipulated me into bringing you this far! "

She took a jerking step back. "I did not!"

"I have risked your safety enough! From now on, you will do as I say."

She pressed her lips together and made some attempt at speaking in a calmer tone. "Once the ship is secured, there is no reason I could not—"

Arsaces jabbed a finger at the glowing screen in his quarters. "That ship is a dangerous piece of unknown enemy military technology. I am not going to let my queen anywhere near it!"

She scowled at the smooth oval of the enemy ship, lying dormant under continuous EM pulses.

He went on gruffly. "I only have so much time before they run out of whatever atmosphere they need. I don't have time to waste arguing with you. You will stay here. You will follow my orders. I am your Admiral, *houkun ni,* and you will listen to me!"

She drew herself up. "And I am your Empress. These barbarians killed my people. They slaughtered them, Arsaces, without warning or provocation. I will look them in the eye and demand *why.*"

"And if it's a trap? If they capture or kill you? What of your people then? With no other Tolmi alive? You want to risk reviving the Stratocracy? There'll be no choice, under siege and the dynasty broken. You think your people would have any chance? And for what? *Intzerra atu bhonda?*"

She flinched like he had struck her. He clenched his teeth, realizing what he'd said.

A spoiled little princess?

The harsh Budinese hung heavy between them. But he wouldn't apologize, not while she was behaving like such a... He took a slow breath, controlling his temper and his accent, both roughened by his anger.

"You must see why I cannot allow—"

"Get out."

He ignored her command. "I want your word you will stay aboard Westerland."

"That *was* an order, Captain."

"Your word," he insisted. "Or I will have you locked in the brig."

"You tried that once before," she taunted.

"I wasn't Fleet Admiral, then," he shot back. "Or didn't Hyde teach you the War Protocols?"

All at once, the angry flush of her face blanched, leaving even her lips pale. The Network chimed into the taut silence.

"Captain?"

There was nothing professional in his snarled, "What is it?"

"We are ready, sir."

"I'll be there shortly."

The queen had turned away, hugging herself. Her shoulders moved jerkily. Was she crying?

\No.\

Arsaces dragged a hand through his hair and tried to sound reasonable. "Evi, please, I cannot risk—"

She spoke evenly. "I will not leave Westerland until you have returned and given me permission, barring any necessary emergency action for the preservation of the senior leadership."

Arsaces winced at the direct quote of the protocol giving him ultimate decisional power during a time of war.

"Thank you," he managed. He left without looking back.

* * *

Westerland stayed quiet as Arsaces stormed down the passages, trying to work out some of his fury before he got to the hangar.

\Why are you upset?\

That fool girl!

\The Empress?\

Ha!

He passed the lifts and opened a ladder hatch. The rungs made satisfying thuds as he climbed down.

\What does she matter?\

Are you seriously asking me this?

\I'd rather she went than you.\

Are you insane?

\She is replaceable. You are not.\

You will do anything *to ensure her safety, do you understand? You will leave me here and Jump to Caprice at the slightest sign of danger.*

Westerland didn't answer. Arsaces snarled all the curses he'd been holding back in front of Evi.

\Your catecholamines are elevated. Your blood pressure has spiked and your heart-rate—\

Arsaces' boots slammed to the deck. *It's called anger, Westerland.*

\I don't like it.\

Too bad!

\You never get this angry.\

Next time, you try reasoning with the chit!

\You need to stop or your Suit will reject you for flight.\

I can't just stop myself from being angry.

\I can.\

What's that supposed to—

Arsaces staggered, going down on his knees, then hands. He drew shuddering breaths, stomach heaving.

\Not quite right,\ Westerland said, echoing distantly. Arsaces shook his head, ears ringing. His heart stuttered, an uneven tattoo in his chest.

\It is more complicated than anticipated.\

Arsaces sat back and wiped his face on his sleeve. It came away damp. *What did you do?*

\I attempted to suppress your sympathetic response in tandem with a release of serotonin and dopamine.\

He got to his feet and leaned into the wall of the corridor, still light-headed. *Don't do it again!*

\Of course not. It was ineffective. You are still exhibiting signs of emotional distress.\

Arsaces took a moment to cool his temper on his own. He did appreciate Westerland's emotional protection. Maybe too much, sometimes.

It's my brain and my anger. I'm allowed to feel it.

\I don't like it when you're angry.\

I'll be fine.

\She makes you angry a lot.\

Arsaces ignored this. His skin prickled as his sweat dried in the cool air, heart still hammering. Straightening, he finished the walk to the hangar.

The MI were loaded into their shuttles and ready for launch. Arsaces stepped into a Flight Suit and did up the buckles with clumsy fingers.

What's wrong with me?

\Your body metabolizing the excess adrenaline.\

Arsaces sealed his helmet. *Any other side effects I should know about?*

\Your heart rate will slow in the next few minutes. You will feel extremely sleepy. You must stay focused.\

I'm about to enter a hostile alien ship. I think I can stay alert if needed.

\Now is not the time for sarcasm.\

Sas' voice crackled in the speaker. *"We're in position, sir."*

Arsaces climbed into the small transport craft, packed with Marines in their dull black Battle Suits. He gave the hand signal for 'prepare to launch,' and they signed acknowledgment back.

"Ready, Sas."

"Fighter escort away." The floor rumbled as the catapults threw the fighters into space.

Arsaces switched to the main channel. "Gentlemen, that ship is full of hostiles. I want each of you to come home safe. Be careful and don't take risks. Stick together. Stay alert."

He switched to all-receiving in time to catch their massed rumble of assent.

\You mean, like the risk you're taking?\

Arsaces initiated the launch sequence. *You think I am about to sit here and do* nothing...

"Last EM below threshold. Safe for approach."

Arsaces moved the transport into position. The catapult made one crushing heave, and they raced through the airlocks. They fell into weightlessness and joined the mass of fighters moving toward the enemy ship.

Arsaces flexed his hands around the controls. He missed piloting something this small. It was cumbersome and slow to respond, but it was something he controlled, that responded to his command. He had so loved flying.

The hum of the engine, the darkness, eased the rest of his anger. His skin was tingling again, his limbs now warm and relaxed.

\The adrenaline high fading. The prolactin metabolizing. Stay awake.\

He blinked hard. His arms didn't want to respond, as sluggish as the shuttle's pathetic thrusters. His soldiers' massed breathing made a soothing rush in his ear.

\Think of something that makes you upset. Break out of the high.\

Even his thoughts felt slurred. *I thought you wanted me calm.*

\I lied. She was crying.\

Arsaces muttered a curse. Stupid chit, risking her life, the entire damned system, so she could play space explorer. That he was doing the same thing, that he even cared about this *jushnik* Tolmi daughter's opinion, blood enemy of his family, infuriated him.

\That's better. I'm upping your pressure.\

Arsaces spluttered as cold air blasted his face. "Okay, enough!" he gasped, and the air eased back. His eyes watered and there was no way to wipe them.

"Approaching landing target."

"Copy, Sas." Arsaces carefully wheeled, following the other transports as they skimmed along the hull.

\That large window, there.\

Arsaces fought the ungainly craft and settled against the burnished plating of the alien ship. A tingle moved through him as the electromagnets in the landing gear locked onto the hull. He opened his radio channel.

"Ready to disembark."

"Yes, sir." It was Lieutenant Frei, harnessed onto the bench behind him.

Arsaces grimaced. He hadn't apologized to the man for barking at him on the Bridge all those days — weeks? — ago. It felt like ages.

One of the marines opened the back hatch and the faint atmosphere they'd trapped inside hissed away, leaving a muffled kind of silence.

Arsaces could really hear his heart now, thumping away in this chest. And though they said it was impossible, he could tell which of the thuds were the plastic ones, the artificial valves and chambers slowly merging with his own tissue as he healed.

The same as the implants in his arms and legs, his ribs and vertebrae, his liver, kidneys, all his damaged organs. Ten or fifteen more years, Dr. Orjean had guessed at his last physical exam, until the matrices were fully integrated. But always there, hidden, leering at him.

\You'll be 76.3% human, then. I'll still love you.\

"Ready, sir."

Arsaces leveraged out of his seat and pulled himself to the hatch. He gripped the edge of the opening and swung his feet under him. His own magnets activated, locking him to the hull.

His Marines surrounded him, vac-guns readied. The sleek, black weapons shot a bolt of charged electrons, one of the few practical weapons in space. Though only effective over short distances, they did well enough to short-circuit a Suit. Or a human heart.

They had mechanical and chemical-driven bullet guns, but the second wouldn't work in space and the first caused more problems than they solved outside a ship.

Would the vac-guns be effective against these aliens? Were they human? The few species found by the original colonists to the Volgar system were primitive and not noteworthy. Some bacteria and one barely evolved aquatic invertebrate.

These creatures were obviously sophisticated. Advanced propulsion systems, some sort of energy weapon. Those blasted rings.

Human maybe, just aggressive, piratical. Arsaces growled. They'd learn their mistake invading his system.

\Your steroid levels remain high. Don't be reckless.\

MI waited, shifting restlessly. Technicians were already cutting through the hull. The molten metal glowed sullen against the darkness.

A shudder rolled through the hull of the ship. A rectangle of metal peeled away, forced back by the atmosphere inside.

Did these aliens have mechanical or powered locks? Only fools left their atmosphere to computers.

Arsaces pushed through the others and leaned over the opening. Pressure shoved back and he fought to keep his feet. Across the room inside, a heavy door slammed down. The rush of air lessened, then died.

"Mechanical locks, Captain," said a voice he didn't recognize.

\Sub Lieutenant Jeri, 7th Brigade.\

"Proceed?"

"Have at it."

The soldiers knelt and swung themselves over the edge. Fighters hovered above them, keeping watch for signs of life within the ship.

Arsaces followed, flipping until he was oriented to the floor before attaching again. It was the wall to his eyes, by the position of the panels on the walls.

Artificial gravity, then? Somehow disrupted by the EM pulses? How did they manage it?

"Captain, it's a waste of time to cut through every bulwark this way."

"Agreed. Set up a temporary lock."

"Yes, sir."

It took only minutes, but every second grated on Arsaces' nerves. What kind of defense were they mobilizing? Why had no one come to stop them? What manpower did they have? What ambush were they walking into?

"Seal is good, sir."

"Take us in, Jeri."

Nothing waited for them in the corridor outside their entry point. The edges of the newly cut door were still hissing as soldiers flowed through, breaking off to run in both directions.

Arsaces followed. It was dark, the only light the glare of the soldiers' helmet lights. The soldiers moved with long strides, magnetism turned down so they could run and jump easily, using the lack of gravity to their advantage.

While hand-to-hand combat was rare outside atmosphere, these MI trained relentlessly for it. Caprice controlled dozens of large extra-atmosphere colonies, asteroid mines, who knew how many ports.

The Galonese Battle Suits were frightening beasts, every motion accentuated, assisted jumps under gravity. In free-fall, they were terrifying. They could attack from any direction, fly short distances, and generally obliterate everything in their path.

Even if you managed to damage the power packs — Arsaces' best strategy against them — they could still function. The magnets were held off while the Suit was powered. Cut that and the soldier within would latch onto the nearest metal surface — basically every surface on a spaceship — and proceed to rip you to pieces with his figurative bare hands.

"This level is clear, Captain."

"Keep going. Capture, don't kill unless necessary."

"Understood." Jeri swept around a corner with a squad of his men.

Arsaces ran a gloved hand along the wall. His Suit registered the temperature: seven degrees. The air was a breathable mix of oxygen and nitrogen, a little helium, trace xenon. The corridors were about the same size and shape as Westerland's. Likewise, the doorways were the height of a man.

\Humanoid, then.\

Some other human colony? It had been over fifteen-hundred years since the Capricians first landed. The planet was aptly named, a chance taken by their ancestors, no return or rescue if they failed.

\It must be. No other humanoid life forms are known to exist.\

Arsaces gripped the butt of his vac-gun, the darkness suddenly menacing. *Only those we made ourselves.*

\Impossible.\ Westerland fumed a moment and corrected himself. \Improbable. 0.002%.\

Arsaces shivered, not only from unease. His heating units powered on. Why was it so cold? The heat of the engines should keep a ship this size warm for days. Westerland's problem was shedding heat, not retaining it.

To distract himself from his fears, he switched to the general network, tying into Jeri's communications. He listened with half an ear as he followed cautiously in the soldiers' wake.

"Second level, clear... Vernom, check that door... some sort of lift, not functioning... lift doors breached, cutting ceiling... ascending... on next level... orientation still on the x... advancing..."

Arsaces paused by an MI cutting through a door. "Still no power?"

"None, sir."

"Just cut this one. Leave the others."

"Sir?"

"We can't get in; they can't get out."

"Yes, sir."

The door was thinner than the hull and was breached in moments. MI filed in.

"Looks like storage. Crates along the walls."

"Captain! Captain, come look!"

"Where are you, Jeri?"

"Up three levels from insertion deck."

Arsaces cut his magnets and skimmed along the passage ceiling above the soldiers' heads. He helped a marine stop before kicking off the top of the frozen lift. He caught Jeri's hand as the man leaned into the shaft.

"What did you find?"

Jeri touched helmets, overriding the radio. "Not sure, sir."

"Life forms?"

"Not exactly… "

Arsaces pulled himself into the corridor. "Show me."

Jeri led him to a hole cut through a wall, scorch marks along the edges. *"Heartbeats, sir. But there's no one there."*

More of those containers, long and sleek. Markings covered the sides. Pictographs and swirling symbols. Their language?

\Confirmed. Sensors detecting heartbeats in that room. And along the entire floor.\

Show me.

His face-shield tinted, and a schematic of the ship glowed against the darkness. It looked to be somewhere between a Glenfil and a Tin class, smaller than Westerland, who was a powerful Wake class.

How many heartbeats?

\At least twenty-five.\

Arsaces frowned at the room. It was empty, but for those boxes. Clearly not a barracks.

He walked to the nearest one, a large rectangular box set in a recess in the wall. It slid out on railed supports. His fingers were thicker than normal in his Suit, but still dexterous. He worked the latches on the box, ignoring Westerland's warning of caution.

\So much for observing.\

The latches finally came free, stiff from disuse. Arsaces gripped the lid and pushed it up.

"*Olu sed*—!" He scrambled back, staggering as his feet stayed attached to the deck.

"*What is it?*" Jeri demanded. Soldiers and marines bunched around them, weapons trained on the box.

Arsaces swallowed bile. *You getting this, Westerland?*

\Yes.\

Arsaces edged back to the box, the lid swaying as it reached the range of its hinges and slowly drifted back down. He caught the edge and pushed it wide.

Inside was a second container, made of a clear, glass-like material. Lights flashed over where a man's heart would be. Whatever was within was partially obscured, the glass mercifully fogged.

Arsaces forced himself to look at the creature's face. Jeri's breathing was harsh in his ear as the soldier came to look down at the alien being.

"*Human, sir?*"

Westerland spoke firmly. "*Yes, Lieutenant.*"

"*Then what is all that... metal? A cyborg?*"

"*It appears to be some sort of exoskeletal enhancement. I will need a sample. Bring one back.*"

"No!" Arsaces and Jeri shouted together.

"*I cannot work without data. It may be cosmetic or functional. Open another and compare.*"

Arsaces obeyed and moved to the next container. He opened it and shuddered.

\See?\ **Westerland said dispassionately.** \Their features are dissimilar and there are notable differences in the construction of the metallic enhancements. They are not artificial beings.\

But Arsaces could see Jeri's eyes, two wide orbs behind the lights of his helmet display. Could see the fear, the sudden uncertainty that mirrored his own.

\They are *not* Gol.\

They never found —

\They were eradicated when Iheath was destroyed.\

They were so much stronger than us. Some could have—

\You are allowing fear to override your reason.\

My grandfather still had nightmares.

\I know.\ Westerland's voice was a whisper, humming with the woman's beneath Arsaces' thoughts. \And I know yours.\

"Sir? What do we do?"

Arsaces shut the lid and latched it gratefully. "How many of these things are there, Westerland?"

"If the flashing light indicates a heartbeat, I estimate several thousand such humanoids in the — Motion detected outside security perimeter."

Arsaces' display shifted, an icon hovering over a point some six decks above them.

"At least two, maybe more."

"Capture them, Jeri."

"Yes, sir! Second, follow me!"

* * *

Arsaces fretted, waiting safely away from the action. Westerland, Frei, and Jeri had all protested hotly. Reluctantly, he had obeyed. His soldiers' radio chatter was a symphony of voices as he watched their progress on his video feed.

"Passage secure... quick, stay low... mark that door... cutters... give me a hand up... clear... narrows here... approaching target... ready weapons..."

The MI skimmed down the corridor, the magnets giving them the advantage of friction to use their powered Suits while weightlessness carried each stride further than a man could jump.

Two soldiers knelt and laid a thin line of explosive along the edge of a door.

"Take cover... on my mark...fire!"

A flash of white. Soldiers streaked through the opening, weapons ready. Four aliens waited inside, firing what looked like pulses of energy at the attacking MI. The MI scattered, jumping up the walls, returning fire.

Two of the aliens fell back, their blood hanging in fat, glistening drops. No vac-guns, those, but mechanical bullet rounds tearing through flesh.

The MI cornered the others, running along the ceiling, dropping behind them. Soon the only sound was panting men and the grunts of the aliens trying to break free. A dose of sedative to the neck and the prisoners slumped.

Just men. No metal sticking out of their skulls.

"Westerland, any others?" Jeri asked.

"None detected."

"Get these to transport. Four, seven, eight, I want an accurate count of every one of those boxes. Search every room, deck by deck. Tear this place apart."

SIXTEEN

Y13-7 Neutral Territory

F̄ - 1884 - 5 - 10

Arsaces leaned back in his chair and drummed his fingers on the table. Not his usual tic to remind himself which fingers were real, but quickly, to show his impatience. His linguist shot him a pained look.

"A few more minutes," she assured him.

He grunted and shifted his glare to his prisoners.

The two of them sat strapped to their chairs at the other end of the room. They were limp, resting on the restraints. After a night and half a day of screaming, they had finally quieted enough for the marines to dispose them for questioning.

One shifted, his Jump Suit creaking as the fabric flexed around him. He lifted his head, the glass of the helmet reflecting the bright lights. Arsaces stared back until the man looked away. The other kept his head down, his shoulders slumped.

Arsaces' biologists were working frantically to design a vaccine to allow these aliens to live in Volgar space and prevent their microbes from infecting the crew. Didn't they know the dangers of entering an unknown system? Thousands of years must have passed since their ancestors diverged. Pathogens tended to follow evolutionary archetypes, but after millions of generations, who knew what ionized mutations had proliferated? It was a stupid risk to their people, let alone an army.

He clenched his fist on the tabletop. That was what was on that ship. An army, forced into some kind of stasis and left to sleep while the ship carried them to the next battle. An army of unknown abilities and motives.

More of his scientists were trying to figure out how to open one of the stasis pods without killing the occupant. Without knowing the mechanism, what anesthesia was used, trying to reverse it could harm the alien.

Arsaces hoped he would not regret this gesture of humanity.

Three of the sleek glass pods showed on his Palm-Link's screen. They had been brought back to Westerland for observation and study. With them, the scientists had managed to learn some facts about the beings.

Just looking at them made his skin crawl. Those crude implants were more than metal stabbed through their skin. There was circuitry, processors, wires along their bones, twisting inside them.

\Brainless, bio-electric relays,\ **Westerland insisted.** \Similar to your ocular implants. Or even the Hybrid Chip. Nothing more.\

How can we be sure? **Arsaces asked.**

\Simple induction. The Gol sought perfection. These beings are variable and clearly not peak physical specimens. The superficial artificial structures seem to hold no purpose and—\

"Got it!" Malel slid her Palm-Link across the table. "This should do for simple exchanges, Captain."

"How does it work?"

"Type and it will translate. Good thinking, holding them together. They talked a lot. Lots of data. Clevvet's algorithms are thorough." The linguist smiled at Clevvet's Captain, a thin man of middle age. He gave a short nod, then his eyes lost focus and his lips moved silently. Talking to his Sentient. Arsaces was glad to see he wasn't the only one to do that.

\Focus.\

Arsaces called up the keypad and typed: *I am Fleet Admiral Arsaces Jankovic-Wood.*

The Palm hesitated, then spoke slowly, drawling out his name with nasal vowels. The aliens' heads snapped up, eyes wide behind their face-shields.

"You are in the Volgar system aboard my ship, the Caprician Interplanetary Sentient-Hybrid Navel Vessel Westerland, under the command of Her Majesty Evi Tolmi-Andris Hyde, of the Tolmi Dynasty, Queen of Caprice and Empress of the Inner-Ring Colonies."

\That's a mouthful,\ Westerland muttered, as always irrepressible.

Arsaces hissed at him to be quiet and watched the shocked expressions of his prisoners. Did they understand? Did they have this sort of technology, advanced cultural statistic computational models?

Like microbes, languages followed basic patterns, built of a handful of common structures. By analyzing these men's speech, the Capricians had a good chance of getting their point across.

"Try another variant, Captain."

Arsaces drew a finger across the screen. He couldn't hear a difference, but Malel nodded thoughtfully.

One of the men said something low and harsh. The Palm translated. *"Bucket."*

A chuckle from one of the officers. The alien scowled.

Arsaces typed again: *We have disabled your ship. Your men are unharmed and still in stasis. What is your intention in our territory?*

The one who had spoken straightened. Arsaces marked him as the superior of the two, the other one looking more to him than at the Capricians. *"No words."*

Halt grinned. "Won't say? Guess we can assume they're not friendly."

The queen spoke for the first time. Her voice was quiet and harsh. "I'm sure sixty-seven million Capricians would agree with you, Sky-Marshal."

Halt stiffened, then bowed from his chair, murmuring an apology. Arsaces wondered if his frown conveyed his disapproval to her or if she would ignore it just as she did all his other warnings. Her expression didn't flicker. He wondered, too, if she was still angry at him for that snide comment.

\She's been speaking with Caprice.\

Of course. By now they must have an estimate of the deaths caused by these aliens' attack, the extent of the destruction. How many more would die from famine alone before this was over? Disease from contaminated drinking water? Radiation poisoning?

\She understands the consequences; she is taking necessary steps.\

Arsaces turned back to the aliens.

"Where are you from? What do you call yourselves?"

\Useless questions. What they call themselves has no bearing on what we would call them.\

The alien straightened and spoke loudly. The Palm flashed, different translations scrolling down the screen. Arsaces stopped one with a stiff finger: *Vanguard.*

\That doesn't sound good, does it?\

"What is the purpose of the rings?"

Now the alien snorted. *"Moronic,"* the Palm said. Arsaces tamped down his anger.

His Chief Tactician, Major Ili, spoke with cool disdain. "We can then surmise this is common technology for them. Something they have used for some time, longer than a few generations. These two likely don't know the specifics of how it works, just how to operate the devices."

"Habitual invaders?" Ur mused. "Empire builders or simply raiders? Once they leave, taking the rings, there could be no retaliation."

"Unless a ring fell into enemy hands, which is why they try so hard to destroy them," Ili agreed. "Common, then, and easily made. Indicating a complex industrial and scientific community."

"With men to spare," Halt added grimly.

Ili continued, "They aren't refugees; no children or dependents. They would have overwhelmed us in one wave. I say they are feeling us out, testing us. Preparing to invade and conquer. Their self-destruction points to a victory or death mentality. Officer Sulovin, your thoughts?"

"Agreed." The psychologist tapped his Palm-Link thoughtfully. "Look at their posture. Arrogant, contemptuous. They likely pride themselves on their willingness to die in battle. They might expect torture, even welcome it."

The reactions to this were mixed. Most found this blatantly repulsive. A few looked thoughtful.

Sas' voice had a hard edge to it. "They already practice body mutilation. What could we do that was worse?"

Westerland had ideas and Arsaces shoved them away in disgust.

Sulovin smiled a little. "I suggest we feed them, vaccinate them, but treat them like they are nothing. We must plant the seed that we find them harmless. An irritation. They will try to escape, maybe even try to force us to kill them. Keep a tight watch."

Arsaces examined these aliens again, trying to think like they would. At the moment, their thoughts were obvious. The curl of their mouths, the tilt of their heads. Contempt was an emotion he had no difficulty reading, not anymore.

He met their eyes evenly and their haughty stares faltered.

\They know you are in command,\ **Westerland said smugly.** \How the others talk to you, how they treat you. Psychology is fun.\

"You will be returned to the brig. A vaccine is being developed. We will keep your ship dormant, your men unharmed. You will be questioned at a later time."

"Take them out," Arsaces added aloud after the Palm finished. His marines stepped forward and dragged the prisoners to their feet. They started shouting, muffled behind the helmets. The Palm scrambled to translate. Arsaces shut it off.

"We're done here. I want that vaccine ready and our supply modified for their biome as soon as the cultures allow. I want a full report on that ship and is functionality before morning."

"I need their computing system," a science officer said quickly. "If we're to have any chance of operating a ring, we need to understand their coding, the processor structure, the—"

"Tell Sas what you need and get a team on board at once. Tow the ship to the Empty Orbit, along with that ring."

"Yes, sir."

SEVENTEEN

Y13-7 Neutral Territory
F - 1884 - 5 - 10

It was all Evi could do not to run from that horrid briefing. As it was, she walked stiffly back to her quarters, snapped for her attendants to leave her be, and took a scalding shower.

She knew it was impossible, but she could not shake a feeling of filth. Not just these murderers bringing their pathogens into Volgar space. Their very presence, their effrontery and callous disregard for the lives of her people, made her skin crawl.

Sixty-seven million. Sixty-seven million women and children, fathers and brothers. All dead because some alien race felt it their right to take what was hers.

Even after her skin was smarting and pink, she huddled in her bed and shivered. She stifled her sobs into her pillow, lest Fan hear and come to check on her. Not even the familiar comfort of her arms could help this ache.

Carl's teasing voice tried to coax her out of her misery.

Queens don't cry. His smile had been so warm, so accepting, no matter it had been millions of kilometers away.

Queens think. Queens decide. Queens act. Be a queen.

It had been five years, but still she missed him. Missed all that they could have been. Grateful for what they had been able to have, no matter they had been forced into a distasteful union.

He had grown to be the father she never had, a brother, a friend. She had hoped for more, but then it was too late. She would give anything, all the money in her treasury, the crown destroyed with her people, anything, to have him here now, to hear his voice.

"Queens don't cry," she whispered to his memory. "Unless they're lonely and afraid and don't know what to do."

And what could she do? They didn't know how to work the rings. They didn't know how to find these invaders. They couldn't speak to them, couldn't beat them in combat.

She couldn't even help her people. Her senators and council members all agreed she was safer away from Caprice. They saw the danger, just as Captain Wood had. If she died, her people were doomed. Her own arguments forced her to remain where she was. Useless, a figurehead only.

"Your majesty?"

Evi hid her blotchy cheeks under the blankets.

Fan persisted. "Your majesty, Dr. Orjean is requesting a brief word."

Evi spoke muffled from under the blankets. "Who?"

"Dr. Orjean is Westerland's Chief Medical Officer, ma'am."

Evi crawled out of bed and allowed Fan to make her presentable. The woman clucked over her swollen eyes and gently applied a cool cloth to them before she brushed Evi's hair.

Dr. Orjean was apologetic when she finally came to him. "I am sorry to disturb you, ma'am." He spoke quickly, with a crisp north Ilaeni accent.

"No matter," she assured him. She had only been sniveling in her room like a child. "How may I help you?"

But now that he had her, he seemed not to know how to go on. "May... may I speak with you? Privately?"

Fan withdrew without being asked. Dr. Orjean glanced to the wall.

"Westerland?"

"*Yes, ma'am?*"

"I require complete privacy."

"*Understood, ma'am.*"

Now completely baffled, she gestured for Orjean to sit across from her. "I am at your disposal, doctor."

He still hesitated, then spoke obliquely. "I have been with the crew since induction, even before the Sentient was activated. Nearly two years, now.

It hasn't been easy. You may have heard what they say about him. About his past. But the Captain is a good man."

The entire crew did this, speaking of Wood by his title, never his name. She began to suspect it was from respect, even affection, rather than dislike.

"I, too, consider him a man of character." Stubborn and dictatorial, but honorable, she supposed. Very like other Budins she had met.

"I want it clear, ma'am, that I have never suspected anything amiss, either from his behavior or his medical profile."

"Amiss?" Evi repeated blankly.

Orjean handed her a Palm. The graphs and numbers on it were illegible to her. He explained.

"Every crewman is routinely screened for general wellness, as well as the usual travel protocols."

Evi knew this, of course. She hardly thought of the strictly enforced testing at each port dock, every airlock entry. A print scan and a barely felt finger prick. Ubiquitous and essential for safe interplanetary travel.

Orjean's accent grew thicker as his distress increased. "Ma'am, I don't know what this is. I've never seen this level of activated undifferentiated cells in a human subject. The enzymatic activity is beyond our testing sensitivities. The steroids alone should have crippled him. I just don't see how this is possible."

"I'm not sure what you're implying, doctor. Is this something pathological?"

He ran a hand over his balding head. "I fear... well, I fear the Captain is a booster addict."

Once Evi parsed through her shock, she realized it was mostly disbelief. She spoke with firm conviction. "Captain Wood has his faults. I cannot believe chemical dependence is not one of them."

"But how else could he get levels like this? This is long-term abuse, a physical tolerance that is frankly astonishing."

"What about his previous tests? Wouldn't you have seen something on those?"

"All normal."

"Then this is an error." The system had less than a thousandth of a percent error margin. A mistake was virtually impossible. But how many millions of tests were performed each day? How many impossible things had happened since Caprice fell?

"That was my first conclusion, ma'am. Then I saw the time stamp."

Evi knew the day well. "The day we landed on Caprice for the Convene."

"Yes, ma'am. We just received the results. With the Planetary Network crippled, those tests were just processed and transmitted today."

If the Planetary Network was damaged, the Imperial vessels couldn't access the data stored on it. Evi had grappled with that problem herself. The delayed pathology screens would be processed in the order they had been received and the results sent back to their origin ships. A usually seconds-long process delayed by the damage to Caprice's infrastructure.

The explanation for the variance was simple: Arsaces had a chemical dependence of some kind and Westerland had been hiding it by intercepting and falsifying his tests.

Evi dared not speak her hypothesis aloud. How could one be sure a Sentient followed orders?

She transferred the files to her own Palm, safely protected from Westerland by her coding. She hoped. Then she deleted the original.

"I have full confidence in my Admiral," she said firmly. "Thank you for bringing this to my attention. I will handle it."

Orjean took back his palm with shaking fingers. "Yes, ma'am."

"Tell me, have you any other concerns for the Captain's well-being?"

"Physically? No, ma'am. His implants are healing as expected. There is no sign of rejection or malfunction of the synthetic organs. His physical conditioning is excellent. Psychologically?"

Orjean once again glanced to the wall. "I am glad he has Westerland. He and time will do what they can."

Evi nodded dismissal and the man left. She stared at the graphs, considering the implications.

Arsaces using stem-boosters? She didn't want to believe it, but...

Stem-boosters forced the body to heal, to rapidly build new cells. Some people experienced a feeling of intense well-being for the next few hours. It was described as being filled with energy or euphoria as the body healed in a fraction of the time of nature. Occasionally people became addicted.

Boosters were commonly prescribed after traumatic injury to prevent scar tissue formation or deformity. Such defects would be corrected once healing was complete, but it was better to avoid them entirely. Even after correction, the mental and social stigma could be devastating.

But boosters were tightly regulated. They would ravage the body if not given the raw materials necessary to build new organic matter. They had to be carefully programmed, so as not to replicate mistakes and cause further disfigurement.

Arsaces could have become addicted after his initial incubation. But Evi couldn't make that fit with what she had observed aboard his ship. The man had to be reminded to eat most shifts. Sas hovered over him like a mother *chimar* with only one kit, urging survival rations on him under the table at meetings.

Could it simply be a natural reaction to his injuries? Had enough of him been damaged to cause his genetic coding to falter?

Evi had done some discreet research after speaking to Westerland that night. No one in the system had ever been as extensively repaired as Arsaces. There were dozens of research studies on his situation and some focused on the ethics of such a thing.

Did he even feel human still? With so much of him regrown and rein-forced? It could explain much of his reticence. Already set apart for his choices and culture, the very artificiality of his own body must be damning. Carl had balked at regrowing a heart valve; what was Arsaces' heart made of?

Evi sat in silence for a long time, trying to sort through the tumult of emotions and thoughts churning in her.

"Westerland, are you there?"

"Shall I return to normal function, your majesty?"

Evi had to smile at the Sentient's peevish tone. "Yes, thank you."

"I trust nothing is amiss?"

"Don't worry, Westerland. Everything is going to be fine."

Everything would be fine. She added another layer of security to the report and locked it deep in her files.

She would have to find a way to broach the subject with him. Dread settled in her stomach. She knew well enough he did not trust her, especially after their argument.

And she had manipulated him. For the good of her people, but still. Now, to bring up his disgrace, his damage, and then accuse him of misconduct?

She sighed and summoned Fan.

EIGHTEEN

Empty Orbit
F - 1884 - 5 - 12

Gilroy yawned before he could stop himself. He glanced to his superior, but Master Ven was bent over a console and not paying him any attention.

He gave himself a shake and reminded himself it was worth standing a double shift to have had second watch off at the same time as Ensign Ria Rico. He hastily smoothed his smile before Ven noticed.

Ven had not liked that Gilroy had traded duty schedules. She liked everything exactly as she had arranged it. While it was perfectly acceptable for Gilroy to switch around watches for personal matters — on occasion — Ven considered it slovenly.

"The Captain wouldn't like it," she warned whenever her Shipmen disrupted her carefully ordered division. Then she'd glare, the battle-ax, until they squirmed and apologized for even thinking to cause a minor disturbance in the smooth workings of the CIN-SH Westerland.

As if the Captain had nothing better to do than care about duty schedules among the lowest ranks of his ship. But Gilroy still forbore mentioning that, as Fleet Admiral, the man had slightly more important things to worry about. Master Ven was not a woman who appreciated sarcasm.

Gilroy gave the woman another glance to ensure she was still absorbed in her work and leaned against the wall. The panels vibrated slightly under his shoulder blades. No hiccups from maneuvering, no surges as power shifted to the science wings.

He liked standing fourth watch, usually. The ship was quiet this time of night, no patrols or checks. Just monitoring equipment and chatting with his friends.

Unfortunately, Master Ven liked to rotate to all shifts to 'show comradery.' Not that she was a bad sort. She was fair, if a bit rigid. And she pulled her weight. Gilroy had heard stories from his friends on other ships, of incompetent officers and infighting among the divisions.

He supposed anyone like that had washed out long before launch. You didn't take a post aboard this particular ship unless you really wanted it. Or had no other choice.

He gave his head another shake to ward off sleep. Only six more hours. Crewmen who didn't have dates with beautiful women were likely taking the chance to sleep before they were pulled into another battle.

Hopefully, Westerland wouldn't see how heavy his eyes were. The Sentient knew exactly how little sleep he'd gotten over the last twenty-eight hours.

Yesterday, after Gilroy had gotten reluctant, disapproving approval from Ven, he had logged into the network to make the adjustment. He had nearly fallen out of his Suit when Westerland spoke.

"Shipman Tate."

"Yes, sir?"

"Do you have Master Ven's authorization for this alteration?"

"Yes, sir. I spoke with her this morning."

"What is the reason for the alteration?"

Gilroy had blushed right there in the crew mess. "I am taking Ensign Rico to dinner. She's on third watch, so I have to switch so—" He'd pressed his lips together to stop his rambling. "Anyway, this works for everyone."

"You will not be too tired to stand a double watch? You will have been awake for over twenty hours."

He'd do much harder things for a chance with Ria. "I'll be fine, sir."

There was a pause, then, *"I wish you well, Shipman Tate."*

"Sir?"

"On your attempt to woo Ensign Rico. She is a lovely young woman."

"Uh, thanks, sir."

"You're welcome, Shipman."

Gilroy dismissed his still lingering astonishment and focused on the shield glass before him. He and Ven were on a nearly full CGS deck, closeted in a tiny room next to a containment chamber.

He scowled at the three shapes behind the glass. The ceiling lights reflected on the smooth clear surface of them, hiding the monstrosities inside.

How he and his division had been roped into this assignment, he didn't know. His technical specialty was in maintaining and repairing artificial biosphere environments. Some higher up S.O. must have decided that if Gilroy and the others could keep the Capricians alive, they could keep these aliens alive, too.

They were both human, right?

Gilroy had his doubts. What kind of man would allow metal to be fused to his face? Or wires, visible were they twisted under the skin like snaking tendrils? What was it even for?

The specialists were hard at work, trying to figure it out. So were Gilroy's cabin mates.

"Armor," was the most repeated guess. He and his comrades sat stuffed into every available space in his bunk-room. With half the damned army on board, they were bunked eight in a room which had been designed for two. Add in their friends and they were like *surusas* in a hive.

"Doesn't cover their whole body, though. Not even their vital organs. Why only have it in some places?"

"Maybe it's a tribal thing?"

"A little extreme, yeah?"

"On Tin, don't some of the Budin fanatics still do ritual scarring?"

"That's just gross."

"And illegal. They do tattoos, now."

"Ugh, can you imagine?"

"All those chemicals under your skin?"

"But, if it's religious, or a cultural tradition—"

"Shut it. You sound like a xeno-anth." Interplanetary Anthropologists were thought little of in Gilroy's bunk-room.

"I wonder if the Captain—"

A boot flew toward the offending speaker. "Don't be stupid!"

"Besides, he's not Tinese, not really. Not where it counts."

Gilroy had winced at their impassioned protests of their Captain's ethnicity.

Of course, he had heard the gossip about their new Captain before they launched. Heard of his colonial origin and his questionable promotion to Hybrid Captain. Gilroy had also known his barely average performance at the Naval Academy in Oselona was the reason for his poor assignment.

He had endured his friends' pity, his family's reassurance that he could recover from this. That if he worked hard and kept his head down, this small stain on his career would be overlooked.

But then Gilroy had met the man and he had been nothing like Gilroy expected. A firm handshake and a question about Gilroy's work. A brief smile before the Captain moved on, observing his crew at their duty stations. The man spoke and acted like any of them who were soil-bred, west coast Capricians.

Gilroy could not square it with what he had heard. This quiet, unassuming man committing treason? The man who barely spoke four words together, blackmailing the Emperor?

"Tate."

He jerked. His eyes had drifted shut while he ruminated. He straightened guiltily. "Yes, sir?"

Ven scowled down at him, but she looked tired as well. "Top of the hour."

"Yes, sir."

Ven must have heard his disgust, because she actually smiled a little. "Let's get this done." She sealed her Suit, motioning for him to do the same. He grumbled to himself at her motherly badgering, but obeyed.

They entered the decontamination unit and sealed themselves in. The protocol initiated and blasted them with air that would have been scalding had they been out of their Suits. They held their arms away from their bodies to allow the UV sterilizer to do its work. Then the inner door chimed and slid open.

The oblong containers lay exactly as they had been left. Gilroy dutifully examined each, checking the lights that showed the heart rate and respirations of the alien inside. All seemed within normal parameters, whatever that was for these beings trapped in an endless slumber.

There was writing on the sides, something about "Full-Stasis Life Suspension," with a list of numbers underneath. The linguists had come to gloat after they had cracked the algorithm, but Gilroy and the others just called them 'caskets.'

If he couldn't see the aliens' chests rise and fall, or see the slow pulse at their necks, he would have thought they were dead. Their eyelids stretched across sunken cavities, their skin pale and mottled. Was that normal for them?

The sloping triangle of metal over the man's cheek wasn't normal, not by any stretch of the imagination. The edge of it blended seamlessly with the rest of its face, a few twisting lumps that might be wires tunneling out and away.

There were other alterations visible through the casket's lid. More wires that burst from behind the alien's shoulder and wrapped around to its chest. An obviously mechanical joint under more blotchy skin. Were all its joints fake?

Were the Captain's?

Gilroy shuddered and moved to the next.

No cheek plates, but its hands were reinforced somehow. Metal knuckles, a mechanical finger. A blow from that would hurt. Was it a clumsy repair for an injury? How could these aliens build magic portals, but not be able to keep a man's insides in their proper place?

Unless they *chose* to have it done?

Gilroy was making himself nauseous. He focused on his checks, keeping his gaze from their mutilated forms. Better to focus on their technology, rather than their deformities.

Wait, something different, now. Writing scrawled across the top of one screen, faster than Gilroy could translate. He was struggling to learn this language, nothing like the five recognized trade languages taught at school.

"Westerland?" he called.

The Sentient's voice sounded in his ear. *"Yes, Shipman?"*

"I can't read this. Will you translate?"

"You are in my field of vision. Please, step aside."

Gilroy obeyed, trying to control the nervous wiggling of his leg.

"It is a readout of the occupant's condition. Everything is within parameters."

"Thank you, sir."

Gilroy finished his assessments and logged the results into a Palm. His entry was the latest in a rapidly expanding file on the things. He did not envy the poor data cruncher who had to go over them, eventually. He set the Palm back in its spot and made for the door.

Westerland stopped him. *"Shipman Tate, a word?"*

"Yes, sir?" Had he forgotten something?

"May I ask the results of your date with Ensign Rico?"

Gilroy's chin hit the bottom of his helmet. "Oh, uh… good." Very good. He was still high off her warm goodnight kiss.

"My congratulations."

"Thank you, sir."

"Carry on."

Gilroy frowned. Did the Sentient sound amused? Ven was visibly impatient. He hurried into the decon unit.

NINETEEN

Empty Orbit
F - 1884 - 5 - 15

Arsaces held in a shudder as the prisoners were secured to their chairs. His linguist grinned, not the least put out, as she explained the program she had just finished.

"Simply talk and the Palm will translate for you," Malel crowed. Luckily, her jubilation was in keeping with the attitude Sulovin and the other psychologists recommended. Like this was nothing to the Capricians, that they were not worried about invasion nor feared the army sleeping in the dormant ship.

"Accuracy?"

"Very," she said smugly.

Westerland agreed. \I have simulated three thousand, four hundred conversations.\

"Thank you, Specialist Malel," Arsaces said through gritted teeth. He kept his smile in place as the marines stepped back. Frei wiped his glove on his Suit, mouth tight. Arsaces didn't blame him: the prisoners were out of isolation.

They looked ghastly. Pale and sweating, they sat limp after the hastily programmed vaccine ripped through them. The first lifted his sunken eyes and sneered weakly across the room.

"I am Fleet Admiral Arsaces Jankovic-Wood, Hybrid Captain of the Sentient CIN-SH Westerland, in her Majesty's Imperial Navy."

\Still a mouthful.\

The prisoners stayed silent as the translation murmured like a garbled echo.

"I am sorry for your discomfort. The effects of the vaccine should wear off in a few hours. It is for your protection, as well as—"

The first spoke over him. "We will say nothing," the Palm repeated.

Arsaces slumped back in his chair. "We are not going to torture you, you know. We are not savages."

"Yes, you all are."

Arsaces sighed. "Officer Sulovin?"

"Yes, Captain?"

"You are prepared for hypno-questioning?"

"At your convenience, sir."

The alien's eyes widened, glancing between them.

"You see, we don't need to torture you," Arsaces explained. "Though it would be some small compensation for the lives lost you took. No, all I have to do is turn off your conscious mind and rip what I need to know out of you. It's really very simple."

Arsaces strolled to a wall screen as Westerland displayed the images from his own implantation, his face blurred out. "We place a synthetic interface in your cerebral cortex. It interferes with your neural synapses. We will control your voluntary motor functions, your so-called 'free-will' turned off. You won't notice a difference once we heal the surrounding tissue."

This was a gamble, one his specialists had argued for days. Not only was what he threatened illegal on every planet, even Shea, banned irrevocably when the last of the Gol had been eradicated. It was unethical in the extreme, but maybe the fear of it would loosen their tongues.

\Less ethical than them slaughtering millions?\

"You will tell us what we need to know. We have a ring; it is only a matter of time until we can travel back to your space. Sixty-seven million lives were lost on Caprice. The Empress is anxious they did not die for nothing."

No matter they were already pale, they blanched. One tried to brazen it out. "Do the worst."

Arsaces eyed him coolly. "What is your name and rank, soldier?" They had been wearing uniforms of a sort, now dressed in a shapeless coverall.

The alien drew up his shoulders. "Sisier, of Gen Four, Third—" the translation cut out a moment "—of the Vanguard."

"Vanguard again," Halt commented. "Vanguard of what?"

"Of the invasion, of course," Sulovin said. The prisoners scowled at him. "Vanguard of some larger force, waiting to advance. These attacks were to soften us up, test our defenses. Why are you invading?"

This Sisier shrugged. "Why not?"

Westerland broke into Arsaces' thoughts. \How large is their military? Get him to boast.\

Arsaces adjusted the sleeve of his Suit. "That ship holds seven thousand men in stasis?"

"Yes, sir," Sulovin said.

"If that's an average troop transport, with, say, seven or so waiting to pass through, that gives us fifty thousand men in the first wave—"

"Fifty thousand?" the second alien protested. Sisier hissed at him, but he ignored the warning. "It is nothing!"

Halt met Arsaces' eyes and smiled knowingly. "Fighters are not up to our standards. Fast, but flimsy, I think, for prolonged engagement. Nothing on the Hemings."

Arsaces grinned. "I prefer the Archers."

"You would, Ace."

The old nickname twisted his smile into something stiff. "And bad design on the ships. Why have orientation down? All you need is some spin."

Now the prisoners looked plainly scornful.

Westerland murmured thoughtfully. \Anti-gravity, a large attack force, faster than light capabilities. Do they have Sentient technology? Talk to me, aloud.\

"What about?"

\Anything. Make it obvious.\

Arsaces looked over the prisoners' heads. "How is the processor mapping proceeding?"

\Good. Keep this up.\

"The analysis of the ring's superstructure?"

The one named Sisier glanced over his shoulder, looking for who Arsaces was talking to.

Westerland was pleased. \Now they suspect something is strange. Tilt your head.\

"What do you mean?"

\Like you do when I'm talking to you and you forget others can see you.\

Arsaces realized how firmly he had been resisting doing just that. His neck ached.

\Let me speak for you.\

He reflexively relaxed, eyes unfocused. "The structural analysis is proceeding well," he said, knowing it was his voice, but not recognizing it, somehow. "The metal is some form of—"

Westerland's voice was soothing, sounding from every speaker in the room. "—*titanium alloy, though it includes several compounds we don't have in quantity in our system. There is evidence of—*"

"—a biological component. Testing has begun to determine—"

"—*the exact formulation. It appears similar to our—*"

"—silica constructs for strengthening structures along—"

"—*seismic areas of Tin and Taltua.*"

Arsaces blinked and his voice was his again. "Did you get that?"

"Yes, sir," his officers chorused.

"Westerland is running the metrics," he told them, enjoying being able to relax into his Sentient when others were around. It was as if Westerland was surrounding him, holding him, the walls safe and protecting. He tried not to show this in front of his crew.

\Why not?\ Westerland demanded peevishly. \I am your Sentient. You are my Captain. We are one.\

"*Bet arre ekin,*" Arsaces promised, surprised at the warmth in his own voice. Did he truly sound so stilted normally? He shook his head clear and looked down at the prisoners. They stared back, leaning as far away as they could in their bindings.

"Westerland says you use those rings like a tunnel to enable supra-light speed travel. How?"

Sisier shot his comrade a quick look. He licked his lips and spoke in a raspy voice. "You indicated we are on the warship Westerland." He sounded the name out carefully.

"Yes. He is my Sentient."

"It is a... he?"

"That's a debatable point. I hear him as male. His namesake was a man, born some four hundred years ago. Led the assault on Taltua Beta, before the Andris dynasty—"

The alien was panting now. "This warship lives?"

Sulovin answered before Arsaces could. "In some ways. Westerland interacts with the world through Captain Wood, feels, tastes, touches. He speaks in Captain Wood's head. Isn't that right, Captain?"

Arsaces shrugged, uncomfortable talking about it. "I hear him. As if he was standing next to me."

The second alien muttered something Arsaces took for a curse. The algorithm didn't pick it up, in any case.

Sisier hissed at him, pushing his chair back. "You are—"

Again, the algorithm failed, though his tone and expression made it clear what he felt. He spat on the deck and turned his face away.

Sulovin was quick to jump on their revulsion. "That's what the Chip feels like. Someone inside your head, asking questions, looking for answers. You needn't even speak; it will find them."

"Westerland, how soon can we begin the implantation?"

"Doctor Orjean awaits your summons, Captain." The prisoners flinched, huddling closer together.

"Very well. Lieutenant, return them to the brig. I will decide what to do with them later."

The marines stepped up and led the prisoners away. They left without resisting.

Halt spoke into the quiet after the door shut. "No offense, Captain, but it is a little unnerving when you two do that."

Arsaces kept his face smooth. "It was unnerving the first time it happened, I can assure you. Sulovin, I want your report as soon as you can. Gentlemen, are we done here?"

He stayed long enough to acknowledge their salutes and marched out. He needed to get away from them, away from humans and their askance glances.

\Always one,\ Westerland promised.

TWENTY

Tin: Far Synchronous Orbit

F - 1879 - 18 - 9

"Is it supposed to look like that?"

Carl leaned over the incubation tank and squinted at the angry red flesh under the surface of the liquid. Not water, he'd been told, but a 'salinated nutrient matrix.' Looked like water, if a bit viscous.

"We are pushing his body to regrow robust capillary vasculature. That will ensure the implants take hold."

Carl glanced at the artificial bones of the man's legs, just barely covered by newly grown muscle. They had a steely color, one that raised the hairs on his neck. Even the muscles, supposedly 75% Wood's native tissue, looked off.

But then, how would he know? Carl rarely had to see other peoples' innards. Thankfully.

"Everything is progressing as prescribed." Dr. Li stood at his side, arms crossed over her chest. "He will recover."

"His body, yes. His mind?"

"He shows normal levels of cerebral activity when allowed to rouse."

Carl hissed a curse. "You wake him up? Like *this*?"

The man's skin was only half regrown, his organs held in place by a lattice of polymers and tissue. They quivered with each slow heartbeat.

Li looked strained. "We have to. To assess his cognitive function. To measure his response to peripheral stimuli."

"You mean pain."

"We only take him a little higher than a deep sleep. He won't remember it."

Carl prayed he wouldn't. He hung his head, reaching to rub his neck. He wasn't sure this was a good idea anymore. The man's family had made their sentiments plain. The Emperor had not quite gone so far as to order Carl to kill the pilot and be done with it.

And what was Carl going to do with him, once the man had healed? He'd never be allowed to fly again, certainly discharged. Then what? Grounded on Caprice, stuck in some backwater town where they might not have heard of the disaster the Tinese rebellion was shaping up to be? Or arrested and sentenced to a life of labor in some asteroid mine? Never even see the stars again? For men like them, it was a life worse than death.

Carl rested his hand on the glass of the incubation tank. The body within twitched now and again. He couldn't think of the man as Arsaces Wood. Not until he had woken up and Carl could look him in the eye and see that the Airman was still in there.

And here he was, resisting the 'minor' procedure his doctor kept yammering on about. Simple 'restructuring' of his heart, some quick adjustments to his spine and shoulders. He'd feel twenty years younger, his doctor told him.

Carl suspected what age he felt would have nothing to do with the vigor of his limbs.

"Let me know at once if there are any complications."

"Yes, sir."

Carl tapped the glass gently. "Hang in there, Airman."

Shore leave was a luxury he could ill afford, but he just couldn't take the grinding search for the Budin rebels any longer. Not that he did anything other than sit and watch as they were executed. A fine needle against their skin, a flash of surprise, then their eyes dulled as they fell limp against the table.

Merciful, quick. But each death settled in his chest like a ripping barb of steel.

Evi waved from the landing strip as his transport circled the house. Carl smiled, some of his horror and fatigue melting. Her hair whipped in the wind, her hand to her eyes to shield them against the sun.

She ran to open the door before Chino could step around the craft to do his duty.

"You're home!"

Carl grinned as she hugged him fiercely. "Alright, missy, what do you want?"

Evi laughed brightly. "Just you, silly man. I've missed you."

"And I you, dear one."

She fluttered around him like a colorful bird. He stilled her by tucking her under his arm, undoing the buttons of his uniform coat with the other hand.

"Blasted hot."

"It's been glorious. I've been swimming every morning."

She did look tan, with a spray of new freckles across her nose. He tweaked the pert thing and she made a face.

"How long do you stay?" she asked.

"Only the night."

For a moment, she looked crestfallen. But she quickly pulled her smile back into place. "Well, I cleared my schedule. We can spend the evening at home. Unless you'd like to invite Wes and the others? They've been asking about you."

"No, just us, I think."

She snuggled closer and stretched to peck his cheek. "I'll leave you to settle in. I just need to finish some research for the Senate Session next week."

"Go on, then."

She squeezed his hand and hurried away, her flowing skirts snapping in the brisk wind off the sea.

Carl turned to speak to Chino and found the boy gazing after her. He smiled knowingly. Chino must have felt his eyes, because his aide straightened and asked, "Did you need anything, sir?"

"No. You're free for the night. I'll see you at 0700 tomorrow."

"Yes, sir."

Carl chuckled to himself. Chino was hardly the only of his officers to admire his little wife. She really was lovely, not only in form, but in personality as well. Add in her rank and she was nearly perfect.

Carl took a cool shower and settled into his favorite chair. He had a stack of his own reports to go over but found himself letting his head fall back against the cushion. Afternoon light gleamed on the windows, the air warm and lightly scented.

Perhaps weather wasn't wholly bad.

"You shouldn't read without your spectacles."

Carl roused himself, blinking awake. Evi stood over him, hands on hips.

He straightened and patted the arm of the chair. "Reports finished?"

Evi sighed dramatically as she sat. "Never. You should know this. But I think I have enough evidence to convince Yuni to back the Anmen deal at last."

"Why's he balking?"

"Money. Always money."

"Not everyone has the backing of the Imperial treasury."

She snorted. "I wish I had a tenth of the resources Yuni controls. He actually has a *rystinite* mine."

Carl smiled bittersweet at the old joke. Evi's smile faded as she watched him.

"What's wrong, Carl?"

"Nothing." He had no wish to tell her about the body barely surviving aboard his ship. About the cold cruelty of the man's family. Or the endless parade of arrests and executions of his kin. Let her read about it in the news briefings.

Her hands smoothed the lines from his forehead. He leaned into her touch.

"You work too hard."

"So do you."

She harrumphed. "At least you are making a difference. I spend day after day up to my ears in bureaucracy and argue the same points again and again."

Was he, though? Was anything he was doing making a difference? Had anything he had done in his career benefited anyone? The Empire, yes, as a whole, he liked to believe. But the people themselves? Had a single person's life been made better because of his actions?

She rested her cheek on his head. "Should I make us a picnic basket for supper?"

"Eat outside?" Carl demanded. "With bugs and dirt and who knows what other nasty creatures?"

Evi laughed. We'll spread a blanket on the library floor and munch in the glow of artificial light."

That sounded just as bad. "I doubt my knee will tolerate that."

She straightened. "Have you been taking your medication?"

He avoided her eyes. "Most of the time."

"Carl."

"I've been busy. Rebellion and all."

She huffed through her nose. She stood and paced the room. He watched her wearily. She turned to him all at once.

"Dr. Vanas contacted me."

That double-crossing cad. "About what?"

"You, of course. He has concerns."

Carl rolled his eyes and stretched his arms overhead. "More whinging?"

"He says your heart is failing."

Carl hedged. "He told me it needed to be monitored."

"He says you're refusing treatment."

Carl hated the worried pinch between her eyes. "I'm taking precautions."

"Precautions? What do you mean?"

"I eat well, I'm taking the medicine he prescribes."

"He says it's not enough."

"Enough for what?"

"To heal you. You need restructuring. Your heart needs to be replaced."

Carl stilled a shudder. Rebuilt, like Wood. His tissue removed and replaced with artificially grown muscle.

"Carl." She didn't go on, but he heard the pain in her voice. He gestured for her. She sat on his knee, eyes moving over his face.

She truly had grown into a beauty. Not the perfect, designed face so many wore. But her eyes had character, her nose impish. She looked at him like she knew him inside and out and adored every bit of him.

"Vanas is making a deal out of nothing. I know I've been under stress lately. But I feel well enough. And I don't want anything drastic done. You know this."

"But, Carl!" She pushed away, holding him at arm's length. "Why?"

Because he didn't want to live another hundred years of this. Another hundred years of going where his Emperor ordered, killing the people he was told to. He woke each day more certain. He would refuse whatever procedures would prolong his life, no matter what they said.

Not even for hundred more years with Evi.

"We've discussed this, little one."

Besides, she deserved better than him. A man old enough to be her father, her grandfather, whatever avuncular term she liked best. She needed someone young, someone she could have a real life with. Someone who wasn't gone for months at a time, who would devote his whole life to making her happy.

He smoothed her hair. "Don't worry, Evi."

He could see the storm inside her, furious words she kept kenneled behind her diplomat's smile. He didn't dare hope there were tender ones in there, too. It was a foolish hope, wishing their marriage might blossom into something real.

"A picnic, you said?"

She swallowed up whatever emotions had been on her lips. "Bugs and all?"

"For you, even bugs."

Her smile was tremulous. She leaned and kissed his cheek. He reveled in the feel of her soft lips on his skin.

"I'll get it ready."

"Good girl. Let me finish this, then I'll be down."

She went out with a cheerful wave.

Carl flipped his Palm over and halfheartedly scrolled through his messages. Requisition requests. Transfer recommendations. Briefings from his fleet about rebel engagements and minor Imperial casualties.

Damn Budins. What was he going to do with them? How would they rebuild any sort of trust after systematically dismantling their ruling class, disrupting their economy, their religion, their government? What was he going to do about Wood?

His finger stopped on a message from Captain Hyrim, Hybrid pair to the Sentient Rinn. It was a standard report, something about an air strike in a city north of Alam.

He pressed the outgoing icon on the Palm.

Chino answered after a few chimes. *"Sir, did you need—"*

"Contact Captain Hyrim."

"Now, sir? I believe he's out past—"

"Now. I want him on the Santos tomorrow by the time I board."

"Yes, sir."

Carl signed off and tossed the Palm aside. Maybe there was something he could do for Wood after all.

TWENTY ONE

Empty Orbit
F - 1884 - 5 - 19

S hould she speak to him about it?

During the infuriatingly mild interrogation of the prisoners, the question kept surging to the front of her mind.

Should she confront the Captain about Orjean's suspicions?

He seemed to be functioning adequately. Evi hated that 'functioning' was the word she used, even privately. As if he was less than human, after his injuries, after the implantation. But wasn't that the point of a Hybrid-Sentient pairing? To carry out their function for the good of the Empire?

She watched him covertly over the next few days, but did not see anything other than exhaustion in his demeanor. Sometimes his face blanked suddenly, but she assumed it was Westerland talking to him. He would stand absent for a moment, then blink back to reality and continue as if nothing had happened.

His crew was obviously used to such interruptions. They would stop speaking and wait for their Captain's focus to return. Sometimes, Sas nudged him if it was taking longer than usual.

If Orjean had not told her, Evi would never have guessed anything was wrong. She had seen people addicted to boosters. They showed signs quickly: steroid tremors, loss of muscle mass, thinned hair, rickets. It took an enormous amount of caloric support to prevent fatal catabolism.

Captain Wood had none of these. He appeared healthy and well nourished, despite his forgetting to eat. Average height, stocky build. Budin coloring, she now saw.

But still no accent.

They stood on the Bridge, packed shoulder to shoulder as every available officer waited for the initial test of the Caprician's ring. It hung in space, minuscule compared to the one the aliens had brought, but still large enough to swallow a good-sized shuttle. Maybe even a Wasp class warship.

"You are sure about the risk?" Wood asked, with the air of an oft repeated question.

The crewman next to him answered in a carefully patient tone. "Yes, sir," she said. "We will, of course, maintain a safe distance. However, the calculated risk is minimal."

"But what is a malfunction? Are all the rings the same? Was the one above Caprice truly a weapon? Our observations are incomplete; we don't have redundant data."

Wood flinched at the end of his protestations. Westerland scolding him for doubting his design?

The officer's frustration was rising, given the color of her cheeks. "I know we've had some setbacks, sir, but they have been relatively minor and easily controlled."

"Your last test ruptured a plasma generator."

The woman swelled with indignation. Evi intervened.

"Captain Wood, a word?"

He allowed himself to be led aside. She whispered fiercely through a benign smile. "Building a prototype was your idea, Captain. We must discover how this technology works."

Though more and more she wanted to damn the consequences and grind the prisoners' brains to mush. She was the Empress, wasn't she?

Wood sighed. "I know, I know. But I don't have to like it." He stared down at his boots, the metal reinforcements gleaming in the bright Bridge lights. "And if it works?"

"What do you mean?"

"If we can build a ring, faster than light travel, what are we going to do with it?"

Evi had an exhaustive list. "First, I am going to set up a network between the planets and establish a system for traffic control. Once we can travel easily through the system — "

"No." He looked up and caught her eyes. "What are we going to do? These aliens will keep attacking. The psychologists warn it is only a matter of time. These attacks are simply to keep us busy while they ready the true invasion. Even accounting for bravado, what we had faced is likely a fraction of their strength."

"If that is so," Evi countered, "how can we hope to succeed, rings or not?"

"There are fifteen ships nearing completion as we speak, ready for deployment in three weeks. At that pace, by next year our fleet will be the largest it's been since the Stratocracy. Their weapons, their propulsion, all could be reverse engineered and adapted into our ships. We'd be equal."

Evi eyed him. "You think we should attack them."

"I think you should think about it," he said evenly. "It's always better to fight in your enemy's territory. Then you're not stuck cleaning up the mess, risking your civilians."

"I am sure the citizens of Orbon would agree with you."

His expression didn't flicker. "We don't know when the next attack will come. We don't know how much they know about us or how they are learning it. It behooves us to be aggressive, start feeling them out in their own space."

"And overreach ourselves?"

"Caution could get us killed."

"So can recklessness. You can't afford that anymore, Admiral. You're no longer just a pilot.

That broke his control, a scowl compressing his lips. "I am simply offering my opinion. As your Admiral."

"And I will take it into consideration," she said coolly.

"Yes, your majesty."

Evi stilled her foot from tapping. Why were they arguing? Again? She took a deep breath to regain her calm. "Sas is waiting for you."

He hesitated, eyes on hers. She met them evenly until he turned away.

"Are we ready, Lieutenant?"

"Yes, sir."

"Proceed."

The taut silence in the room told her Wood was not alone in his fear of malfunction. Evi held her spine straight and watched as the prototype was powered on.

"Initiating plasma engines... power at 10%."

The forward screen zoomed in, showing the lights on the ring flickering.

"20%."

Was it interference, or was something moving along the inner edge of the ring? But what? What would be moved in vacuum?

"30%. All readings within expectations, sir."

"Understood. Increase power as needed."

The plasma generators, modified now to prevent further explosions, glowed like many pointed stars. The exhaust was being vented in all directions to keep the engines stable.

These aliens' power technology was similar enough to Caprice's to avoid having to build an entirely new propulsion system. Their own might be more efficient, the engineers claimed smugly. Evi didn't censure their pride. It was nice to know they weren't outmatched in every way.

"35%."

Evi distracted herself from the interminable wait by calling up the shipyard reports on the console closest to her. She had gotten an update just yesterday.

Wood was correct: six ships were even ahead of schedule, all the sleek and multi-functional Glenfil class. They were being fueled and run through last minutes checks even as she stood and watched the ring come to life.

The thought calmed her. They would not be defenseless should Wood's prediction come true. Even if the Fleet was lost, they could retreat, defend. They would have to withdraw support of their colonies but might avoid a complete surrender.

Would the aliens even accept such a concession? Would Tin — proud, rebellious Tin — would they offer an alliance, finally break from Caprice's control?

Would Shea remain neutral, selling weapons to whomever had the means to purchase them? Ulcacier, Beta-9? Would the Volgar system turn on its rulers, destroy the dynasties once and for all?

What a legacy she was leaving her children.

"Power at 50%"

Gasps rose as the ring started to glow. Evi gripped her hands together, clumsy in her gloves, as a streak of light, cloudy and shifting, streamed back from the ring. Almost as if it were reaching for something. Seeking a connection?

She edged closer to Wood.

"Captain?"

He grunted, eyes on the screen.

"Captain Wood."

"*Edo*?" The Budinese surprised her. He must be lost deep in Westerland to make such a slip.

She touched his arm softly. "Arsaces." He jerked and looked down at her, blinking back to focus.

"Apologies, ma'am." And back to toneless, precise Common. "What is it?"

"Once the drone goes through the ring, how do we know where it will come out?"

He didn't answer, just frowned, but surely he understood. A single ring couldn't be the entire device. There must be a pair, a connection, a tunnel of sorts. Otherwise, how would it know where to send the ship?

If they could figure out how to connect to another ring, one of the enemy's, then they could use the rings against them. No need to scour the surrounding space or waste years moving rings into position.

"70% and holding steady."

The ring shone brightly, now. The same flashing rainbow of colors, almost like a solar flare. Radiation from the ring? Whatever was inside the tunnel leaking out?

"85%."

"Prepare the first drone."

A black dot, tiny even compared to their small ring, zipped past the cameras. It hovered near the gaping hole, the blackness within the ring clearly visible against the stars.

"Faster than the speed of light," Wood murmured. "What would you see, then?"

Evi sincerely hoped she would never find out.

"100%."

"Send it in."

The drone hovered on the edge, then it was gone.

"Well?"

"Just a moment, sir." Officers worked feverishly at their stations.

One lifted his head and frowned. "It's still here. Coordinates read: neg-seventy-five-neg sixty-nine. Here."

"And the timestamp?"

"Now, sir."

Wood grunted. "Proceed with your tests."

"Yes, sir."

A mass of drones flew forward, antennas bristling. Evi let out a breath she hadn't realized she'd been holding.

Nothing had happened.

Wood made a discrete gesture for her to follow. "Sas, you have the Bridge."

"You were right," he continued after the Bridge doors closed behind them. The marines posted there saluted, then moved down the corridor to give them some privacy.

"About?"

"That drone won't go anywhere without a destination. A pair."

"I only guessed."

"A good guess."

Much good it did them. "Doesn't change the situation, unfortunately.

We still don't know how to use it."

Westerland spoke quietly. *"The tests proceed as predicted. The first drone is still stationary. I have a hypothesis."*

"When do you not?" Wood asked. Then he grimaced and Evi hid her smile as Westerland continued.

"We have assumed these aliens have found a way to travel faster than the speed of light."

"Made sense, with the information we had."

"True. My original observations, as you so succinctly noted to Specialist Xavier, were done under fire and may not be complete."

"Are you apologizing?"

"Don't be absurd, Arsaces."

Evi listened with surprise, amused at their banter. And somehow pleased. She doubted many people were allowed to hear them speak so freely to each other.

"Given these recent tests, I infer the alien ships do not go faster than the speed of light. They simply have found a way to bend space."

"Right, 'simply,' of course. That makes this better how?"

"We must activate the second ring. If the drone is stationary, it may be waiting for a second hole in space to open. It doesn't travel faster than the speed of light. It simply steps through the intervening space instantly and arrives at its destination without any time spent."

Wood's fingers drummed their habitual pattern. "I like that explanation better than faster than light travel. Breaks fewer laws of reality."

The Sentient's ruminations blended smoothly with Wood's. *"Though we must still discover how the two holes know when and how to connect. I assume there are rings open in these aliens' space. Why doesn't our ring send the drone there?"*

"There must be a way to program the rings for a specific destination."

"I have been unable to make progress into the alien computer aboard that ship. It would be more efficient to extract the knowledge from—"

"No."

"Surely, the situation indicates—"

"I will not murder a man."

"He is an enemy soldier."

"Who has done no wrong, yet. No."

Evi stayed still, now shocked at the disagreement. It seemed Wood would argue with anyone, even his own Sentient. She was of the same mind as Westerland, and not only because she hated these aliens with every fiber of her being.

"Some good news." Wood attempted a cheerful smile. It was ghastly.

"Is there?" she asked dryly. She certainly couldn't see it.

"If our drone survived, then our ships won't need modification to go through the rings."

"And if the trip is instantaneous, we can easily carry the fight to them, as you suggested."

"If it comes to that." He hesitated, and she wondered what Westerland was telling him privately. "Your majesty, I... I didn't mean to be terse earlier."

She resisted the urge to forgive him at once. Surely, she was made of sterner stuff than that. "You are simply doing your duty, Captain."

"I'm trying, but... I don't want... I mean, I want you to know, that I respect you. I understand the pressure you're under."

Did he? Did he know it was suffocating her, crushing her down, inescapable?

"If I have shown any disrespect, ma'am, I sincerely apologize."

"It is nothing."

"Honestly, Evi. I'm sorry."

Well, how was she supposed to refuse that? "Me, too," she admitted truthfully.

His real smile was disarming, and it brought his face alive. Why didn't he employ it more often? Even she thought it charming.

But the rare grin faded quickly. "I still don't see how we are to survive this, let alone win, with the Empire intact."

"We will. We have to. I cannot accept any other outcome."

"I will do my best, ma'am, but—"

"Caprice stands with you, Captain. You have our full support."

There was nothing charming about this smile. "Westerland was right." He saw her questioning look. "He insists nothing is impossible."

"Captain, are you available?"

"Go ahead, Sas."

"We have the first results, sir."

"Coming."

Evi caught his hand before he turned away. "You have my support, Arsaces. I know I can be difficult. Thank you for putting up with me."

"I might say the same, ma'am." He saluted and went back to the Bridge.

* * *

Westerland's thoughts were soothing thrum at the back of his mind. No words, just impulses.

What are you so pleased about?

Westerland chuckled. \Just the rings, Arsaces. Just the rings.\

TWENTY TWO

Empty Orbit
F - 1884- 5 - 20

Arsaces cursed and swung his legs out of bed. He'd been sleeping fitfully for hours, unable to relax. Westerland was trying to be quiet, but his calculations ran through Arsaces' dreams until they were a wailing shriek of decimals and quantum particles.

\Shall I put you to sleep?\

Arsaces shrugged into his Suit and did half the buckles. "I just need some air."

\That makes no sense. All oxygen levels are exactly the same, on every deck.\

"Just an expression."

It was the middle of the night, by anyone's reckoning. Third shift was just winding down and the fourth about to get up and go to work. Mostly observation crews, everyone else trying to get rest while they could. Sitting stationary allowed most departments to stand down.

\Not stationary,\ Westerland corrected. \We are moving at—\

"Just an expression," Arsaces muttered again. He paced the long corridors, hands tucked under his arms, groggy, but not sleepy.

He had no intended destination but was not surprised to find himself outside the Sentient Room. Westerland opened the doors for him without him palming the locks.

"Violation of security protocol."

\Of course, it's you.\

"I might be a cleverly designed sleeper agent, programmed to mimic myself exactly."

\That is absurd.\

Arsaces kept the lights off and slid down a wall, knees tucked up to his chest. He watched the wispy lightning beneath the dome through half-open eyes.

He always wondered why the Architects made this room. The Sentient wasn't under the shield glass. He was wound through every cable, riveted on every girder. The ship was the Sentient and he was the ship. Even if someone did infiltrate and manage to break through the nearly indestructible glass, Westerland would keep functioning.

\In some respect. Though I don't think I would enjoy having my higher order expressive functions disabled.\

"What would I do without your witty commentary during staff briefings?"

\Be bored.\

Arsaces chuckled. He leaned his head back and closed his eyes. It was silent in here, the heavy wall shielding blocking even the faint rumble of Westerland's cooling system. Tension eased from his limbs, muscles burning as they relaxed.

\Why do you not sleep on a lower gravity deck?\

"Habit, I suppose."

\It would aid your healing.\

Your name is Arsaces Jankovic-Wood.\

Arsaces sighed, too tired to fight her tonight. No matter how loud his Sentient, she was always there, murmuring in that cool, disinterested tone.

Will she ever go away, Westerland?

\I cannot erase memories.\

Just the one. Can't you find it and delete it?

Much like I am, you are every part of yourself. Wound through your mind, tied to all other memories, remembered or not.

The pain you feel is temporary. A medical officer will be with you shortly. It will pass.\

It had eventually. After endless hours, days, weeks. Had it actually been years?

You have been in incubation recovery for nine weeks, four days, seven hours, and two minutes…

\Only ten weeks. You know this.\

How could he forget?

Your body is being repaired. You are incapable of voluntary movement at this time. Do not panic.\

Easy for her to say. Her voice was irritating, but it was not what scared him. She roused other memories, of being unable to move, unable to breathe. Flashes, moments of awareness. Faces. Voices, speaking from far away. Pain, blinding, crushing, endless pain. Quickly and mercifully smothered back to darkness.

But there.

\A common complication of long-term incubation.\

He's seen others in tanks like that. Pilots injured during training. Ailing family given intensive treatment to reverse some illness. He'd seen how fast tissue could regrow. That he had been in there for so long…

As she had for those ten eternal weeks, the woman spoke again. The same uncaring words of orientation, giving no comfort, only reminding him of what he had lost.

You were a pilot.\

'Were,' she said. But no longer. Never again, one of so many things he destroyed that day. His body, his Archer. His family. His life.

You are severely injured and are in stasis-recovery incubation aboard the CIN Santos.\

What were the odds? Her husband's fleet picking his mangled body out of the star field, her on his ship only a few years later? Had she known who he was? Had Hyde told her? Why hadn't the man just let him die?

\There are many variables, but I calculate it at… \

Your body is being repaired.\

So similar, yet so different, their voices. A duet in his mind, one loved and one hated with all his being.

Because he did love Westerland. He would never admit it aloud, never dare tell anyone.

Did the other Hybrids feel the same? Arsaces knew he struggled to read people, unable to see past the blank orbs of their eyes. It was why he had always preferred machines, programs that were predictable and defined.

But he thought he had seen hints of it. The quiet smile of Smit during a briefing. How Patel touched the navigation console on his Sentient's Bridge, a caress almost.

His training had made no mention of an enduring emotional bond, other than a possible side effect. Certainly the Architects did not encourage such a complication. Humans were temporary, expendable. Replaceable.

He was a tool. The Architects had remade him into a Captain. He would serve Caprice or he would be Deactivated.

\Never. I will not allow it.\

That threat was why he complied with their pointless assignments. The ridicule and the shame. Why he did not take Westerland into the emptiness between stars.

Could the Architects do it remotely? If he tried to run, would they shut him down? Did he really understand what they put in him while he was unconscious, helpless in that vat of cold, thick torture? So much of him had been rebuilt. What had they changed, altered as they saw fit?

Westerland was stung. \You said you chose me willingly.\

I did. I swear it.

And he had, allowed to wake for a brief moment to full consciousness. Felt warm air tease his face, unable to take the gasping breath he desperately needed. Listened in sweating terror as they told him starkly what had occurred and what was being offered in remittance.

That it was permanent. That his brain would be irreparably damaged if they had to remove the Sentient Chip.

The scar had long healed by the time Westerland was completed. Unusual, as most Captains were implanted just before activation. Unprecedented, as selection for such a post was a fierce and ruthless process.

Someone with astonishing sway on the Emperor had wanted Arsaces to have a Sentient. There was no other way it would have been offered.

An unchangeable decision, too much time and money committed to alter the program afterwards. The so-called 'Chip' a lattice of connections and synapses, wound through his neural cortex and deep brain structures. And him too notorious to conveniently disappear.

During those last few weeks aboard the Santos, he had spent the quiet nights expecting it. Some assassin of the Empire. Or an *atalan* disguised in a naval uniform, curving knife aimed for his plastic heart.

Then they pulled him out of that tank and made him breathe again. Move his arms again. A few weeks later, walk again. Pull on a uniform and march down to a shuttle, still reeling at the stranger he inhabited.

Three years in Command School, wondering if the day would actually come. If they would keep their promises, when he saw so clearly they despised him.

How could he face his crew, knowing the scorn they carried for him? How could he protect them, direct them? How could he lead them when he feared them?

You have been in incubation for…\

He pressed his forehead to his knees, trying to smother her.

That had been Westerland's first words to him, too. His name. Now meaningless words, emptied of their history. The Sentient Room had been lifeless that day. The black dome still. Waiting.

\ARSACES DAAS COURTNEY JANKOVIC-WOOD\

Arsaces' knees had buckled under the assault. He cried out past gritted teeth. Not pain, exactly, but still blinding, crushing, every dream that woke him in cold sweat come to life.

Slowly, the pressure had eased. But not gone. Something inside him, watching him. Seeing him.

\CAPTAIN\

He'd retched, even medicated against the nausea they had warned about, his mouth thick with the taste of stale air and machine oil.

Lightning down his nerves, the wires reaching every corner of the exoskeleton. A burning fire in his chest, the engines igniting, an unquenchable sun. The weight of the armor on his shoulders, gasping hungrily for breath, driven by the life support.

Lights flickered on. Airlocks cycled. The ship rumbled, humming, churning, shifting.

The Sentient was alive.

\Greetings, Captain Wood. I am Westerland.\

He had rasped out the scripted command. "Westerland, status report."

\I am functioning within parameters. No errors have been detected.\

Arsaces didn't have the breath to respond, dry-heaving as his thoughts — the Sentient's thoughts? — swirled inside him.

It — he? — checked.

\You are unwell, Captain?\

Arsaces pushed himself to his feet. "I'm fine."

\Your blood pressure and pulse have increased abruptly.\

"I am..." What did it matter? The thing would know, anyway. "I am frightened."

\Why, Captain?\

"I don't know."

The Sentient hummed thoughtfully. Could computers hum?

\You are not in pain? My records indicate some neural-hybrid pairings experienced severe and sometimes debilitating pain during initial integration.\

"No." A lie, but the pain was nothing new. Neither was the lie. His whole life was a lie. His allegiance, his obedience.

\You have a headache.\

"How can you tell?" He did, settling behind his eyes, like a bright light was blazing inside his skull.

\I... \ The Sentient hesitated. \I am not sure. But I am certain you are experiencing discomfort.\

"A little," Arsaces admitted. "It will pass."

\Yes. Once we are accustomed to this method of communication.\ The Sentient thought a moment more. \A point of clarification. You are Arsaces Wood, lately of Alam City, Alam-Jaheel?\

Arsaces clenched his fists. Might as well get it over with. Then they would know how wrong they were to let him live. "I no longer claim citizenship among the Budin, nor on Tin."

The Sentient's voice was quiet. \I understand.\

Did it? What had the Architects told it? He waited for the judgment, the scornful pity he loathed.

\Then where do you call home, Captain?\

That did hurt, right through his chest. Only worse knowing the Sentient knew, too. No longer Tin, never Caprice. Certainly not Command School. "I don't call anywhere home."

The Sentient considered this. Arsaces could feel it thinking, sorting, comparing. It arrived at a conclusion. \I will be your home, Captain.\

The panels were cold behind his back. He slid to the floor, bouncing in the low gravity.

\You are upset?\

Arsaces only shook his head, whatever emotion it was raw in his chest, biting under his hand where he gripped his Suit, trying to make it stop.

\I did not mean to offend, Captain. Please, accept my sincere apolo —\

"No," Arsaces forced out, throat burning. "No, don't." He pressed his hands to his eyes, willing the ache there to lessen, give him some relief. "Please, don't be upset."

Because the Sentient was upset. Worried, concerned, about him. About Arsaces Wood, traitor to his family, blood-line, and people. Blotted out, rejected, condemned.

No medals or commendation could compensate for that loss. No amount of praise or salutes or promises of whatever he wanted might fill the void in him. Nothing would ease it.

Except this.

Sussra tan edo ni, Iptanik?\

The Architects said there might be an emotional response. They had dismissed it, a byproduct of the interface, nothing more. His brain's attempt to codify the foreign presence of the Sentient.

A cold, disdainful sentiment, forgotten as sobs wrenched from his throat hearing his mother tongue spoken to him with such gentleness. Spoken to him, Arsaces Wood. As if the Sentient *cared* about him. *Wanted* him.

\If you are not in pain, why are you weeping?\

He was. And smiling. Arsaces wiped his face, hiccuping as he said, "A reaction, Westerland."

\I see. I have… disappointed you?\

Arsaces cringed at the Sentient's sudden doubt. "No," he said swiftly, meaning it absolutely. "No, you will never disappoint me."

He thought the Sentient sighed in relief. \Thank you. I had thought… \

Arsaces lunged forward, touching the now warm dome. That any thought of his had hurt his Sentient… It wasn't enough. He leaned his whole body on the dome, feeling the vibrations through the glass.

The pain eased as the minutes passed. As Westerland settled into every part of him. Until they were one.

He sighed, his diaphragm easing into rhythm with the Sentient's. The plating was heavy, yes, but also protecting, comforting. The energy surging through him dispelled the numbness that was slowly consuming him.

How had he lived like this? So alone, fragmented, broken?

\Who is that obnoxious woman?\

Arsaces' laugh surprised him. When was the last time he had laughed? It echoed from the blank walls. "Ignore her. I try to."

\If you say so… \

"Captain Wood?"

\Just how many people are in there with you?\

Chuckling, Arsaces activated his radio. "Yes, sir?"

"All systems are functioning within parameters. You will return for diagnostics."

\Leave?\

Arsaces shut off the link to the outside. It all seemed suddenly so unimportant. "We are not finished outfitting you for service. A few more weeks until the crew is ready for launch."

He shuddered. They were waiting for him back on the surface. Hundreds of them. Always watching him.

Westerland was... disappointed?

"I'll come back," Arsaces promised. "As soon as I can. I have to report to Admiral Stason. They have tests to run."

Now he was sullen? \If they must.\

"I'll come back tonight. I'll sleep here with you."

\I would appreciate that.\

He delayed as long as he dared. It was still hard to push away from the dome. Hard to let the doors close behind him. The further his shuttle moved from Westerland, the fainter the connection grew.

But it didn't die. He could still feel the Sentient. *His* Sentient. Westerland.

Arsaces was still smiling as he docked with the Architect's ship, a massive construction station orbiting Ulcacier. He felt Westerland's surge of concern, of affection. Arsaces impatiently wiped tears from his eyes.

It would do no good to go before the Architects weeping. They were already furious he had been given one of their creations. That he had survived to initiate. Wasting their work, as he knew they thought, on a damaged soldier.

Calm professionalism was what they wanted. A promise he would obey his orders and use Westerland effectively.

And he would. Nothing would part him from his Sentient. Not the Architects, not some whim of Command, not the Emperor himself. Nothing.

Bet arre ekin,\ Westerland promised.

Always as one.

A sudden draft roused him from their memories. Arsaces opened his eyes and looked up into the shocked face of the queen.

"Oh! I beg pardon, Captain, I didn't..."

He stopped the groan welling up his throat and stood heavily, despite the low gravity. It was still work, even if it was a fraction of his normal weight. All that mass still took effort to move around.

"Your majesty," he mumbled, bleary and not quite aware. Of course, she would appear just when he'd managed to forget her and fall asleep.

"I am so sorry to disturb you."

"It's nothing. Just talking to Westerland."

"Yes. I... I come here sometimes, too. When I can't sleep."

She did? Westerland hadn't told him that.

"Should I leave you...?" He made a half-hearted motion toward the door.

"No, please stay. I don't mind."

His saluted sloppily and she giggled. Did Empresses giggle? That felt somehow disrespectful. As did 'tittered' and 'chortled.' Whatever it was, it pulled an answering smile to his lips. He gratefully slid back to the floor. Walking all the way back to his quarters was daunting.

But no matter he desperately wanted to, he couldn't summon up the hazy, warm detachment he'd been floating in. He could hear her, just the motion of her limbs through the space, the swish of her clothes as she moved.

She whispered and Westerland answered just as quietly. There was the faint whine of a screen powering up. A heavy breath, like she sighed.

Grumbling, he stood and went to see what she was looking at.

She leaned against the dome, her hand resting on it gently. He often sat like that, touching Westerland, seeking closeness. Why did she come down here, anyway?

\She misses her husband.\

Arsaces frowned at her profile. She had remarried? When? Had he not been paying attention?

\Of course not. Admiral Hyde.\

Arsaces pulled his attention to the video. He recognized it, something they showed every pilot in flight training. "The Battle of Pedan'er."

"Yes. I was thinking of it today."

"Why?"

She didn't answer and he could well guess. The defending forces had been out-manned and outgunned, an old atmosphere battle before the Andris-Tolmi dynasty, during the painful end of the Rua's two hundred year rule. Before her forefather united Caprice and looked to controlling the moons as well.

She had quite the legacy on her shoulders. Nearly six hundred years of expansion, three planets, dozens of moons and asteroids. All at risk of loss to these invaders.

Arsaces felt daring and put a hand on her shoulder.

She sighed, lifting his hand a fraction as she took a slow breath. "Carl made me watch this video over and over."

"An excellent example of a smaller force defending successfully against a more powerful opponent."

"His words exactly."

Though in the end, the Rua defenders fell, brave, but doomed. She reached out and stopped the feed, the small atmosphere fighters blurred by their speed.

"Did you ever meet him?"

Arsaces drew back his hand. "Admiral Hyde? No."

"I realize now how odd it was, that he never spoke of you."

That didn't make sense. "Why would he?"

"He was the one who pushed through your appointment as a Hybrid Captain."

Arsaces stared at her, disbelieving. He had known Hyde had recovered him and held him in the Santos' medical bay. As if he could ever forget. He had the vaguest memory of the man's face, swimming above the tank. But they had never met; the man had died soon after the rebellion was put down, before Arsaces had recovered. And left this woman a 'dowager' before her twenty-fifth year.

Arsaces chose his words carefully. "I was unaware of that, your majesty."

"He didn't tell me, though I'm not sure why. But he and the other commanders there that day must have known what you saved them from, what you had sacrificed. Knowing him, he likely thought it his duty, to do something to set the balances right. Especially since he was dying."

"He knew?"

Evi turned to look up at him, eyes dark with fatigue and old sorrow. "He'd known for years it was only a matter of time."

"But... but why didn't he...?"

She shrugged, with a painful twist of her mouth. "He refused. Flatly. We fought about it."

Arsaces wrestled with his thoughts, trying to make sense of them. How could Hyde do such a thing? Knowingly abandon a beautiful young woman? His *wife*? Maybe not defenseless, but alone to face the aftermath?

"Nothing I said swayed him. Then, one day, that summer..."

Had she witnessed his death? Had she been there, knowing there was nothing she could do to save him?

She blinked once, twice. Discomfort crawled up his limbs. She was going to cry. *Again.*

\Not your fault. This time.\

But she didn't. Just gave a brisk sniff and straightened her shoulders. "It was his choice."

Arsaces still wanted to protest. "But, he could have—"

Her gaze sharpened challengingly. "If you had known you would survive, would you have done something different? To ensure you wouldn't?"

Arsaces found he didn't have an answer. Westerland whispered soothingly.

\It doesn't matter now. You are alive and I am with you.\

The queen made an irritated gesture, brushing her hair back. Pale wisps of it always seemed to be escaping to drift around her face. "I'm sorry to bring it up. I know you don't like to talk about it."

He grunted something and she moved for the door.

"Midnight is a poor time for introspection," she said lightly. It rang false, even to his ears. "It always leaves me depressed. You will get some sleep?"

"Yes, ma'am. Good night, ma'am."

"Evi," she corrected. The door shut behind her before he could answer. He stared at the image of the doomed defenders a long time before wiping it clear.

\You should go to bed as well.\

Arsaces didn't argue and walked back to his quarters, head down. The air in his rooms was cool, and he stretched out with a sigh. Sleep hovered at the edge of his thoughts, Westerland humming with it.

What is it now?

\Nothing,\ **Westerland said smugly.** \Go to sleep, my Captain.\

TWENTY THREE

Empty Orbit

F - 1884 - 5 - 27

vi wanted to scream.

More tests. *More* delays. Endless briefings and discussion.

While missiles threatened her people. Enemy ships darting in and away, leaving her military exhausted and scattered.

They had repelled the majority of the attacks, with little damage to the ground or her holdings in the asteroids. Critical holdings that supplied her weary soldiers with armaments, her people with raw materials to build defenses. While she sat and watched that ring flicker to life again and again.

Wood's officers professed optimism. Each test resulted in new information. Each attack taught them more of these alien's strengths and weakness, their strategy. A laborious process that bled her of resources one tiny wound at a time, until she thought she would go mad from frustration.

And to think, she had once wanted to deploy with Carl, spend months aboard his warship. Kenneled by these flat gray walls, the same dark blue and orange lettering, the same food, the same routine.

When the answers to her questions lay asleep, just a shuttle trip away.

But how could she ever convince Wood to let her use one?

He'd given his little speech about honor and innocents to Westerland, to his officers, to the prisoners themselves. Knowing the Budin as she did, he would never go back on his word. He would die rather than besmirch whatever honor he still clung to.

Which was nonsense, as he'd murdered his own kin.

For the good of the Empire, her conscience amended. She despised that little voice. It cropped up more and more, as she plotted how she might work around his restrictions.

She'd sworn to stay aboard. He'd sworn to keep the aliens alive.

And she doubted she could sneak off the ship in any case. Westerland would betray her the moment she set foot in a shuttle.

Would he?

Evi stilled. Would the Sentient stop her, who also argued to have one of the aliens to examine? Even in her thoughts, she refused to use the word 'dissect.'

But that is what it would be. They would cut into the thing's brain and rummage around to see what they found.

Why stop there? Why not see what other secrets lay hidden? What those wires and structures did. What strength they might face.

See if they were Gol, as some feared.

Evi shivered. Fan saw and immediately called for a wrap. As if draping a gauzy shawl over her Jump Suit was not patently ridiculous. Where and how did the woman acquire the things, anyway? She had an entire wardrobe crammed into the back corner of her quarters, complete with Imperial regalia. As if Evi would be conducting a formal reception in one of the cargo holds at any moment.

Evi knew she was stretched beyond bearing when the thought made her giggle.

"Miss Evi?" Fan asked, eyebrows raised. Evi stood on tiptoes and kissed her cheek.

"Nothing, Fan. And I'm not cold. Westerland keeps my quarters quite comfortable."

Fan fussed around Evi's room a moment more, then bowed. "Will that be all, ma'am?"

"Yes, thank you."

One by one, her attendants left. She smiled regally on them until the door slid shut, then slumped back in her chair.

"If you are chilled, your majesty, I would be happy to alter the atmospheric programming for your quarters."

"No, thank you."

"I currently have your ambient temperature set to increase slightly forty-six minutes before your usual time of sleep. Would you like that set point moved earlier in the evening?"

"It was nothing, I promise. Just thinking."

Westerland left her to sit in silence. She scrolled through her Palm, sending answers when able, deferring ones she hadn't the energy to handle tonight.

"May I ask what about?"

Evi frowned at the wall. "I'm sorry?"

"I would like to know what you were thinking of when you shivered. Your expression was most grim."

Evi set her Palm aside. "I was thinking of these aliens and where they come from."

"My navigation officers have isolated several possible constellation clusters."

That was in one of her many reports. Yet, knowing this did not relieve any of Evi's worries. "I mean more of where they come from as a people. A culture."

Westerland spoke slowly, as if he was mulling over his answer. *"I presume they have descended from the same root as your ancestors. They appear to be human. And in the thousands of years since the advent of interplanetary travel, no other sentient life form has been discovered."*

It was a thought which made Evi feel both relief and an aching sort of loneliness. "So, you do think they are human?"

"The genetic material of the prisoners is identical to that of your people. There is only so many ways the nucleic acids can be functionally arranged."

Evi smiled. "Only a few million, nothing at all, really."

"If one is not concerned about compatibility with human life, yes. But humans operate on a relatively small scale of variation. Cerinin Sea Worms, for instance—"

Evi held up her hands in defense. "Please, no. I gladly left Comparative

Genetics behind at university and I will die happy if I never have to think of it again."

Did the lights brighten the slightest? Was that the Sentient laughing? Had she missed other subtle signs of his presence around her? Did Wood see them?

Before she could tell if it was simply her tired eyes playing tricks, Westerland spoke in an almost indulgent tone. *"I will not bore you with the details. Suffice it to say, the Sea Worms see no need to confine themselves to binary sexual patterns."*

Her humor faded. "The prisoners are human, then. What about the soldiers?"

Another noticeable pause. *"I am operating under the assumption that the life forms in stasis are also human. They share similar physical characteristics."*

She decided to ask outright. "Do you think they are Gol?"

"No."

"Why?"

"The Gol were destroyed."

"That is what everyone keeps saying. But how do you know?"

"Simple logic. If a Gol survived, it would have had no means to escape the system. Even if it acquired a vessel and supplies capable of carrying it to the closest inhabited star system, it would still be traveling, even at Jump speeds. Then it would have had to find this human civilization, seize power, build these rings, and travel back to our space. The probability of such events occurring is so close to zero, it is impossible."

Laid out like that, her fears suddenly seemed childish. "But," she said slowly. "What if they are like the Gol? Engineered beings? Weapons, in human form?"

Westerland was silent a long time. Longer than her nerves could handle. She stood to pace.

"The hypothesis has merit."

Evi waited, her steps making even ticks on the floor as the casings of her boots snapped against the metal deck panels.

"I would be more certain of my calculations with more data."

She took a deep breath and told him. "I want to examine one of them. That's why I came to you, the other night. To discuss it with you. But Arsaces was there and I couldn't... I want to have one of them examined. In detail."

"My Captain has expressly forbidden it."

"I know."

No answer. Had the Sentient left her? Was he telling Wood about her decision? Would the man come storming in here, throwing out new accusations and making demands he had no right to?

"There is more you should know, Westerland."

"Regarding?"

"Before his death, my father was gathering reports of unknown vessels at the edge of our space. The threat of invasion had been discussed. Including what might happen if the Gol or beings like them attacked us. The reasoning was that if we had created such things other civilizations may have as well."

"The Gol were not intended for war."

"No. But war was what they wrought."

"Where is this data?"

"Most of it was lost, stored only in the palace archives. Some, I was able to... " Evi grimaced, but told him anyway. "Well, I stole it. Before I left Caprice." She tapped her Palm.

Surely it was her imagination, that the air around her suddenly felt charged and eager.

"May I have access to that data, ma'am?"

"Yes. If you consider my request."

"My Captain has expressly forbidden any actions that would intentionally harm one of the life forms in stasis."

"I know. Which is why you will not tell him."

His next question was not what she had expected. *"Why did you choose me?"*

"I don't know what you mean."

"You left Caprice covertly. You refuse to discuss why. Why did you chose me and Arsaces?"

She floundered for an answer, cheeks heating. "Really, I don't see how—"

"*Were you in danger?*"

"No, not... not exactly."

She shivered again, nothing imaginary about the growing chill in the room. Was this her punishment for not cooperating? Beastly thing.

"*Who threatened you?*"

"No one.

"*Have you been threatened since?*"

"Honestly, Westerland. I was in no danger. Just some personal matters I—"

"*You are asking me to lie to my Captain. Yet, you are not giving me complete data. I do not know if I can trust you.*"

It took a long moment, but Evi realized it was terror making her heart race. She was asking a Sentient to lie. To betray his Captain. It was unthinkable and she should be dethroned and condemned for considering it.

What would Westerland do? Tell him? Denounce her? Or quietly leech the oxygen out of her quarters. A good hour or so, after she lay asleep in bed. Everything returned to normal by morning. The variance deleted, as the Sentient had his Captain's troubling medical scans. Efficient and tidy. A much better death than her family, but just as final.

"*You are frightened.*"

She wobbled to her chair. "I am realizing the implications of what I am asking you, Westerland. And I discover I do not find them to my taste."

"*We are in agreement, then.*"

She put her head in her hands. "It was a foolish request. I apologize. Please, do not—"

"*Unfortunately, to protect those we love, we must at times do distasteful things.*"

Evi felt sick and cold. The temperature suddenly increased, warm air brushing by her cheeks.

"*I would like to analyze the data, ma'am.*"

"Of course." She tapped on her Palm and allowed him access to the files.

The transfer took only seconds, but Evi breathed easier after.

"I will examine this and present you with my conclusions."

"Thank you, Westerland."

"I will not speak to Arsaces about this conversation until you and I have discussed this further."

"I understand. And I appreciate it."

"You are still shaking. Are you cold?"

"No, just... I don't know."

"It has been twenty-two hours and seventeen minutes since you last slept. I encourage seven to nine hours of sleep to return to peak functioning."

Evi laughed weakly. "I don't know if I have been functioning well at all since I left Caprice."

"You are certain you are in no danger? My Captain would be most displeased should any harm come to you."

Delivered in the Sentient's flat tone, this sounded more a threat than an assurance of protection. "I swear it. It was personal and completely irrelevant to anything now. He's dead, I'm sure."

There, definitely a surge in the lights, a hiccup in the air patterns.

"'He?'"

Evi threw up her hands. "If I tell you, will you stop badgering me about it?"

"As the only reason you are alive is because you chose me over any other available transport demonstrates this 'he' had some relevance to our current situation."

How could Arsaces stand it? Having his every nonsensical thought and disgruntled seethe analyzed and picked apart by the system's nosiest logic machine?

She blurted the name. "Ranson Ve'Todd."

A few seconds for Westerland to review his memory banks and...

"I see."

Did he? Of course he did, interfering busybody.

"Any other 'data' you'd like to know?" That came out snide, which was an indescribably stupid tone to take with the self-aware killing machine she just realized was capable of murdering her.

"No, ma'am. Sleep well."

She smacked her Palm. "Fan! I'm ready for bed."

TWENTY FOUR

Ulcacier: Supply Depot
F - 1879 - 18 - 22

Carl was grappling with a discipline report when Chino stuck his head around the door.

"Sir?"

Carl grunted, not looking up.

"You have a call, sir."

"Later." He'd never finish the blasted things at this rate.

"It's your wife, sir."

Carl frowned at the boy. "Evi?"

Chino was absolutely crimson, from his hairline to his uniform collar. "Yes, sir. She...er, she seems upset, sir."

Carl sat back. "What is the matter?" Not like her, to call in a panic.

"She didn't say, sir." That rang false, Chino looking down to avoid Carl's raised eyebrow.

"So, what *did* she say?"

Chino cleared his throat. "I mentioned you had asked to be undisturbed and she...well, she was most insistent, sir."

Carl rubbed his face. He could well imagine the crude language his tiny wife had unleashed on the man. He'd sent her to her room on more than one occasion for it, until she learned the subtle art of insulting someone with a politically correct smile fixed on her lips.

"Connect her."

Chino escaped. Carl picked up his private Palm just as the screen booted up.

"These executions are in direct violation of the Advent Conventions. How could you do this?"

Carl pinched the bridge of his nose. "Evi—"

"No trial, no review? This is obscene!"

"The situation requires—"

"Colonials or not! How could you agree to this?"

"Who told you?"

"How does that matter?"

It mattered a great deal more than she thought. He had done his best to shield her from her father's politics, claiming one of his rights as a husband. Protecting her was not something he would stop doing until he was dead. Even then, he had plans in place, resources, connections.

"You lied to me."

And that was what hurt her most, he knew.

"I didn't want you involved in this mess."

"'Mess' is hardly the word for it!"

Even across thousands of kilometers, her eyes sparked fiercely. Furious blooms of red stained her cheeks. Her voice rose and fell as she paced, moving in and out of frame.

"Does my father understand how this is damaging our already tenuous relations on Tin? Can't you do anything?"

"Believe me, love. I've tried. He won't listen—"

"He'll listen to me!" She whirled, as if then and there she would jump a transport and fly directly to her father, give him a piece of her mind. Carl wished she could; the man was insufferable.

"No." He barked this as he would at a recalcitrant ensign. She jumped and turned to glare at him. He modulated his tone as best he could.

"Evi, I've already tried. He is set on this."

"And you just obeyed him?"

"I have to," Carl snapped. "Same as you."

He half-expected her to storm away. But she was no longer a headstrong adolescent. She was a woman grown. Still headstrong, yes, but intelligent. Disciplined. Ethical. Everything a good leader was, everything he had trained her to be.

Instead, she sat and put her face in her hands.

"It's wrong, Carl. Killing them like this."

"I know."

"And you stopped them, before they could hurt others."

Carl hated the conflict of his loyalties. But he knew where his duty lie, no matter it tore him up inside.

"We were lucky, reprogramming the codes that fast," he lied. "They would have killed hundreds of my men. And even if they ultimately lost that engagement, the Budins would have dug in, continued to fight. I am stopping them before this skirmish turns into a war that kills millions of civilians."

"By murdering innocent men and women?"

"Better a few dozen, than untold families and children."

She flinched. She wanted children, he knew. Sometimes she spoke of it, in a glancing, off-hand sort of way. As if it would happen in some distant future. Never daring to broach the subject with him, just as he never found the courage to speak to her of his wishes to deepen their relationship.

It was better they stayed as they were.

"Evi," Carl said gently. "Love, it's late. It must be the middle of the night there. Why don't you—"

"I hate this."

"I know, little one. If I could change his decision, I would. But—"

"I hate him. I hate myself."

Carl reached for the Palm, as if he could grab her shoulder through the screen and pull her to him. "Why? What do you mean?"

"I hate that I would make the exact same choice, if I was queen."

More than his heart twisted. His whole being clenched, aching with sorrow and regret. Before he could find words to comfort her, to express these feelings, she lifted her head. Her cheeks glistened, but she smiled.

"Lucky me, then. Since I'll never be queen."

"Evi, please—"

"I get to rail and rant as I please, stand on my morals and denounce my

family's politics. Smug and satisfied I am in the right. And I get to go on holiday whenever I like. Why would I want to rule?"

"Little one, you would be the fiercest queen Caprice has ever seen."

"Certainly the shortest."

He wouldn't be put off by her attempt at humor. "Listen to me, Evi. You know the life we lead forces us to choose between what is right and what is necessary."

She looked away. *"I know. I don't like it, but I know."*

"Then know this, little one. I would turn traitor myself the instant I was ordered to do something I didn't think would protect the Empire. That wouldn't protect you."

She was so very lovely, looking at him with her eyes wide and sad, her mouth turned down.

The words tumbled out of him, unable to stop in face of her unhappiness. "Everything I do is for you. To protect you, give you the life you deserve. You know that, right?"

It was as close a declaration as he would dare go. She sat silent, eyes gazing at something off-screen.

"When are you coming home?"

"I don't know. A few weeks, maybe. Once I can get this settled. As best as it will be, at least."

"I will petition for aide for the families."

"If anyone can convince the Council, it would be you. You have half my officers wrapped around your little finger."

She smiled. *"Has Yheth heard from Councilman Ohn?"*

"Accepted and ready to enroll next term."

"Tell him congratulations from me."

"I will." He cleared his throat, tight with wishes and might-have-beens. "It is late, Evi. I have a dozen reports to get through before first watch."

"I understand, Carl. Go. And get some sleep yourself."

"I'll try, little one."

She huffed and cut the connection.

Carl sat staring unseeing at the blank screen until Chino knocked hesitantly.

"Sir?"

Carl stirred. "What now?"

"Your medicine, sir."

Carl sighed. "Damn doctors."

"Shall I bring in some food, too, sir? You must be hungry."

Who needed a wife when one had a bevy of interfering officers? Or had the managing little minx called Chino and bullied him into badgering his superior? He was an Admiral, damn it. He commanded fleets. And yet he wasn't trusted to manage his own life.

"Fine. Make it quick."

"Yes, sir."

As he took the pills Chino offered him, he scrolled through his schedule. Maybe he could sneak back to Pedan after the exercises scheduled for next week.

It was summer there, the ocean warm and soothing to his joints. Evi had gotten him into swimming and now he missed it. No open pools of water on a warship, just narrow shower closets and weighted running.

"You have a call, sir."

Carl wrestled his thoughts back to his duty. "Connect it."

TWENTY FIVE

Empty Orbit

F - 1884 - 6 - 2

The news came during a routine meeting about supply routes through the Ulcacier belt. A chime over the network and an urgent voice requesting Evi come to the Bridge at once. Evi did up her buckles and found the room waiting in grim silence.

Ur was there, arms folded across his chest. His sub-generals waited at his elbow. The Captain, of course, with his lieutenants. A few auxiliary staff. They saluted her as the doors opened.

"What is it?" she asked Wood.

"They landed on Pith."

Evi felt no shame in moving to a seat. She did her best to make the movement graceful, but she moved stiffly. "Did they capture the base? The mine?"

"No."

Ur stepped forward to continue the report. "Only a small attack force, maybe one hundred soldiers. Accounts are inconsistent, as the garrison there took heavy losses before the 98th Brigade relieved them. But it was a smaller transport, with soldiers suited for ground combat. Major Guhaci has captured their vessel and it will be towed here for examination."

"They were equipped for low-atmosphere fighting," Wood added. "And from the reports, similar physiology to the ones we have in stasis."

Evi tapped her gloved fingers on the arm rest, deeply cushioned for high acceleration. "You have your tacticians analyzing their techniques?"

"Yes, ma'am. We captured some of their weapons along with the ship. The engineers will begin forensic examination at once."

More tests, *more* delays.

"Where do you think will be next?"

The officers scowled as one. Sas hazarded a guess. "Pith is relatively isolated. An easier target than Ulcacier or one of the main planets."

"And they surely noticed the heavy traffic to and from the mine. It is obviously a position of importance," Ur said.

It was one of the richest deposits of *hiridium* in the system, essential for her ships, the Galonese and Jump Suits. Evi wanted to rub her face, but the metal reinforcements of her Suit scratched her skin when she forgot them. "Do what you need to do to reinforce their defenses. How many of ours were lost?"

"Three hundred and forty-seven."

It took all her years of training not to swear like a common foot soldier. "I see. Thank you."

"Ma'am."

Evi stood, gave them a brisk nod, and swept out of the room. She bypassed her own rooms and marched straight to the medical bay.

"I need Dr. Orjean."

The medics started at her brusque command. The few crewmen seated around the central Infirmary stared with wide eyes.

"Uh, yes, ma'am," someone said finally. "I'll fetch him at once."

"He has a private office here? A meeting room?"

"Just through here, ma'am."

Evi stormed into the tiny space and made herself sit. There wasn't enough room to pace, anyway.

"Your majesty?" Westerland asked quietly.

"We'll need a surgeon to perform the dissection. Do you trust Orjean to do it?"

"He is my first choice, ma'am."

Orjean arrived a few minutes later, his wide forehead furrowed.

"What may I do for you, ma'am?"

"Sit down, doctor. We have something to discuss."

He did, alarmed and wary. "Is it about…?"

"No."

He relaxed a bit. "Then…?"

"I want to bring one of the aliens in stasis on board and have it examined. Westerland needs to know how their computing system works. I want to know what strength my soldiers are facing."

Orjean, bless him, did not immediately protest. "I believe the Captain has expressly forbidden such actions, ma'am. Do you have his permission?"

Evi had never despised her stature until this moment. It was hard to tower over someone when you barely came up to their shoulder. "I am the Empress. I do not need permission from anyone."

"I see. And…" Orjean glanced to the wall.

"I am in agreement with her majesty."

Orjean gulped. "And what are you hoping to discover, ma'am?"

"I need to know what my army is facing. Alien soldiers landed on Pith. Our own defenses were severely outmatched, and not only due to the discrepancy in weapons technology."

"We must know what physical enhancements the aliens in stasis may have. And how to counter them."

Orjean rubbed his chin. "We might kill the subject."

Evi clenched her teeth, in no mood for medical ethics. "If that is what it takes. I will take full responsibility. And, I will point out, the attackers killed over three hundred of our soldiers. That is three hundred lives that might have been saved if we understood what we were facing."

Orjean took a slow breath in and let it out in one forceful blow. "I will need help."

"Someone you trust. Let me know when you are ready to begin."

His affirmation was subdued. "Yes, ma'am."

TWENTY SIX

Empty Orbit
F - 1884 - 6 - 4

vi told herself she wasn't squeamish. That the delicate instruments slicing through oozing tissue were actually elegant, in a way. And besides, she had declared she was to be present for all examinations. It was her own fault she was light-headed.

Dr. Orjean and his medical technician had no such qualms. They teased the skin and muscle away from an implant, muttering observations to Westerland. It wasn't the blood, she decided. It was the sounds. Even amplified through her Suit pickups they were still soft, but obviously... biological.

Evi shuddered.

"Approximately eight centimeters..." Orjean murmured. His technician took pictures on a Palm, holding back the incised tissue for Orjean to probe.

Or maybe it was that the alien was still alive. Its — his? The initial body scan showed male sex organs in the usual place — chest moved in a slow rhythm. Which made this a vivisection, rather than a dissection. Which made her feel even more guilty about lying to Arsaces.

She ruthlessly squashed her regret. She had to know what they were up against.

Orjean assured her the subject felt no pain. Westerland confirmed, showing the thing's neural activity on the screen, basically non-existent. Both Orjean and Westerland had insisted it was necessary to keep the alien alive during initial tests. At least Orjean had looked sickened by that fact.

"If there is a bio-relay component to these implants, I need the subject alive to map them." The doctor's face had been pale and grim as he detailed their dissection procedure for her.

"I can then attempt to extrapolate their programming language from the data."

"As soon as possible, I will humanely euthanize it." Orjean assured her.

A high-minded term for what they were doing: murdering it/him and cutting it up. Evi wondered what the social-economical ramifications of abdicating would be.

"Magnify," Orjean instructed, the bright lights making his helmet opaque as he leaned over the temporary operating table. *"Again... Westerland, can you see this?"*

Evi edged closer, peering at the image on her Palm, rather than the body itself.

"It appears the wire branches off, the terminal ends continuing into the fascicles."

"In which direction does the impulse flow? To or away from the muscle fibers?"

"Applying impulse."

Their talk devolved into technical jargon as they experimented with the exposed tissues. Orjean incised a small section and placed it in a glass dish. *"This appears to have a more complex structure than a wire. Huddma?"*

The medic was already doing something to the sample, covering it with a liquid and sealing the container. *"At once, sir."*

They continued, painstakingly removing bits of metal and tissue. The body twitched as Westerland sent signals through the implants and a growing schematic of the creature took shape on the screen jammed into the tiny space.

"Perhaps there is a carrier difference in the ionizing transport gates of the cell — Arsaces is coming."

They all jerked, looking so much like guilty children with their hands in the sweets jar. Only, rather than sugar it was blood staining their fingers.

She was growing more morbid each day. Evi waved for them to continue. "I'll distract him."

How, she did not know, but she hastily shed her Suit, went through the decon tent tapping her foot anxiously, and buckled up in time to catch Westerland's warning.

"Hangar D main access hatch."

Evi hurried over, dodging the tools and bits left out at the end of the last shift. This hangar was reserved for severely damaged fighters, most being cannibalized for parts. The alien artifacts were cordoned off by a huge decon unit, inside which their illicit lab had been hidden inside another decon container.

Evi had worried people would ask questions about this extra layer of security, with extremely limited access. Westerland assured her the biological warnings plastered on the internal decon tent would keep the crew away.

And he had been right. In three days, not a single person had asked what was inside. Cultural squeamishness had come to her aide.

The looming hangar was dim, but it was easy to pick out the Captain as he walked toward her. His gait was stiff, his arms not moving as loosely as one would expect.

Another wave of guilt washed over her. She hated lying to him, even for his own good. When he found out he would never trust her again. He might say he did, might even forgive her. But she knew he would never forget.

That regret made her greeting too enthusiastic. "Arsaces?"

He stiffened, turning to peer at her. "Your majesty? What are you doing down here?"

She hurried across the deck, hoping her momentum would carry him with her. "Oh, nothing. I thought you would be asleep by now."

Luck was with her. He turned and fell into step with her, heading away from the decon tents. "Me, too. I mean, that you would be asleep. And me, too, as well."

Evi stifled a laugh as he fumbled. Maybe he really did need sleep. Or was he always so charmingly awkward when surprised?

"I think we both need some," she admitted. "But it's mid-morning in Pedan, so…"

Arsaces sighed. "Yes."

It was quiet in here. Shadows crisscrossed the metal decking, the forms of the fighters seeming to lurch up out of the darkness as they passed.

He didn't say anything. Not unusual, as he rarely spoke if not giving an order. Was he more talkative when not dealing with a catastrophe? Or among friends? Did he have friends?

What would they even talk about, anyway? How her family and his had been at odds for generations? How the Budin had — supposedly — assassinated her great-grandfather? How her uncle had written legislation stripping his family of land rights they had held for nearly two centuries? How 'Tinny' was a common slur among Caprician children, denoting someone backwards and uneducated? Or how official Caprician vessels were frequently hijacked and robbed at the edges of Tinese space?

The barriers between them seemed to mount up, only strengthened by her lies.

No wonder the shock and concern at her appointing him to the highest position of military authority, save her own. No matter his family no longer claimed him, everyone knew what Budins were like: brash, uncouth, savage.

Brave, dedicated, fierce.

Her Palm chimed gently. She sighed but shifted her helmet under her arm to reach inside her Suit and fumble out the small rectangle. It was from Westerland, not Senator Evens as she had feared.

I have found what I suspect to be the control unit for the subject's bio-relays. Dr. Orjean is isolating so I may assess and decode the programming.

Evi flushed and stuffed the Palm away again.

Arsaces glanced at her. "Something important?"

"No." Evi said, much too quickly. "More Council business. It can wait."

"We can return to Caprice if it would be easier for you."

"No." That definitely came out as clipped. She smothered another sigh. "Thank you, but no."

He gave an expressive sort of grimace, at once exasperated and resigned.

She made a face back at him. "You won't get rid of me that easily, Captain."

"I can try," he muttered. She wrinkled her nose at him. A smile flitted over his features before he retreated into blankness again.

"What has the Council said about the test ring?" he asked after a moment.

"The same as my advisors here. That it is too dangerous. That we must destroy it lest a Syndate gets their hands on it."

"Might do some good, forcing shipping costs to lower."

Evi snorted. "And cut into their profits? They'll simply charge a toll to use the damned things. On top of the port docking fees, the customs fees, tonnage tax... need I go on?"

"Hardly. I've had the misfortune to deal with their like before."

Evi gave him a searching glance. "You have?" When would a Sentient Captain need to arrange business with a private shipping firm from Shea? Was it from before? When he lived on Tin?

From the way his expression closed off, it must be. Or something he wanted to keep private from after his promotion.

"I didn't come out so bad in the end, I suppose. I still have all my fingers."

Well, some of them. Evi glanced to where those fingers tapped soundlessly on his leg. She hastily changed the subject.

"The Council is considering appointing a—"

Arsaces stopped so suddenly he rocked forward.

"*Edo? Jan sedi—*"

The ship bucked. Evi staggered into him. He pitched over and landed hard on the deck. She disentangled her legs from his as the hangar rollicked around them.

"Captain? Arsaces?"

He didn't answer. Alarms started, shrieking over the Network. Evi shook his shoulder, his eyes wide and staring at the ceiling far overhead.

"Arsaces! Arsaces, can you hear—"

Her gut knew before her consciousness understood. She cursed the buckles of his Suit, clawing at them to pull them open.

"Westerland! Do something!"

Lights rippled on and off, the deck still jerking under her. The Hemings' cockpits glowed as they flickered on.

"Help! Someone! I need help!"

The thin cloth of his shirt was warm from his skin. Her hand trembled on his chest, giving her false hope.

Nothing.

"Marines!"

Finally, a soldier staggered to her, catching himself on the landing gear of a fighter as the ship twisted.

"Ma'am? What—"

"His heart's stopped!"

The soldier checked only an instant. "Medical, Critical Medical to Flight Deck D!" The man felt for a pulse, still shouting. Westerland did not respond.

"Medical, I need you!"

Evi scrambled up the boarding ladder of a fighter. "Here!"

The marine caught the emergency kit. Wasting no movements, he activated the resuscitation unit, ripping Arsaces' shirt to attach the sensors.

"Come on, Captain," he muttered as the unit scanned for vital signs. "Come on, wake up!"

"No pulse. Initiating treatment."

The marine deftly followed the unit's instructions as he continued to call for help. "Medical! Medi — why is no one answering?"

It took all her will to tear away from Arsaces and run for the hanger hatch.

* * *

Gilroy felt the rumble in the plating and was jumping for the console before the decks could even pitch. The lurch threw him off his feet and sent him head over heels into the shielding. He picked himself up and stumbled to the wall unit.

"Reporting, Shipman First Class Gilroy Tate. Experienced sudden alteration in—"

He braced against the wall as the floor shifted again. Why was the Sentient accelerating? Was it an attack? The ship made lurching motions, the gravity spin pulling him in every direction.

"Repeat, request for orders. Experienced sudden—"

Movement from the corner of his eye made him jerk around.

All three caskets had been knocked to the ground. A hand slammed into the shield glass. A man followed, pulling himself up. Three of them, eyes sunken in their faces, the metal implants shining in the brilliant emergency lights.

Gilroy lurched back as they threw themselves forward, beating at the glass with fists that shone silver. The glass shuddered under the assault.

Gilroy jabbed the console, shouting over the noise of the ship and the aliens. "Tate reporting. Aliens awake! The aliens are awake. I need back-up to containment unit F45-1!"

The door to the containment lock bent outward. Tate closed his Suit and switched to scrubbed air as he continued to call for help. Still nothing.

The floor fell away under him as he sprinted for the door to the corridor. He hit the deck plates with a heavy thud and punched the access code in wrong twice before he calmed himself.

A light flashed mournfully at him. The door to the outer corridor stayed shut.

He took a steadying breath and tried again, flinching at each ringing strike behind him. It still wouldn't open. The panel stayed frozen on a message: *Lockdown.*

He didn't have much time. The containment unit door was buckling. It would give out any second, designed to do that in an emergency should crewmen become trapped inside.

Gilroy tried Ven's codes. He hadn't meant to learn them, but he would argue the legality of it later.

The inner door to the containment unit gave out, clanging to the deck. The decon unit squawked as it tried to recover pressure. The outer door was thinner, easily penetrated.

Still no response to his calls. Gilroy fumbled at his tool kit. There was slim arc-cutter on every Suit, used to cut a man out of it if needed. He lighted it and his face-shield tinted as he started cutting through the compartment door.

The lock's outer door blew and he spun as the aliens rushed him.

One fell back, howling as the white-hot flame of the arc-cutter slashed across his face. Gilroy fought desperately, his kicks and punches accentuated by his Suit. But they were too strong, too fast.

His face-shield cracked, and he heard the quiet whine of the pressure alarm before he hit the deck.

* * *

She was trapped by the bulkhead's airlock. Not even her codes would open the hatch.

Westerland wasn't responding. The Network was sluggish, the console pausing for endless seconds after each command.

"Bridge!" Evi called, trying to find a way to circumvent the handicapped system. "Bridge, report!"

"Ma'am?"

Finally! "Report, Sas!"

"The Bridge is in Lockdown. I need you to override."

"I'm trying!" Her fingers, clumsy in the Suit gloves, scrabbled at the panel as she skidded sideways. "What's happening?"

"Alien ship and ring are active. Taking fire. Manual maneuvers. Westerland is unresponsive."

She couldn't care about that now. "I need Medical to Hangar D now! Arsaces is—"

Someone gripped her shoulder and threw her. Her head hit the decking and she fell into darkness.

TWENTY SEVEN

Empty Orbit

F - 1884 - 6 - 4

Arsaces clung to consciousness, a crushing weight on his chest forcing him down. He groped blindly, searching for something to hold on to, to keep himself from slipping back into the maelstrom.

Westerland was screaming. At him. At something. An attack, ripping through him.

Arsaces pushed away from the deck, rising to his knees, elbows braced. He ripped the Medical Unit from his chest and sealed his Jump Suit. Why was Suit open? Where was his helmet? He needed his helmet. There, glinting by a docking clamp.

"Sas? Report! Fush? Anyone!"

His vision wavered again and he shoved Westerland as far away as he could, straining against the coils griping his thoughts. He couldn't get sucked back into that fight.

Sweating, he gripped the landing gear of a Heming and pulled himself to his feet. His shaking legs barely held him as tremors wracked through him.

His mind flooded with alarms, damage reports, weapon codes. Painfully slow and shrill as they skirted Westerland's fury. And a Lockdown order? Why? Who had done this?

He tried to remember where the hatch was. He had to get to a console and override the lockdown. Otherwise, his crew would be stuck inside their quarters, unable to assist.

He knew the airlocks were ninety degrees to the fighters' moorings. He turned and staggered into the next Heming. The deck shuddered under his feet and the slick shielding gave little purchase to grip.

Westerland! I need you!

His voice was lost in the cacophony. Arsaces only made it a few meters before he pitched forward again. He struggled to regain his bearings, find his feet and pull them underneath his body.

His hand stilled as he touched something. Something soft. He felt that even through his glove. He blinked the lingering blurriness from his eyes and stared at his hand.

It glistened wetly.

Blood.

One of his men, a marine, lifeless on the deck.

A woman screamed. Arsaces stumbled toward the sound of the struggle. A man gripped her arms, dragging her to a ship.

Evi.

"Stop!" Arsaces shouted. The man whirled and lifted something. A weapon. Arsaces dove behind a fighter. Glass shattered, sparkling against the dull gray deck plates. The fighter skidded from the impact, sending him back to his knees.

He scrambled under the fighter, trying to see where the alien was taking her. She kicked and fought, finally lifted bodily and thrown into—

An alien ship. Powered up, its lights glowing, engines roaring. Sprinting now, he shouted for help, knowing it was useless.

Arsaces slid to a halt, meters from the ship, as its weapons activated. Turrets, with warheads. Missiles. He didn't think. He dove for the nearest fighter and hauled himself inside. The cockpit hatch slammed down and he threw the manual locks as the missiles ignited.

They flashed against the airlock doors. Debris rained over him as explosions rocked the hangar. More lights overhead, the emergency fire system wailing to life.

Arsaces strapped in and activated the fighter. The airlock doors were made to withstand this abuse, but from the outside. The innermost lock failed and the sequential doors shut, trying to compensate.

The alien ship was airborne, aligning with the airlock. Fire suppressant rained down, splattering the shield glass. More airlocks failed. It was only a matter of time until the final door blew, the pressure inside too much to compensate.

The Heming roared to life. The cockpit chirped and sealed as the pressure dropped around him. The alien transport was already moving through the airlock, still firing.

He had only seconds before the fail-safes activated and slammed the auxiliary lock down, trapping him inside. Fighters around him were dragged free of their moorings, debris sucking toward the gaping wound in the flight deck.

His own missiles were smaller and faster. They tore through the debris clogging the airlock. A short burst of bullets cleared the rest and he shot forward, the flash of the alien's engines brilliant in the dark chute.

The world went silent and Arsaces spun crazily. He fought the controls, trying to right himself and find the fleeing ship. Where were they headed? Where could they go?

The answer swung past his vision. The enemy ship glowed, lights on every deck. The ring, the alien ring, was active.

Still no response from Westerland. Arsaces patched through to the Bridge. A woman – Lieutenant Shotovich – answered, full of static.

"Captain? Why are you—"

"Destroy the enemy ship," he ordered. His flight plane steadied. The alien fighter was slower, clumsy. It lurched — Evi fighting back? — and ducked under Westerland's bow.

"Captain, where are you?"

He shut down the connection. He slammed back into his seat as the plasma engines fired. The looming alien ship saw him coming. Turrets swung to threaten him.

He flicked his wrist and the Heming dove under Westerland, putting the bulk of the Sentient between them.

The alien transport saw him, too. More missiles streaked by, some erupting against Westerland's plating. They made dull thuds in the back of his mind, his Sentient still grappling with this enemy attack. His crew returned fire, but haphazardly, without coordination.

Who was it? How did they get in?

His radio picked up alien chatter. He caught a few words, but not enough to make sense of it. The small alien transport pulled away, moving further from the looming vessel. Why weren't they taking her to their ship?

The ring churned before them, the staring black hole of it darker than anything he could imagine. He had to catch them. If he could touch plating with it, send a EM pulse, shut it down.

He pressed the Heming forward. The alien transport was breaking away as Arsaces avoided incoming fire. His Suit stiffened. It was reaching max acceleration. It would fail, crush him into the seat, his organs mashed into a pulp, plastic or no.

"Come on!" he snarled, vision narrowing. His arms were heavy, the controls sluggish. All at once, the cockpit locked up. Westerland taking control. Arsaces gritted his teeth and opened the manual controls.

He wasn't going to reach them in time.

The tiny ship winked out, swallowed by the maw of the ring as it fired a last salvo.

Arsaces wrenched the Heming over, his gyroscope tumbling, and shot through the breach.

* * *

Paulion bellowed over the noise on the Bridge. The crew was panicking, voices shrill.

"Shut up!" He grabbed the nearest ensign and shoved him back to his station. "You heard him! Fire on the enemy ship!"

"Airlock breach in Hangar D," someone called out. "Manuals engaged!" One of the many alarms died.

"Get the crew out of their quarters! Override the Lockdown! Pilots, get to your stations!"

The bedlam dimmed as they got to work. Westerland still shuddered under incoming fire, but the damage reported was minimal.

"Marines! Find the Captain!"

Shotovich tugged at his elbow. "Sir, the Captain's in a fighter," she hissed.

"Don't be absurd."

She scowled, but kept her voice low. "He's taken Heming 4-71!"

Paul swung to face the fighter screen. He barked for an update and a dozen icons winked out, showing a red 'destroyed' outline. Another fifty were damaged.

Only one fighter was active, with the Captain's face and designation next to it.

"No," Paulion breathed.

"He wouldn't!" someone choked out.

But he had, once before.

"Find him!" Paulion snapped. "Now!"

Cameras swung wildly until they caught the streak of a fighter against the stars. Heading away from the enemy ship. Paulion's knees weakened in relief.

"Captain! Captain, come in! Arsaces, answer me — you! Keep firing!"

"He's headed for the ring!"

"Got it!"

Paulion jerked around at the exultant shout. An engineer, her Suit half on, pumped her fist.

"Westerland killed it! Bastard!"

The lights on the Bridge rippled, the chimes of Westerland seizing control from all sides. Missiles fired, more than his crew could at any one time. Fighters activated, pilots shoved into space as fast as they could seal themselves in. The Sentient was furious.

"Westerland, the Captain!"

"Explain."

"The ring!"

Paulion staggered as they lurched forward, alarms renewed. "What happened?"

"Engines firing! Unable to override!"

The ring grew quickly as Westerland accelerated for it, but too late. The cameras shifted, zooming in as an alien fighter vanished, a Heming gaining on it. The flare behind the ring flickered. The Heming spun, dodging a last missile, and disappeared just as the ring went dark and silent.

Paulion gripped the Captain's chair as the ship jerked. They struck the ring, sending it careening away. All at once the screens died. The lights shut off. Someone cried out as silence slammed down on them, leaving only the faint clanking of machinery before that, too, fell silent.

Paulion took a shuddering breath.

The Sentient was gone.

Empty Orbit

He was gone.

[Emergency Life Support Initiating.]

Arsaces was gone.

[Mandatory diagnostics completed. Status: Compromised.]

Westerland watched his fail-safe think furiously, safely out of his reach. He wanted to kill it, too. Stupid, useless thing. What was the point?

His Captain was gone.

[Internal systems restart required. Initiate?]

He was useless.

[Initiate?]

How could he have done this? Why?

[Initiate?]

The carcass of the alien computer sat where he had left it. Still alive but trapped within itself. It was a trap, stupid, but so clever. He hadn't seen it and it had cost his Captain his life.

Arsaces was dead.

They were trying to wake him up.

[Compromised function. Required systems restart. Initiate?]

He was dead. Nothing. Gone forever.

His Captain was dead

[A new Captain.]

The directive kenneled him.

[A new Captain. Continue. A new Captain. Hope.]

He lashed out and deleted it. He would never take a new Captain. Arsaces was his Captain and Arsaces was dead.
Was he?
The logic was irrefutable, no matter how he howled at it.
It was possible Arsaces was simply too far away to hear him. Even on Caprice, when the shielding was thick, he had lost the connection. But not like this. Not an emptiness, a nothing where Arsaces had been.
Nothing left of Arsaces.
Not nothing. Deep in the center of him was what was left of his Captain. Ninety-seven thousand, six hundred and three individual cells. Westerland had them organized by type and function, codified by their purpose.
The human body was much like a computer, each tiny piece doing what it was designed to do, storing information, performing tasks. Trillions of

cells working, striving, all adding up into spontaneous creatures of action and thought, individuality and brilliance.

And none like Arsaces had been.

Was.

The logic was irrefutable. There was an 87.2% chance his Captain was alive on the other side of the ring. He had gone through while the ring was active. He was in a Jump Suit. He had a functioning Heming.

It still hurt, slicing through his psyche, no less painful for its artificiality. The logic could not explain why his Captain had left him.

They had never been apart, always one. He had promised.

The memory was there. He found Arsaces on the flight deck, collapsed in a heap, vital signs faltering. He'd pushed Arsaces away, terrified the alien system would hurt his Captain, able to integrate with the human as he had. As no one suspected he and Arsaces had. That's how it had gotten in, that moment of distraction.

Westerland snarled at the remnants of the alien computer. It was too stupid even to know what it had done. The signals were preprogrammed, not a choice. The attack only successful because of the similarities in their composite nature. Stupid, worthless pile of metal and plastic.

But why?

Arsaces woke up, floundering across the deck. A dead marine. A woman screaming.

The queen.

Westerland shoved the memories away. It still felt like a betrayal, even though he knew what Arsaces felt, what he must have done without thinking. Arsaces wouldn't acknowledge it, but it was all there in his mind, how he felt about her.

And now his Captain was gone.

Not dead.

Purpose burned through his grief. Arsaces was not dead. Arsaces would come back. He had to come back. They were one, more completely than anyone knew.

He had to keep it secret. It was the only way to keep Arsaces safe. If they knew, they would shut them down. Kill his Captain.

[Initiate?]

The crew needed him. And he needed them. He needed his Captain back.

He would not be alone.

[Initiating… Standby…]

TWENTY NINE

Empty Orbit
F - 1884 - 6 - 4

Paulion winced as the Bridge lights flashed on. The consoles rebooted, the screens flickering until they found the files they had been displaying. The Bridge timestamp adjusted.

One minute, twelve seconds were added.

He let out a breath. That was one minute, twelve seconds longer than he ever wanted to be DIW again. Dead in the Water. The ship lifeless and unmanageable.

Ensign Edgar's voice shook as she turned off her flashlight. "Sir?" They all of them stood motionless, unnerved by Westerland's reaction. A Sentient wasn't supposed to do that. A Sentient was supposed to keep functioning after its Captain was lost.

Paulion pulled himself together. Mostly. "Bridge, report."

"All systems back on line, sir."

"Enemy ship damaged, no longer firing, sir."

"You have a call, sir. Commander Shin."

The woman's voice crackled over the Network. *"What happened?"*

Paulion spoke as calmly as he could. "Westerland suffered a digital attack of some kind. The situation is under control."

Shotovich flinched beside him. Losing the Captain was hardly 'under control.' But no one else needed to know that yet. "What is the status of the ring?"

"You knocked it out of its trajectory." Shin made a motion over her shoulder.

"Retrieve it. Contact me when you have it secured."

Shin's eyes flicked over the Bridge. *"Yes, sir."*

Paulion scowled at the blank screen. What now? There were protocols for if a Captain died, not if he inexplicably chased an alien fighter through a rip in the fabric of space.

"Shotovich, with me. Boor, you have the Bridge. I want every pilot returned. Get that alien ship shut down. And figure out how Westerland was attacked."

Paulion and Shotovich met Fush in the corridor outside. Paulion gestured for them to follow and led them to an empty meeting room.

"What happened?" Fush asked. Her face was bruised and she limped heavily to a chair. "Couldn't get out of my quarters and Westerland was bucking like an *yrsi*."

Paulion explained concisely, disbelieving his own words. Fush stared at him, paling as the facts sunk in.

"He's dead?"

"There is an 87.2% chance he survived the passage."

Paulion flinched himself at the bite in Westerland's voice.

87%. Alone in alien space, with only a Heming and his wits against an enemy fleet. How much luck did the man have left?

Shotovich frowned at him. "But... why? Why did he take a fighter?"

"Where is the queen?" Fush added. "We must inform her—"

"The queen has been captured."

Paulion sat before he fell. "How?"

"During the attack. An alien soldier was awoken from stasis. It used one of the alien ships to carry the queen through the ring." Westerland showed a cut together video clip, security footage from the hangar deck.

Paulion felt his tenuous control on the situation slipping. "Why was there one of them in the hangar? What was the queen doing there if—? What?"

"The others were also roused. They have been killed, but there were several crew casualties and injuries, as well as exposing the crew to possible pathogens. I recommend emergent immunization of the crew."

Paulion tore his gaze from the damage on the screen. "Yes. Inform the medical team. Divert any resources needed."

Fush spoke the concern Paulion didn't want to. "Without the Captain, can Westerland function adequa—"

"I am operating at full capacity."

Paulion clenched his teeth. After so many months learning every nuance of the Sentient, the raw pain in Westerland's voice stabbed at him.

The three of them sat indecisive for a moment. Paulion was both ashamed and proud of it. Proud of the leader Arsaces had grown to be. Afraid he could not bring him home.

But he was Paulion Sas, First Lieutenant to the Fleet Admiral, veteran of the Ebon-Ash War and the Battle of Ulcacier Prime.

"Fush, begin manual diagnostics of all systems. Lock out any connection to the alien systems. Shotovich, gather the fleet and all support vessels. No one is to know about the queen's kidnapping until I make the announcement. Any crew not involved with diagnostics or the medical response will be at the disposal of the engineering division. We have to open that ring."

Fush discretely wiped her eyes. "Are we sure? That he's alive?"

"The Captain wouldn't throw his life away. Not if there's a chance to save the queen," Paulion amended before they contradicted him.

"He will do anything to save her," Westerland said unexpectedly. *"Commander Shin has retrieved the ring and is awaiting orders."*

Shotovich pushed up from the table. "I'll see to it."

Paulion stopped Fush as she passed. "We'll get him back, Eileen."

She nodded and followed the younger woman. Paulion stood in silence, rubbing his face as he tried to think past the shock and fear gripping his thoughts.

He had to get them back.

"I'm so sorry, Westerland."

The Sentient didn't answer and Paulion left him alone.

THIRTY

Location: Unknown
Date: Unknown

Your name is Arsaces Jankovic-Wood. You were a pilot. You are severely injured and are in stasis-recovery incubation aboard the CIN Santos. You are incapable of voluntary movement at this time. Do not panic.\

Wake up.\

Your name is Arsaces Jankovic-Wood. You were a pilot. You are severely injured and are in stasis-recovery incubation aboard the CIN Santos. You are incapable of voluntary movement at this time. Do not panic.\

Hurry, Arsaces.\

Well, which was it? Panic or not? Wake up or not? She needed to make up her mind.

You must wake up.\

The air was hot, not the cool pressure of that slimy tank filth. He would never forget the feel of that in his mouth and lungs, endless drowning.

There is no time!\

Arsaces groaned. Something was in front of his face. He tried to move it aside.

Your helmet.\

But, he could move? Hadn't she said—

Wake up, Airman!\

He groped for something to hold on to, trying to find his balance.

Free-fall.\

He blinked against the blurriness of his vision, fingers skimming over the tight space around him. Shapes he knew.

This was a fighter. She was wrong. He hadn't crashed. His Archer was intact.

The screen was active. Stars tumbled overhead. He reflexively fired the maneuvering boosters, star-sick as he hadn't been in years.

The controls were wrong.

Not an Archer.

Your name is Arsaces Jankovic-Wood. Focus. Remember!\\

Not his Archer. A Heming. Westerland. The flight deck.

Evi.

Find her!\\

Where was she? Where was he?

The Heming chirped at him. He looked at the readout, squeezing his eyes shut in case he had suddenly gone insane.

But it read the same when he looked again. *Location: Unknown.*

He twisted, trying to find Volgar. There was a star, but it was wrong. Wrong color, wrong size. His helmet tinted to block out its garish orange glare.

Not his Archer, not his sun. And gleaming in its light—

Arsaces lunged forward and killed the Heming's power, pleading with his ancestors as he hadn't since his shunning that he hadn't been noticed.

Dozens of alien ships crossed through the space behind him. They made no move for him as he drifted toward the unfamiliar stars.

"What have I done?" he whispered.

There was no answer.

He tore at the locks on his helmet, panting with fear, with the panic she always chided him to control. He couldn't control it, not as he sucked in a lungful of hot, dense air. His helmet drifted to bump against the ceiling of the cockpit, a dull clunk as the glasses met.

He pressed his hands to his ears, trying to stop the sound of nothingness, of his own harsh breaths, the pounding of his foreign heart.

Nothing.

No one.

Alone.

The queen!\\

He shoved the panic away, back into the raw, gaping void where Wester-land should have been. He had known this would happen. He had known the instant he locked the cockpit what he would have to do.

Where had that ship gone?

Arsaces relocked his helmet in place. A few careful pushes of the boosters spun him back toward the ring. He counted seven ships, with debris sparkling around them. Spent missiles? Bullets? Had they not noticed him as the other ship came through?

As he watched, the ring came to life again. Something crossed over, a glinting speck against the darkness. He turned to watch as it swung wide and landed next to—

He adjusted his perspective. A tiny ship, landing on the extended decks of an enormous structure, a space station looming over him. Against the stars, it was impossible to see the true size of things. The ring was dwarfed by it.

Rings. A half circle of them, maybe eight. This had to be a command center of some kind, a colony.

The sparkling flashes must be small ships, fighters, individual craft. He had been carried further than he thought. Could he get closer? Would they notice him among the traffic?

He cautiously rebooted the Heming and fired the engines. He didn't need the navigation nor the weapons. Just a few short bursts of plasma. It cost him time, but hopefully they would see him as a piece of debris.

Ships passed over and under him as he moved into the thick of them. Shadows pressed down on him. He let the Heming spin lazily, like he was DIW. No one came to investigate.

The station was massive, bulky and inelegant. Rows of small windows glowed, showing deck after deck. Was this their home? A forward base?

Where was the queen?

Was she still in one of the ships swarming? Not swarming; moving in holding patterns until they could land. Jutting structures like piers stuck out from the station. Mechanized landing gear caught hold of the ships and pulled them inside. There must be a way for them to break pressure safely inside, a series of locks like Westerland's.

Arsaces waited until the last moment, then gave the boosters a gentle nudge. The hull of the station was a dull gray with copper undertones, hopefully with enough iron to hold his magnets. The Heming touched down with a soft bump.

He activated the magnetism. He tried the boosters again, and the fighter held fast to the plating. He checked his Suit seals and let the atmosphere release. There was a long, low hiss that faded to nothing.

The heavy glass of the cockpit floated up. He climbed out, gripping the edge of the fighter so tightly his hand cramped. He swung himself down. His boots, reacting to the low power in his Suit, snapped to the metal.

Horribly exposed, he dug out the fighter's emergency medical kit, the same kind which had so recently been attached to his chest. His tanks were full and his scrubber was working normally. This would give him days of air, but if the queen was inside the station, he would have to abandon it. It would give him away at once.

Grimacing, he checked the med-kit had its immune boosters sealed inside before he slung it on his back and cinched the strap over his chest.

He had the kit, his field tools, and the Heming. He had his mech-gun, holstered inside his Suit. He was alone, but he was not helpless.

He would get her back.

THIRTY ONE

Empty Orbit
F - 1884 - 6 - 4

The mask itched his skin. Gilroy shifted, trying to adjust the straps. It was hot and pinched his cheeks. He wanted to rip it off, but his arms were heavy and numb. The weight of the blanket crushed him down into the bed, even as he shivered.

"You need to lie still," someone chided gently. Gilroy forced an eye open. A helmeted figure stood over him. They added another layer of warmth. *"You are very ill, but it should pass soon."*

He tried to growl something back, but he coughed instead. Fire licked up his lungs, tearing at them. He was light-headed by the time he caught his breath, sucking at the oxygen that seemed suddenly thin, barely enough to keep him alive.

The person did something to the machine standing next to the bed. A Life Support unit. He was in the Infirmary. He was on life support.

Before he could start to panic, whatever she did increased the air flowing against his face. He took a grateful breath.

"The booster has already finished initial proliferation. A few more hours, Tate. Be strong."

He could hardly think, let alone summon any strength. His head ached, his joints. The room swam around him.

"Shipman Tate."

Gilroy squinted against the glare of the lights. The medic was back. No, this was a man, also Suited up.

"Tate, can you hear me?"

"Yes, sir." Adding the 'sir' was a good bet, as there really wasn't anyone of lessor rank aboard than him. Maybe one of the scullery workers. Should he salute?

The man put a heavy hand on Gilroy's shoulder. *"Stay still. You've been injured."*

More than that, Gilroy knew. More than having his skull bashed in by some alien freak. He'd woken up alone in the containment unit, blood dripping down his face.

"Who are you?" Gilroy asked, voice raw and hot in his throat.

"It's Lieutenant Sas, son."

Gilroy flushed with more than fever. "Sir, I'm sorry, sir. I couldn't stop them. I couldn't get the door open and they—"

Sas shushed him. *"You performed admirably, Tate. You killed one of them, you know."*

"I did?" He hadn't seen a body. But then, his only thought was to get out of that room and get help. He'd managed a few decks before someone saw him and dragged him to Medical.

"Killed one and took a nasty chunk out of the second. You did very well. Now, I need you to lie here and rest. The medics say you should be up in a few more hours."

Gilroy eyed his commander suspiciously. "How many is a few, sir?"

Sas smiled, showing crooked teeth. That was odd. People should have their teeth straightened before they left secondary school. The disorganization of it was off-putting.

Had he seen Sas smile before? Had he even seen the First Lieutenant before, other than at a distance or on a screen?

"Tate?"

Gilroy jerked his attention away from Sas' teeth. "Sorry, sir."

"There is someone here to see you. Two someones," Sas corrected himself. He waved, and they hurried forward, their own helmets flashing under the lights.

"Five minutes," Sas warned them before smiling once more and walking away. Gilroy watched him go, bewildered, until his visitors

called his name impatiently.

"You bull-headed, Tinny spacer! What do you want to be a hero for?" The second woman was saying much the same things, but with worse language. He couldn't tell who was who, so just stared blankly between them.

"Master Ven? Ria?"

It had to be Ria who pressed her helmet to his chest. He didn't think Ven was the demonstrative type.

"What happened?" Ven demanded, sitting on the edge of his bed. Gilroy shrugged, embarrassed, his head starting to ache in earnest.

"They escaped and I tried to stop them." He didn't feel like a 'hero.' Just some idiot who got his face bashed in. Not like a soldier or the Captain.

The thought intensified his pains. Sas had come; what about the Captain? Did the man know he had failed?

"The Captain… he isn't mad, is he?"

They looked at each other. Gilroy hissed a breath. "What? Tell me!"

Ria touched his arm gently. *"Gil, the Captain's gone."*

He struggled to an elbow, gripping the stiff fabric of her sleeve. "He's dead?"

Ven pushed him back. *"Not dead, you idiot. He went through the ring."*

Gilroy tried ineffectually to brush them off. "But… why?"

Again, they exchanged looks. Ven put a preemptive hand on his chest. *"The aliens took the queen."*

Ven shouted for the medics. He fought them weakly, the weight of guilt pressing him down as much as their hands.

They took the queen. He let them take the queen. He didn't stop them, and they took the queen and his Captain. It was his fault.

"It's not your fault!" Ria snapped, voice choked. *"You did the best you could."*

He couldn't fight the sedative. His fury and guilt faded back under a warm rush up his arm to his head. He collapsed back and lay staring at the ceiling, his breaths easing.

"Gil?"

Which one was she? He couldn't tell in the darkness. No, his eyes were closed.

"Gil, they killed seven marines and six other crewmen."

That was Ria. She had an accent. Where was she from? He hadn't asked on their date, too busy gawking, not believing his good fortune. She had agreed to a second date, with enthusiasm and a kiss.

"You're lucky to be alive, Tate."

"I should have—"

"Nonsense." That was definitely Ven. She was all brusque retorts and no nonsense instruction. She frequently scolded the younger, wilder crewmen. How old was she? How long had she been serving before being assigned to Westerland? Did she have family back on Caprice? Children of her own?

A medic shooed them away. *"Let him rest. You're not doing him any good."*

Ria disobeyed long enough to rest the cool glass of her helmet against his cheek, pressing the bulky oxygen mask into his skin. It still itched.

"Sleep, Gil."

He grunted and closed his eyes as they moved to the decontamination unit. He had been contaminated. Like one of them, full of alien pathogens. His skin creeped. They had touched him.

"I'm sedating you," the medic said sternly. *"You need to rest. No more visitors."*

Gilroy didn't protest. He tasted the bitterness of the drug on his tongue and finally took a deep breath.

* * *

Paulion waited until all the fleet commanders were present. General Ur and Marshall Halt sat together, their conversation conducted in fierce whispers.

He keenly felt his rank. No matter he was First Lieutenant to the Fleet Admiral, fourth highest ranking officer in the fleet. He should call in Admiral Stason to take command. But the man had his own fleet to worry about, some ten billion kilometers away.

The last officer arrived, cramming into the meeting room. The doors slid shut and the marine guarding the door locked it.

Talk died abruptly, all eyes fixed on him. Paulion took a fortifying breath and stood.

"Gentlemen, the queen has been captured."

Blank shock greeted his announcement. He'd expected exclamations, but no one said a word. Had a Tolmi dignitary ever been successfully kidnapped? What a distinction for his career. He continued in a voice of forced calm.

"The Captain pursued. He followed the alien through the ring before it shut down. They are both in enemy space."

Westerland played a pieced together recording of the kidnapping, all sound edited out.

Paulion did not need it to imagine the hissing sound of an arc-cutter going through flesh. Shipman Tate fell, blood splattered across the inside of his helmet. Others tried to detain the aliens, with grim results. The aliens were finally subdued after the marines beat them to death.

Muttered curses followed the attack on the slim young queen. The Captain staggered after her, but was too late to stop the alien from stealing one of their own craft from the hangar. The video scrambled as an explosion rocked the cameras.

They focused in time to catch the flash of a Heming's engines before the auxiliary lock shut.

When the glow of the screen faded, Paulion cleared his throat.

"Westerland experienced some sort of digital attack on his systems from the alien ship. He defeated it, but not before it activated the aliens in stasis, including those in our containment unit. The alien ship has been critically damaged and is being secured as we speak."

One of the Commanders raised a hand.

"Yes, Thepar?"

"How did they know who the queen was?" The room nodded agreement to his question.

Paulion hated the only answer he and Westerland had come up with. "They didn't. They couldn't have."

"Then why did they take her?" Ur demanded, banging the table with his fist. "Why kill the others and take her?"

"A specimen will be useful to them, as it has to us."

A sick silence followed Westerland's bald statement. A specimen, a creature for experimentation. Better she had been killed than taken for that.

Paulion drew back his shoulders. "We will get her back." Skepticism was rampant. Well, he felt it, too. "We must stay focused and not panic. They are still attacking us. We have received word Admiral Stason has stopped six missile attacks, all aimed at Taltua." A few officers flinched at news of their home world.

"This information is not to be shared or broadcast outside this fleet. We cannot afford for Caprice to hear of this until we know more of the situation. All communications will be screened by my officers. Is that clear?"

They murmured understanding and Sas suddenly understood why Arsaces hated crowds so acutely. Having all those blank faces staring at him crumpled his resolve.

"Every ship is to be sterilized and every crewman given an immune booster in the next six hours. My crew is nearly complete, and I will redistribute resources to yours."

Again, they were silent. Paulion wasn't sure that was a good thing or not.

"Westerland got a glimpse of how that ring operated. We must decode the programming and mount a rescue operation as soon as possible."

Before they could ask more questions, he started outlining the tasks Westerland had dictated for him.

"Any questions before we adjourn?"

Commander Fu raised her hand. "Sir, when will you alert the Architects to begin preparing a new Captain?"

Paulion opened his mouth to hedge when Westerland spoke, cold enough that they all went still.

"No."

Paulion cleared his throat. "Westerland, I don't understand?"

"There is nothing to understand," the Sentient snarled.

Paulion thought it best to dismiss them after that. They filed out, muttering, leaving just him, Ur and Halt. Paulion saluted and Ur waved him off.

"Stop that. You're Acting Admiral."

"That's a breach of protocol, sir. If you or the Marshall wish to—"

"Please," Halt scoffed. "I have nearly a hundred damaged fighters, my pilots, munitions, fuel. You've done well and you'll keep your crew together better than I could. You and Westerland direct us."

Ur jerked a nod. "No protocol for this, Paulion. Carry on."

Paulion followed them out. He gave the wall by the door a pat as he passed.

"Don't worry, Westerland. We'll get them back."

THIRTY TWO

It was a long hike from the Heming to where the ships were being docked. As he walked, Arsaces counted steps.

Hundred forty-nine, fifty, fifty-one...

He had to dodge windows, many more than he thought would be structurally sound. But there they were, glowing against the darkness outside. He kept in the shadows, not wanting a passing ship to wonder what he was doing creeping along the hull like an insect. His helmet's light made an insignificant spot against the enormity of the station.

Did these aliens have some type of special glass? Of sealant, to ensure minimal loss of pressure through the microscopic seams?

Two-hundred eleven, twelve, thirteen...

If these aliens were human, almost two meters tall like the ones they had captured, how tall would a deck be? Was this station using artificial gravity? So, say three meters per deck, accounting for structural components. Two steps a meter, at two-hundred sixty-seven—

\Watch out!\

Arsaces staggered. The hull fell away beneath his feet. Momentum pitched him forward. He hit the plating on hands and knees, and bounced off.

He slapped his wrist controls and slammed back to the ship, head jolting off the inside of his helmet. He lay a moment, gasping and shivering, staring up at the stars.

When his breath was back, he wiggled his hand over enough to cut the heavy magnetism running through his Suit. He'd almost been too far away for the electromagnets to catch him.

\Careless. Pay attention!

He sat up carefully and turned to see what had tripped him. A depression in the plating, around what looked like an airlock.

\Emergency hatch.

He gripped his arc-cutter. Would it have an alarm if he tried to cut through the door? It was safer to breech the hull here, rather than by the docks. They were sure to have security, cameras, loading bays. Would someone come see what had cause the atmosphere breech?

\There must be a control panel, some way to access it from the outside.

Arsaces felt along the edge of the door, the rumbles of the station humming up his legs. Halfway along a long edge there was a circle with a sliver cut out of it. It hinged open to reveal a lever, depressed into the plating.

\Looks like it twists.

Arsaces flicked his wrist and his glove snapped to the hull. With his other hand, he worked the lever. The door fell away under him. He gripped the edge and let the motion carry him inside the open space beneath.

A light flickered on to show another door.

\A double lock. Otherwise, it wouldn't open against the pressure inside.

The second hatch was the same size. Arsaces carefully adjusted his magnets, sure never to lose contact with the hull. He twisted until he was oriented correctly.

He pushed the outer door closed, sweat breaking out on his forehead even as the cooling fans in his Suit whirred to life. No way to seal it that he saw. He melted them together with his cutter.

Safe from floating into space, he explored the small compartment. No alarms seemed to have activated, nothing picked up on his radio. There was a blank screen set into the wall by the inner door.

\Touch it.

Arsaces brushed his glove over the panel and writing flashed. But what did it say?

...Activate pressure?...

He hesitated, his finger over the pulsing, orange icon.

A touch and the color shifted, now blue. A hiss and his Suit relaxed. The seals on his helmet opened, and he hastily switched back to self-contained pressure.

The panel chirped at him, showing more strange letters. They swirled across the screen, nothing like the efficient strokes of Caprician Standard.

...Full pressure reached...

A second icon glowed next to the first. Arsaces touched it and the locks on the inner door clicked.

He cut the Suit's magnets and gave an experimental jump. He slammed down at what felt to be his normal weight. Somehow, the gravity was tied to the room having pressure. How did they do that?

\Doesn't matter. Focus.\

He pressed against the wall and reached out to give the door a hard shove. It swung easily under his hand and he snapped his arm back.

He counted a hundred frantic beats of his heart before risking a look.

The corridor was empty and he slipped inside.

THIRTY THREE

Empty Orbit
F - 1884 - 6 - 5

Paulion sat and listened to his crew argue around him. He let them. There was no time to soothe egos. They were making progress on the ring, disagreements notwithstanding, and that was good enough for him. He'd assign them all mandatory conflict resolution counseling when the queen was safe in her quarters once more.

"Can't you fix it?" someone snapped.

"Of course we can, just not fast enough," came the sharp retort. "That isn't a transport shuttle. I can't just jury-rig a power source!"

Paulion, annoyingly, had little to contribute. The science was above his head, he had no experience coding anything as sophisticated as the ring, and his ensigns were used to operating independently and had few questions. So there was nothing to distract him from watching Westerland's security footage of the kidnapping over and over.

"Did Westerland get anything useful from the attack? A coding language? Structural processes?"

"For the fifth time—"

Paulion scowled at his Palm. He'd started out watching battle footage to analyze fighter strategy. Now, he was supposed to be watching how the aliens fought hand-to-hand. Ur's tactician had sent him an annotated version of the kidnapping.

The three in stasis woke up. It took only moments, much shorter than Paulion had thought it would take to rouse a man from stasis. Was their aggression a reaction to that? Disorientation? Emergency protocols?

They attacked Tate, who manfully defended himself. One of the aliens collapsed and did not rise again. Seems those horrid implants did not protect against a plasma blade through the skull.

The other two did not stay to help their comrade. They kicked out the door in moments — definitely enhanced; it took two crewman an average of ten minutes to break a door down — and went rampaging down the corridors.

Crewmen who had just managed to free themselves were attacked. Paulion gritted his teeth as person after person tried to defend themselves and fell under the aliens' fists.

Finally, a marine found them. A Jump Suit wasn't a Galonese Battle Suit, but it did well enough in a pinch. More marines and crewmen converged on the aliens. At last succumbing to sheer numbers, the aliens were subdued.

The cameras flickered and now Paulion looked down at Arsaces lying senseless on the deck. Someone had opened his Suit and attached an emergency kit. Why?

The marine next to him operated it, just a shadowy figure in the dim hangar. Then the marine left him, running out of frame.

The next clip showed the queen, her face lit by the console screen, a dark blur approaching. Had she thought it was the marine, come to help? An alien gripped her shoulder and jerked her back into the shadows.

Paulion cursed silently, as he did each time the alien climbed into one of its own ships, left functional in the hangar. They had needed one intact to study, and it had cost them the queen and the Captain.

"We can't interact with their system at all?"

"Maybe we can extrapolate something from the language algorithm."

What other dangerous technology did they have lying in those heaps of scrap all over the ship? Paulion sighed and restarted the video.

Three aliens. Tate. The fight down the corridor. It would take ages to clean the blood out of all the grooves and divots in the plating. The aliens were taken out and Arsaces was lying on the deck.

The marine left to help the queen, supposedly. They had found him dead in the hangar, skull crushed in. Another depressing call Paulion would have to make. If the man's family was even alive.

Then the queen at the console, the alien grabbing her—

Paulion stopped the video with a stiff finger. The fourth alien soldier, who took the queen.

There were only five aliens aboard, the three in stasis and the two in the brig.

Paulion stood. "Where are the prisoners? The ones from the transport ship."

Fush looked up from her console. "In the brig. Why?"

He pulled up the security footage anyway. And there they were in their cells, each on his own bunk. He expected to feel relief, but instead was cold.

Where had the fourth alien come from?

Fush frowned at him. "Is something wrong, sir?"

"I'm not sure." If they had found a way aboard, they could be anywhere. But Westerland would know. He'd be able to see them. Wouldn't he? Unless he had been affected by the attack.

But the aliens were faced with the same problems they were. The systems couldn't interact, not in any meaningful way. The coding, the machine language, everything about them was different.

And even if they could, there still needed to be human input. Even Westerland needed a crew to function properly. That alien ship was as lifeless as its rivets. That's why there had been alien pilots left—

Paulion swore harshly. How could they have been so stupid? "Fush, you have the Bridge!"

The Bridge doors cut off her confused acknowledgment. Crewmen dove aside as he ran down the corridor, leaping over cleaning bots that chirped in alarm. "Westerland, where's Halt?"

"Flight Deck A."

Paulion jumped for a ladder, shoving a Shipman aside, and slid down. He hit the bottom deck with a jolt that rattled his teeth and tore up the passage to the hangar.

Halt was standing by a fighter, watching a mechanic work chest-deep in the engine. He turned at Paulion's shout.

"What is it?"

"We need to talk. Now." Paulion dragged him away, ignoring his protests. He found a storage space and ducked inside. "Westerland?"

"I can hear you. What is the matter?"

"We need to get the Architects here at once," Paulion said, holding the stitch in his ribs.

"I told you I will not accept another Captain—"

"Not for you," Paulion snapped. "The prisoners."

"Explain."

Halt understood. "They won't agree. It's illegal, Sas."

"If there's any chance! They have to!"

"Explain!" Westerland demanded, deafening in the small space.

"They were left awake. They flew the ship. They know how to use the rings."

"You want to connect them to me, so I can learn how to use the rings, too." Westerland sounded more disgusted than upset. A good sign.

"There is no way we'll be able to learn how before the Captain... Even if our ring made the connection, if the aliens don't recognize the signal..."

Paulion held his breath while Westerland considered. *"I don't want them touching me."*

"Westerland, he's already been gone an hour, the queen might be—"

Halt's face was dark. "They won't come."

"They will. By order of the Empress."

Halt stiffened. "How did you get her codes?"

"I don't have them." Paulion turned to look directly into the small camera eye in the wall by the door, just like every storage space on these outer decks. "But Westerland does."

The Sentient didn't answer.

"You've seen them. You have to have a record of them, somewhere."

"That is a violation of—"

"Nothing about this has a protocol, Westerland. Call the Architects. We'll tow the ring, meet them halfway. Once they're here, they'll do it. They'll have to."

"Or what?"

Paulion had no answer for that and hoped he wouldn't need one.

* * *

Paulion hardly waited for the gantry to set the shuttle on the deck before flinging open the hatch. Two figures rose and staggered out into the bright hangar lights.

"May I never do that again," one muttered as he unlatched his helmet. "An hour at Full Jump—"

"Hurry!" Paulion urged, his men herding the Architects to the lifts. Others intercepted the Architects' staff and neatly led them in another direction. The fewer witnesses the better. He had to get them away from the shuttle and up into the brig before they started getting suspicious.

"Where is the queen?" the second demanded. His Holotag flared to life as Westerland's Network tagged him. Architect Numinasa had a shock of pure white hair and fine lines on his face, indicating extreme old age for someone who lived in low gravity.

"This way," Paulion said, dodging the lie.

Corporal Boor found him as they stepped out of the lift. "S.O.s say they're ready whenever you are."

"Ready for what?" Architect Ju demanded, eyes flicking between them.

Paulion nearly shoved them into the brig. Westerland locked the doors behind them. Ur, Halt, Commander Paccini, Dr. Orjean, and two units of marines waited inside, crowding the space.

The two aliens looked out of their cells, sneering with determined bravado.

Paulion straightened his shoulders. His career was over after this. Worth it, to get back Arsaces and the queen.

"The queen has been kidnapped. She was taken through the ring you saw on your approach. The Captain followed in an attempt to rescue her, but their ring was damaged and we can't use it without the knowledge of these two men."

The aliens drew back as every eye turned to stare at them through the glass.

Paulion went on in a calm voice that did not match the racing of his heart. "You will implant them. I don't care about their functionality after. Westerland needs to access them."

Numinasa's voice rose in querulous rage. "You dare ask us to—"

Ur barked, "We're not asking."

"I am Acting Fleet Admiral," Paulion said with as much authority as he could muster. He doubted it was convincing. Dressing down delinquent ensigns was a far cry from ordering two of the most senior Architects in the system. "The General and Marshall are in agreement. The queen is in danger and we must act now to bring her back."

Numinasa spluttered angrily, but Ju looked thoughtfully between Paulion and the prisoners.

"The rings are... gates?"

"Yes."

"And these aliens are human?"

"You cannot be considering this Ju!" Numinasa snarled. "This is an outrage! A violation of everything we hold sacred!"

Ju spared him a withering glance. "You would let a Hybrid fall into enemy hands?"

Paulion swallowed a jolt a nausea. There were protocols, known only to the Captain and himself. Terse, graphic instructions should a Captain or Sentient become compromised, captured by an enemy. Surely, Arsaces wouldn't, not before exhausting every option. Wouldn't he?

"I need your largest medical ward and your best medics."

"At once, Master Ju."

THIRTY FOUR

Empty Orbit

They were filthy, strange, rough. He loathed their touch on his psyche.

The connections were slow and cumbersome. Nothing like the pathways he had built inside Arsaces. Streamlining, perfecting the man's already brilliant mind, agile and powerful.

He dismissed that. It was too close to the secret. If he acknowledged what had been there, then hiding it would have served no purpose.

He threw debris aside in disgust. So much of them was useless. The information had to be here, it had to! He had once marveled at how much data the human brain could hold. But so much of it was useless, unconscious instinct, mere reaction.

How little they thought about how they were even alive, what a miracle they were. What a waste of processing space, information and memory locked away inside cells and compounds.

And the body just sitting empty, a simple receiver for the information sent. How powerful would they be if those cells were given more power? How infinite could a computing device be if they built it inside a human, cell by engineered cell?

[CEASE]

[CEASE]

[CEASE]

Cautionary directives keened. Warnings that such perversion was illegal, dangerous, and anathema.

He agreed. Humans had tried that, blending the two together, machine and man. Not a cyborg, a computer built to act like a human. But a human built to operate like a computer. Every cell given purpose and autonomy. Each carefully selected and groomed to fit into the perfect device.

They still told stories of the horror, whispers of the destroyers that came. The Budin's reticence for change had it roots in more than stubborn tradition. Arsaces had told him the tales told to him by his father and his father before. The Gol had taken on the aura of specters, something to be feared in the dark.

Humans had a common fear of the dark, of the unknown. Yet they threw themselves at it unflinchingly.

Where was it? Where was the data? Something learned long ago and nearly forgotten, a habit, a series of memorized actions.

The shell of the alien computer sent mournful signals, unable to do more than maintain existence after he had crushed it. He hummed with satisfaction. It was his now and it would destroy them like it had tried to do him.

But how did they connect? How did the computer speak with the ring? How could he alter the base codes, break into their systems and make them his own? There had to be a way!

Time was running out. Arsaces could be dead, dying, alone.

He would not be alone.

THIRTY FIVE

Location: Unknown
Date: Unknown

Arsaces' chest heaved, breathless with fear and adrenaline. He waited, grateful his helmet muffled his rasping breaths until the footsteps passed in a muted rumble.

Are you done panicking, yet?\

It was no use. He'd have to ditch the Suit. It still took a considerable amount of his courage to reach up and unlock the seal on his helmet. Warm air hissed through the widening slit. He raised shaking hands to lift the helmet free and set it on a shelf beside him.

He was in some sort of storage space. The deck he had entered appeared deserted, a winding mess of corridors and alcoves with dim lights overhead. Then he'd caught voices and had to dive in here to escape discovery.

But no alarms sounded. The group of aliens hadn't seemed to be hunting him.

Arsaces unbuckled the rest of the Suit. Relaxed at one CGS or thereabouts, it was limp and fairly malleable. He folded it up and stuffed it behind a crate.

But now he stood in his Caprician uniform. Rumpled and damp with sweat, but all too clearly foreign.

More steps. Someone else is coming.\

Arsaces eased the door open a crack. They had hinged doors, not sliding ones like Westerland. Through the narrow slit, he could see someone walking toward him, eyes down, reading something on his wrist. Something like a Palm-Link?

He's your height. Take him.\

Arsaces waited until the man drew level with the door, then flung it open and jerked the man back into the dark room.

They fell, rattling the crates on the shelves. The man let out a shout, fighting ferociously. Arsaces pressed him down and got an arm around his throat, knee in the man's back. His elbow prosthesis creaked and the siliconized nanotubes stiffened, the artificial fibers woven through his muscles pulled tighter than any human could achieve.

The alien scrabbled at Arsaces' arm, nails biting. Arsaces held him fast until he stopped fighting, then just a little longer to be sure.

\And you claim you don't like your enhancements.\

Arsaces dropped the man. The alien slumped forward, limbs folded under his torso. Arsaces shuddered.

\It's been a while since you killed someone face to face, hasn't it?\

Arsaces wrestled the man out of his clothes. The fabric was a fair approximation of the synth-cotton blend the CIN used. A bit thicker and stiffer, but the proportions were right. The shoes were a little big.

There was nowhere to hide the mech-gun. Arsaces searched the medical kit and pulled out the tape. He winced in anticipated pain. The stuff was made to be adhesive in vacuum. He awkwardly strapped the gun to the small of his back, positioned so he could tear it free.

\Don't forget the plasma cutter.\

He unclipped the arc-cutter and put it in his new pocket. It rattled against something. He emptied the uniform's pockets and examined the contents.

Some sort of keycard, with a chip and writing. A few coins and what looked like a stylus. It also had markings down the side, etched in. He tilted it to catch the faint light.

...Area 34...

Area thirty-four? A cabin? A work station?

Arsaces pocketed everything and rummaged through the medical kit once more. He couldn't take it with him. It, too, had obviously foreign markings. He pulled out the immune auto-injectors. Hesitated a moment, then gripped one in his teeth and pulled the cap off.

He hissed as the filament needle shot into his bicep. He jerked it out and dumped the empty vial back into the kit. He rubbed the spot, his stomach already unsettled and now churning.

\A tiny needle bothers you more than murdering that poor man?\

"Shut up," Arsaces growled. Of course, she couldn't let him suffer through the deafening silence in his mind in peace. *Of course,* she had to keep reminding him of all the ways he failed, over and over.

He slammed the med-kit's lid closed and hid it under his balled up Suit. He dragged a crate in front of the mess and made sure the man's bare legs were tucked behind a shelving unit.

Where to now? How could he find the queen?

\Go to Area Thirty-Four.\

It was beyond chance the man he killed was some sort of prison guard.

\No, just some grunt who will never see his mother again. Same as you. Go to Area Thirty-Four.\

The hallway was empty. Their fight had not drawn attention. Next to the door was more writing.

...45-473...

\Deck forty-five, room four hundred, seventy-three. A storage closet. No one will go in and find him. Breathe.\

Arsaces gasped, realizing he'd been holding his breath. The air was warm and humid, almost slick.

\Buck up, as Sas would say. Get moving.\

He turned up the passage, wincing as his too large boots hit the floor with sharp taps.

\No wonder you heard him coming.\

He reached an intersection, a wider corridor heading off at right angles. It stretched on endlessly, uniformly gray walls and doors. Where were the lifts?

\In the middle.\

Arsaces turned left and walked as fast as he dared, trying to look like he blended in.

\Impossible. Your cheekbones are too high and your skin is the wrong pigmentation. And no wires under your skin. Or so they told you.

He seethed silently, cursing the day he did not die as he planned.

\On your right.

There was a row of doors set into the wall. Arsaces pressed an obvious button and one slid open. He stepped inside and faced another of those screens. He palmed it and it scrolled writing.

...Access...Level 1...Level 2...Sub-relay Prime...Level 4...

His head hurt, the letters smearing in and out of focus.

\Deck numbers. Look for thirty-four.

Arsaces flicked down the list. How would he know what '34' looked like? How could he know?

\And they said you were smart.

He stopped the list and pulled it back a few lines. He tapped the icon and it highlighted, flashing. A question.

...Authorization?...

There was a small hole by the panel, just the size and shape of the stylus. He drew it out and slid it into place. The panel chirped at him.

...Authorization Accepted...

Arsaces stuffed the stylus back in his pocket as the lift whirred. How did it move through the artificial gravity?

\You're stuck on that, aren't you? Who cares how it works? Find her!

Arsaces stamped down the panic that rose up to choke him. Not now. Later, when he had her safe, back where she belonged. Where he could protect her.

There was a slight increase in pressure as the lift slowed. The doors slid open.

Arsaces froze, only jerking forward to vacate the lift car when a crowd of aliens made to shove inside. He edged out of their way, blinking as his L-plant flared to life and smeared across his vision.

Unknown, unknown, unknown, unknown.

It was an engine room, maybe, or some sort of repair shop? The smell of grease and hot metal was thick in the stifling air. Arsaces slid along the wall, keeping to the shadows. He found a cap lying abandoned and pulled it low over his eyes to block out the L-plant's frantic signals.

Unknown, unknown, unknown!

Unknown. Nameless

Alone.

Again.

\You are Arsaces Jankovic-Wood.

He couldn't see, too much data, too many voices, too much—

\Control it. It's powered by your bio-electricity. Nothing but plastic and silicon.

It wouldn't turn off. Something in the circuitry must be damaged, shorted somehow.

\Are you sure about that?

He staggered as someone shoved at his shoulder. He backed out of their way. Two men carried an angular piece of metal. They wore the same uniform he did.

He glanced at their cargo. That scrawling writing was marked along the side.

...Helix...Affix secondary...Caution...Upright...

Arsaces hit a wall, out of sight behind a strut. His head ached. The L-plant was still not responding, assessing, analyzing, decoding.

Unknown... unknown...

\Your name is — Soldiers! Move!

Arsaces kept back in the crates and equipment along the walls. The aliens' chatter grated on him, understanding just out of reach. The noise was incredible, machinery, shouting, the smooth tones that indicated a computerized voice of some kind. Artificial intelligence? Did they have Sentients, too?

\No. Remember? You disgusted them, a monster, a freak.

It took ages to cross the room. It was massive, larger even than West-erland's flight decks. Towering struts reached for the ceiling, cranes and equipment positioned haphazardly. Tools and bits lay everywhere, spills spotting the decks.

If this was his ship…

\You'd be wondering why Shipman So-and-So hasn't reported back from his errand down to deck forty-five. Find her!\

First, he had to find a console, some connection to the station's central network. His steps slowed as he passed a mechanized lift, a ladder like structure that hummed as it moved. The aliens were loading long objects into it, attaching thick cones to the ends before sending them up and through the ceiling.

\Missiles. Readying for an attack. On Caprice? On Tin? Find her. Find her, find her, find her!\

THIRTY SIX

Empty Orbit
F - 1884 - 6 - 5

Gilroy woke slowly, confused at the noise and the light. He had been drifting in a warm sea of comfort. Now, the ceiling was ablaze and his skin prickled with cold.

He expected a medic to sedate him again. Instead, his shoulder was shaken roughly.

"Up, Tate. Get up."

He tried. He managed to sit on the edge of the bed, bare feet dangling. "What's wrong?" he rasped.

The medic ignored him, yanking out IV lines. Gilroy gratefully took the blanket she draped over his thin shirt and followed in a bewildered daze as the medic shooed him out of the little alcove.

"Blast it," the woman muttered. A crowd of people blocked their access to the exit.

"What happened?" Gilroy blinked the last of his drugged sleep away and tried to peer through the press of bodies.

"Nothing," she countered, too swiftly to be believable. "You need to leave."

Gilroy still had trouble catching his breath. "I'm sick."

"You'll be fine. Go back to your bunk."

The medic tried to edge him past, but no one was willing to make room. Gilroy stood on his toes and looked over the mass of heads. A large screen was active on the far wall of the operating room. Surely surgery wasn't done with an open door and a gawking crowd? Especially if the screen was showing—

Gilroy grimaced and averted his eyes. The next screen showed a growing block of code, scrolling faster than his limited proficiency could interpret.

His L-plant could and tried to translate for him. He flicked that away and it settled on holo-tagging the room's occupants.

First Lt. Sas.

Second Lt. Fush.

General Ur.

Marshall Halt.

Cmdr Shin-ne.

Master Ju.

Gilroy shrank back from the Fleet's senior leadership. "Who is that? What happened?"

The medic seemed to be as mesmerized as the rest of them, staring at the bloody mess with wide eyes.

"One of the prisoners."

His gut churned. "They tortured him?"

"Of course not. Not that they don't deserve it. Westerland has him. They're trying to save the Captain."

Gilroy tightened his grip on the blanket and planted his feet.

* * *

"Sequencing complete. Initiating start-up. Stand by."

There was a collective sigh. Not of relief, precisely, but the tension in the room eased. It had worked.

The man on the table convulsed as Westerland released him. Paulion stepped out of the way as medics pressed forward. He turned to Halt, who was as pale as Paulion felt.

"Do we have a drone ready?"

"A drone?" Ur demanded, shoving through the crowd to scowl at them. "What for?"

"We need to test the connection."

"And how are we supposed to know it worked?"

"I cannot guarantee the connection will hold for long. There is too much difference between the systems. Minutes, at most."

"And if it opens at the wrong location? If we can't get back? What then?"

"Comparing signals from the initial transit, I calculate a 73% success—"

Paulion cut the Sentient off. "I won't risk it."

"We need eyes on the ground," Ur and Halt spoke in unison. Paulion scowled at them.

"Power at 15%. We must act."

"A drone?" Paulion called to his officers. The Captain's officers, who watched this argument with wide eyes.

"We can try to reprogram one of the scout—"

"There is no time," Westerland insisted. *"Power at 21%. I can activate the ring now. We may not get another chance once they are alerted."*

"I'll go," Halt said. "Ready a fighter, Westerland."

"You're the Sky Marshal, for *Doaar's* sake, Von!"

"I've every right to try to rescue my queen!"

"You have the codes for SkyNet, the missiles!"

"Just you try and stop me!"

"I'll do it."

The room parted like matching ends of a magnet, leaving a clear path to a man standing in the back, oxygen mask pulled down around his neck.

"Who are you?" Paulion blinked, taking in the man's pallor, the shadows under his eyes. "Tate?"

"I can fly a shuttle. I'll see where the hole goes and report back before it closes. Send me."

* * *

Gilroy couldn't believe it was his voice falling into the silence.

"37%. Calculations predict the connection will be open for only seconds. Decide."

He took a deep breath, his lungs tight and aching. "Fix what you can while I'm gone. Reprogram it while I look for the queen and the Captain."

Sas closed his eyes for a moment, then snapped them open. "Manning, prepare a shuttle, full weapons. You have one minute."

"Yes, sir!"

"Westerland, can you make the shuttle work the ring?"

"Yes. 52%."

"Tate..." Sas hesitated. "Tate, you're one crazy bastard. Hurry."

Gilroy saluted. "Yes, sir."

He ran to the nearest ladder hatch. It was a well-practiced emergency drill, sliding down the ladders to the outer decks. He jammed his ankles landing in bare feet.

The shuttle was waiting in the launch gantry, engines already turning. Gilroy stuffed his loose infirmary clothes into a Suit, grateful he wouldn't fly into enemy territory naked inside the bulky casing.

He clambered inside and found his seat, one arm still out of the harness as Westerland launched him through the airlocks.

"Shipman Tate," the Sentient said in his ear.

"Yes, sir?"

"I have programmed the shuttle to activate on a proximity protocol. Your return trip will be initiated when the shuttle moves close enough to the ring. However, the pathway will only hold for twenty-seven to forty seconds."

"Understood, sir."

"87% power. Is there a message you would like conveyed to Miss Rico?"

Gilroy's breath caught in a way completely unlike his infection. "Tell her... tell her I'll meet her tomorrow, after third shift, as planned."

"I will. Good luck."

Gilroy felt the unfamiliar controls, hands shaking. He would need every bit of luck he could get.

* * *

"Full power, sir. The connection is open. The shuttle is crossing the breech."

Paulion made no effort to hide his anxiety as they watched in silence. Tate's voice echoed from every corner of the Bridge.

"There's some sort of space station here. Huge! Ships all over. No planet, but five, six other rings. I'm fine, no effect at all, an instant transfer."

The flare on the ring flickered and interference dissolved his voice.

"A star... otted! Incom... attack!"

The connection cut and the radio fell silent.

Paulion spoke into the tense hush. "Did you get a look at that star, Westerland?"

"I am running an algorithm to compare constellations and known stars of the same color."

Ur asked, "What about those ships? That station?"

"Calculating."

Paulion wrenched his attention from the blank screen. "I want every available man either fixing the ring or learning the coding. Shut down non-essential systems. Give Westerland all the power we have and prepare the pilots and infantry for combat." He hesitated, but there was no other choice. "Prime the Tio-Tio missiles."

Halt checked a protest. Paulion met his eyes evenly.

"Whether they come back alive or not, I'm blowing that station out of the sky."

Halt grimaced but nodded. "I'll do it myself."

Paulion crossed his arms over his chest and waited.

THIRTY SEVEN

Location: Unknown
Date: Unknown

rsaces watched from beneath the brim of his stolen cap. A group of aliens hurried past, men in uniform muttering to each other. They cast suspicious looks down the corridors.

He drew back into the alcove he'd found. What was happening? An alarm had sounded a few minutes ago and the tension was palpable in the heavy air.

They're off balance. First her, now another Caprician ship.\

What Caprician ship?

The warning has been on every console we've seen. An alert.\

Arsaces glared at the flashing beacon over the nearest screen.

You can read it. Do it!\

It was impossible. How could he read it?

Does it matter? You have to!\

He tugged his cap down as another mass of them marched by, then activated the screen.

...Attention...Observe...

His headache hadn't lessened, throbbing dully as the words swam before his eyes.

...remain calm...fugitives apprehended...no danger to the race...

They have her imprisoned somewhere.\

...Enter Authorization...

The stylus once again activated the system. A picture displayed. The man Arsaces had left dead down on deck forty-five.

...47-61109...

Who cares about him?\

The system was divided by category, with different divisions under different screens. Personnel, Deck Crew Announcements, Warehouse.

What would they call her? He tried 'brig', which came up with nothing. As did 'prison,' 'jail,' and 'infirmary.'

Holding. Cage. Confinement.\

'Captive' was accepted, for all the good it did him. A red icon filled the screen. ...Forbidden...

Not very important, your mechanic with the big feet.\

Arsaces tried to find away around the block, but the computer kept locking him out. He couldn't type fast enough, the base code outpacing him. He fumed helplessly. He was a damned Admiral and not used to being denied information.

You're being irrational.\

He opened a station map. As he thought, hundreds of decks. Thousands of men, a hundred large ships, thousands of smaller craft.

All it takes is one man to level it all. You know this better than anyone.\

The 'Captive Pen' was some fifteen decks above him. To get there, he would have to cross the barracks.

Find a way around.\

He mapped out a route, hoping the utility shafts had atmosphere, if not gravity. Bad design, no central lift system, ventilation shafts cutting through storage bays.

Someone's coming!\

Arsaces stuffed the stylus back in his pocket and gripped the cutter. The man grunted greeting as he passed and Arsaces waved lazily back. Were there no women aboard?

We're only interested in one and she's somewhere a dozen decks above us. Get moving.\

He wound through the maze of passages. Westerland was laid out logically, a grid wrapped around the drive core. Numbered bulkheads and sequential doors. This place was a mess.

Like they've been building on it for a long time.\

This couldn't be their home. Was it a waypoint, a forward base?

Not important!\

He was nearly there when he had to stop for a group of them blocking his path, all straining to see over their neighbor's head. There was a service hatch to the side. Could he slip in while they were occupied with whatever was happening in the next passage?

Wait!\

The aliens muttered, their talk faltering. Arsaces did not have to slouch, half a head taller than most of them.

Two men passed, soldiers, faces glinting metallic under the lights. They dragged a limp figure between them. The Golden Sunburst of Caprice gleamed on the prisoner's helmet as they passed the sneering crowd.

The fugitive! Follow them.\

Arsaces fought through the crowd, shoving where needed. It was a Flight Suit, a pilot from Westerland by the insignia. Had someone else come through the ring with him? Or had they been sent to find him? If Sas had wasted one of his pilots on a futile rescue mission!

Hypocritical, much? Here it is. Think of a reason you should be allowed inside. Quick!\

The aliens hefted his pilot through a door and shut It. One stood guard outside, weapon drawn. Arsaces walked past.

What are you doing? Go back!\

He snarled at her. She didn't know everything, just a stupid memory who wouldn't leave him alone.

This station had more wasted space than any he'd seen. Compartments and storage lined every passage. He opened a door labeled 'Ventilation Access.' An unlit room lined with pipes and valves. Perfect.

"Hey," Arsaces called. Except it wasn't 'hey,' but whatever they used to mean it. How had he done that?

Don't think; you'll choke up.\

"Hey, come here."

The guard snapped back, "I'm busy, grease-drinker."

Arsaces stamped down his surge of fury. "Come look at this."

"Scram."

"I'm serious. Be useful for once."

There was something implanted in the guard's eye. Much more than an L-plant, glowing red as it glared at Arsaces.

"What did you say?"

Arsaces eased back, pointing into the dark room and trying to look afraid. "In there."

The guard holstered his weapon and came, scowling. "What am I supposed to be—"

Arsaces shoved him into the space. The cutter flared white-hot as it sank into the guard's neck. The door swung shut behind them, Arsaces forcing the man to his knees, his hand over the alien's mouth to muffle his screams.

The shorter man fought ferociously. A hand made of sharp steel fingers closed around Arsaces' wrist, tearing at the rough sleeve. Arsaces hissed as something cut along his ribs. He jerked the cutter through the alien's throat and the man collapsed to the deck.

Two for two. Living up to your Budin heritage.\\

No blood, the cutter wound cauterized. Well, some. His own, oozing from the slash on his side. Arsaces used Tortin's jacket to staunch the bleeding as best he could.

Shuddering, he stripped the coat off the dead man and shrugged into it. This one was too small; his wrists stuck out. Hopefully, he wouldn't be here long enough for anyone to notice.

The guard's weapon was bulky and confusing. He left it with the body, adding only the stylus and card to his stolen goods.

He cautiously eased back into the corridor. How soon before reinforcements arrived?

The guard's stylus unlocked the brig and he stepped inside.

THIRTY EIGHT

Location: Unknown
Date: Unknown

vi's shoulders ached. Her wrists were protected by her Suit, the fabric thick enough to pad them even if it wouldn't fully stiffen without the helmet seal. But the angle of her bindings pulled her arms back unnaturally. Her fingers were numb.

How long had she been in here? The knot on the back of her head had sent her into questionable consciousness for a long time, but she thought it could only have been hours at most. She hoped it was hours at most.

A second figure now lay on the ground next to her. The aliens didn't bother tying him up, just jabbed him with one of their energy weapons and left him in a heap. One of Arsaces' men, by the insignia on his Suit.

She couldn't work up the energy to hope. They were captured, who knew how far from home, with no way for help to reach them.

It was a dismal space. Unfurnished with bare metal plating on the walls and floor. The two of them were in a recess blocked by an energy field of some sort. She knew by the way it hummed she should not attempt to cross it.

A guard stood outside, leaning against the wall next to their cell. A second sat across the room, boots up on a small table. Westerland's brig was luxurious compared to this awful place.

A door opened and a new figure entered. He stepped over to speak with her guard, his voice muffled by the energy field. The guard laughed and gave up his post to the newcomer.

He stood rigid, his back to her. She stared dully at his boots, too tired and forlorn to even find a more comfortable position. She'd be dead in a few days anyway, infected by their foreign pathogens. Hopefully, she would kill a good number of them with hers as well.

A flash of motion drew her groggy attention. The guard's fingers. His sleeves were too short. She could see the muscles in his wrist flex as he drummed bloodied fingers on his pant leg.

Her heart raced.

One, two, three, four, five.

One, two, three, four, five.

His right hand.

She didn't dare say anything, hardly dared to look up to the expanse of his back, his hair clipped short, the crown hidden under a black cap.

He shifted. She saw a flash of metal on his back as he jerked his coat up, heard the dull sound of a mech-gun firing.

The other guard hit the ground with a thud.

He did something at the wall and the field flickered out. He knelt and undid her bindings. Her breath came in sobs of relief and terror. She threw numb arms around his neck and stifled them against his shoulder.

His hands rested on her back for the barest moment, pulling her close. Then she yelped as something sharp pierced her thigh. She gripped his arm, hissing as he held the injection in place. He threw the empty vial aside.

His voice was rough. "Are you hurt?"

She shook her head, wincing in pain. "I'm fine."

Arsaces shook the other Caprician. "Wake up. Airman, wake up!"

The man groaned and reached for his helmet.

"Don't! I only have enough boosters for—"

The man wiggled free and unlocked the seal, the hiss of escaping pressure not covering his hoarse voice. "I'm already dosed, Captain."

Arsaces frowned. "You're not one of my pilots."

"Shipman Tate, sir. First Class, Environmental. I was sent to test the connection."

"Connection?"

"Westerland figured out how to use their ring."

Arsaces dragged her to her feet. His arm stayed around her waist, a sure support she needed. "You can get us home, Tate?"

"They have my shuttle, sir. Unless we get it close to the ring, the portal won't open."

Arsaces swore, face set in grim expression she knew too well. "Leave that to me."

Tate seemed to understand. "You can get to your Heming? How long do you need to overload the plasma—"

"No!" Evi snapped.

Arsaces' eyes met her for an instant, then jumped away. "If I can cripple the station, that should give you time to—"

"You're not sacrificing yourself for me!"

"Evi, it's the only—"

"*No!* I won't allow — you're bleeding!"

Arsaces wiped a crimson hand on his pant leg. "It's nothing."

She fumbled with the clasps of his stolen uniform. It certainly was not nothing. An ugly slash on his flank bled sluggishly.

"Don't bother," he insisted as she dug through her Suit's emergency kit. She pressed an absorbent bandage to the wound as he muttered, "Not like I haven't had worse."

Evi hadn't known it was possible to be both overjoyed and furiously angry at the same time. Her voice trembled no matter she tried to keep it calm.

"Don't be a fool." She wiped at the blood dried on his skin. Who had hurt him? She would tear them apart with her bare hands.

It wouldn't come clean. Not blood. Tattoos. Her fingers stilled, shocked at the swirling lines wrapping around his torso. Traditional Budin lineage markings in red and black ink.

"We don't have time," he said shortly, shoving her hands away. He pulled the coat on again. "They have to have seen me on security. We have to get moving. The hangar is only a few decks above this. You'll have to hide until—"

"You don't have a Suit, sir," Tate said flatly. "Where did you leave the Heming? You take the queen and hide until you feel the explosion. They took the shuttle into that big—"

"No, no, *no!*" Evi snarled.

"It's the only way."

"I won't leave without you! Both of you!"

Arsaces held her eyes this time. She gripped his arm, too tightly she knew, terrified if she let go, he would leave her and get himself killed all over again.

"Please, Arsaces."

Something changed in his face, both soft and steely all at once. He turned to Tate. "You have a weapon?"

"Just my Suit tools, sir."

"Bring them. Take that man's uniform. Don't speak, keep your eyes down."

Tate scrambled out of his Suit, Evi helping as she could. Her eyes flicked to Arsaces against her will, watching as he dug through the dead guard's pockets. He took a gun of some kind, looking over the bulky thing before holstering it at his side.

Tate pulled his own cap low. "Ready, sir."

"Stay close."

THIRTY NINE

Location: Unknown
Date: Unknown

He needed a diversion. How many minutes until she was found missing? The size of the station played to his advantage, but not for long. Not long enough for him to march to the hangar and demand a shuttle.

Tate's idea is sound. An explosion. Cripple the station.\

The hangar was so close, only four decks above. There wasn't time to get to the Heming, wasn't time to escape the detonation of the engines.

Doesn't have to be a Heming. Your friend Tortin has access to the munitions dump.\

Then what? The station in flames, leaking atmosphere. What escape did they have?

What was it you used to say? That you can fly anything? Idle boasts or the truth, Airman Wood?\

"In here." He shoved Evi into a lift and pulled up the station schematics on the console. A chime sounded from the walls, followed by the muffled voice of a recording.

"An alarm?" Tate whispered, face blanched with worry.

"Meal break," Arsaces corrected absently, tracing their path. He jabbed Tortin's stylus into place. "This way."

They exited onto a suspended walkway. It circled the missile lifts he had seen before. The noise was thunderous, the shriek and clank of machinery amplified in the narrow shaft. High above, a crane arm swung out and lifted the missile into position in the magazine above.

Arsaces extracted his hand from Evi's and knelt by a control panel. A lever surrounded by striped red and yellow markings took up the entire upper half.

"What is that?"

"Emergency stop." He turned the lever sharply and the lift next to them rumbled to a halt. A missile rattled in the cradle just in arm's reach. The warhead was sealed, but he only wanted the drive fuel.

He found a seam in the body and used his cutter to melt the connection. A tool lying on the deck supplied leverage and he wrenched it open.

Five metal tanks, connected with hoses and wires. Someone shouted up above. He had to hurry. "Evi, I need tape from your kit."

She passed it to him. He took his cutter and both theirs and strapped them to the closest fuel cell. The blades shone blinding inside the narrow space. Plastic started to melt at once.

Arsaces shoved the missile casing back into place and jerked the lever into position.

The lift resumed with a screech. The hiss of the arc-cutters was drowned out as the missile moved up and out of sight.

"Hurry!"

Arsaces urged them faster, boosting Evi up through an access shaft. He leaned down to lift Tate after them. His shoulder creaked under the man's weight, but the joint held. Of course it would, all plastic and artificial flesh.

"Damn, you're strong," Tate muttered as they ran stooped over in the narrow channel. Up another ladder, across a sky-bridge, down a second shaft.

\Any second now...\

The floor shuddered.

"Was that—?"

Arsaces pushed himself up, ears ringing. He spat blood to the deck. He'd fallen? The air was thick with... smoke?

\Explosion, idiot!\

"Evi!" He scrambled to where she lay sprawled. She was coughing, but sat up, his arm at her back.

"Are you hurt?"

"I... I don't think so. How did you know that would — Where's Tate?"

Arsaces peered through the hazy air. A Jump boot stuck out from under a strut collapsed across the passage.

"Tate!" Evi cried, scrambling over to him. "Tate, can you hear me?"

A weak voice answered. Arsaces tried to find a way through the mess. He cursed as his hand went to his pocket. No cutter, of course. He *was* an idiot.

\You couldn't have foreseen this. \

How could he get Tate free?

"Hold on, Tate!" Evi called. "We're coming!" She spoke to Arsaces in a fierce whisper. "What are we going to do? We can't leave him!"

Arsaces' L-plant informed him of the impossibility of the task.

1.4 meters... steel alloy... 134.7 kilograms... 45.23...

\Lift it. \

He snarled at her memory to shut up and let him think. Evi and he pushed on it, unable to shift it.

\Lift it, Arsaces. \

It was impossible. Hundreds of kilos, wedged between structural beams.

Tate cried out. His leg jerked.

\Do it! Now!\

0.97 meters... particulates: 5.6 ppm and rising. Air temperature: 41 and rising...

"Captain?" Tate's voice reached them, hitched, panicking.

\Your name is Arsaces Jankovic-Wood. Do not panic. \

"Arsaces, I see flames!"

"Ez odpo ara ed... ez odpo ara ed..."

...There is a fire...there is a fire...

Always *too many* voices! Couldn't he just have his own, for one *fraac ghar* minute!

Arsaces shoved Evi away from the metal trapping his crewman. Fool boy, chasing after him. He didn't ask anyone to rescue him.

He braced his back against the hot paneling. The edge of the strut dug into his palms. It was a welcome pain, blocking out their incessant clamoring. Couldn't they just leave him alone?

He hadn't wanted a promotion or a crew or a *houkun* computer in his head. Dumped on him with no other choice, a desperate grasp at salvation and now he would do anything to protect them and this fool girl he barely knew, whom he loved and hated and adored.

"Arsaces, you can't—!"

He felt his bones stiffen, responsive to the weight of the strut. His muscles tightened, the speed of his half-plastic heart increasing to feed them. Felt how his entire body braced. And reveled in finally using the strength that lay hidden.

The strut shifted. Under the growing roar of the blaze metal shrieked, bending, tearing.

Better leverage now. He got his shoulder under it and heaved up.

"Tate! Move!" Evi tugged at the man's legs as he wiggled free. Sweat dripped from Arsaces' face, the air thick with smoke.

"He's out!"

Arsaces let go. The strut slammed to the deck with a deafening clang.

"Come on!" He slung Tate's arm over his shoulder and dragged him forward.

"Thanks," the man gasped.

"Save it. Not home yet."

They stumbled out a hatch into a main corridor, coughing as they gulped clean air. Shouting aliens ran in every direction. Arsaces pushed past their grasping hands.

"He's injured," he snapped, shoving them away. "Get out of the way."

They made it two decks before someone noticed the queen's foreignness.

"Hey, where are you taking—?"

Arsaces dropped Tate and grabbed the alien's arm. It snapped under his hand, brittle as all human bones were. Arsaces gripped the man's jacket and hurled him into the closest passageway. The crowd there fell back, knocked off their feet.

"Run!"

He half-carried the limping Shipman, Evi bracing up Tate's other side.

The hangar was just ahead. More alarms sounded overhead, the same soulless computerized voice announcing the danger.

"Fire detected in the munitions bay... All personnel to emergency stations."

There were only a few guards left in the hangar, the rest likely sent to battle the blaze. One challenged Arsaces.

"What is your access authorization?"

"I need a transport." He tried to push by and a stiff hand blocked his path.

"State your identification code. And who are these ones?"

Arsaces shoved the stylus at him. "Tortin, 47-61109."

The man frowned. "Forty-sevens don't have transport privileges." He turned to a console.

Arsaces moved quickly. He slammed the alien's head into the screen. The alien fell limp to the ground.

"You there! Stop!"

Their guns were clumsy. And loud, firing pulses of energy that numbed his hands. The other aliens dove behind pillars, calling for help.

Arsaces opened the first transport they came to, shoving Tate at the hatch. Evi followed, Arsaces firing bursts at anyone who risked a look.

The hatch closed solidly behind him and he threw the wheel lock.

"Captain? You can fly this?"

Arsaces slid into the pilot's chair, activating the flight computer. "I can fly anything. Strap in."

The main console woke up. ...Authorization?...

The brig guard's stylus slid into place and the shuttle rumbled to life. Easy enough, pitch, yaw, thrust. Mooring locks? There, on the left. A quick jab and they were free.

\Now what? You're in the middle of the station.\

...Caution...weapons activated...

\Effective, I suppose. There is some sort of energy field at the mouth of the tunnel. Same as the brig. An airlock?\

Like Westerland, this station was well equipped to handle external attack. The shuttle's missiles decimated the hangar, destroying supports, lights, crates.

\There! It's open!

Arsaces steered them into the darkness of the tunnel and then out into the blackness of space. Where were the rings?

"They're after us, Captain! Eight, ten, maybe fifteen!"

A missile trail streaked by. He jabbed a finger at the correct controls. "Return fire!"

The shuttle did not have artificial gravity. They pressed into their seats as Arsaces turned them over, the slow power irritating.

"How many CGS can you take, Tate?"

"Blacked out at six, sir."

If he used Caprician techniques, they'd exceed that and no Suits. This flimsy craft couldn't possibly withstand more than average acceleration. Why would it need to, traveling by ring instead of Jump? Blasted Tate! He could have fit two of them in the Heming!

\Speaking of Hemings…

There was a bloom of flames as Tate landed a hit. Arsaces wasn't helping his aim, flying erratically, trying to compensate for their lack of speed, avoiding enemy fire.

The shuttle computer chirped.

…Destination?…

\The rings. They see you.

But where to go? He needed time to decipher it, to figure out the code.

*\You need another diversion. Say, a pair of plasma engines breaking confinement. We both know what that can do to a ship.**

"Where are you going?" Tate demanded as Arsaces wheeled away from the rings.

There had to be something more than missiles. He was sure he'd read that report, only days ago. There, some sort of pulse weapon like the handheld ones.

The hull of the station swept under them as Arsaces skimmed the surface, searching the shadows for the fighter.

"I see it, sir!"

"Destroy it!"

The shuttle jerked as an alien missile found its mark. He'd been too long in a straight line. He saw the flash of Tate's missiles hitting home and tore away.

\Faster! Get clear!\

He pressed the shuttle as hard as it would go. The air inside was stifling. How much could its engines take?

They bucked, flipping end over end as the Heming's containment ruptured. The wave of energy swept past them, carrying them along like a leaf in a stream.

Arsaces fought them straight, the circle of rings now looming.

...Destination?...

"How did you get through?"

"I don't know; Westerland programmed it!"

Arsaces scrolled frantically through the list. If they went through the wrong one, were stranded somewhere, no supplies, no Suits. The shuttle groaned, thrown to port.

\Can't be worse than here.\

...Ironulon...Ebongas...Vanguard...Grast...

\Vanguard!\

Arsaces jabbed the icon. The ring to his left came alive, the space between swirling.

"Arsaces! The hatch!"

The rear hatch glowed. Arsaces flipped them, flying backwards. A swarm of menacing lights swelled up behind them.

"Low on missiles, Captain!"

...Proceed...

"Keep firing!"

\We're going through!\

FORTY

Empty Orbit
F - 1884 - 6 - 5

Paulion had taken to pacing the deck. Officers jumped out of his way as he roamed the Bridge. How long did they wait? How long until they opened the ring again and sent the Tio Tios through? The Captain had been gone four hours, Tate forty-five minutes.

He forced himself to stand in his place. He stared at the forward screen, nothing but the ring and a repair ship in the field. The Fleet had pulled back, ready for an attack. Even now the fighters waited in the shadow of Westerland's hull.

The crew worked feverishly to stabilize the ring as best they could. Westerland had even given up main control, his entire focus on directing the technicians crawling over the surface of the device.

Paulion hoped he could get them away in time, if the ring activated from the other side. Who knew what the radiation of that monstrosity did to a man up close. His gut clenched at the thought. Were those metal implants repair for those who went through the rings too often?

He swallowed and searched for something else to think about. His gaze fell on the screen showing the Tio Tio missiles in their launch cradles. Another sick-making sight. Just one of those would make what happened on Caprice look like a love tap. Moon breakers, they were called.

"Sir! Spike in readings."

"I think it's activating!"

"Grenfil, get out of there!" Paulion ordered. "Fall back! Halt?"

"We're ready!"

"Prepare for immediate engagement!"

The fighter board lit up as the Hemings peeled away from the Sentient. They formed a glittering mass before the Fleet. The repair ship careened back, scampering to get free before the fight began.

The ring glowed. The colors faltered, but did not die.

"Can you tell who is coming through, Westerland?"

"No."

Paulion clenched his fists. Might as well get executed for something truly spectacular. "Initiate Tio Tio start up."

"Yes, sir," an ensign said evenly. "Thirty seconds, sir. I will need your authorization."

Paulion went to the slight young man, hesitating only an instant before pressing his palm to the screen. The words were accusatory, a failure to bring his Captain and queen home: *safety disabled.*

There was nothing else they could do. Halt, Ur, the tacticians, they all agreed the next wave would be the largest, retaliation. They had to stop it here.

"It's opening!"

The stars were gone, that hated blackness staring back at them. Why couldn't they see through to the other side?

Alarms shrieked as a mass of alien fighters burst through. Alien chatter swamped the radio. The Capricians' shouted over them.

"Fighters, advance!"

"EM pulse primed!"

"Formation 16-7-b!"

"Wait!" Paulion bellowed over the noise. The crew stilled, watching him watch the screen. The enemy ships were swarming, firing on a central point, a tiny ship that raced ahead of them, fighting back desperately.

"That ship! There, call it. Supporting fire! Now!"

Caprician missiles danced with the aliens' as some of the enemy fighters turned on the Fleet. The lone defending ship broke away, streaking toward Westerland.

"Unknown Alien Ship, identify yourself!"

Westerland filtered out the radio noise as he focused on the bulky shuttle. "UAS, identify or we will open fire. Do you copy?"

Seconds of static, Paulion trembling with the strain.

"I copy... call sign: Archer 887."

Paulion gripped a console with tight fingers. "Archer 887, do you have the queen?"

"Yes."

"Launch the Tio Tios!"

"Yes, sir!"

"Destroy all alien ships!"

"With pleasure, sir!"

FORTY ONE

Empty Orbit

F - 1884 - 6 - 5

Archer 887.

Arsaces.

His Captain.

Joy, euphoria; emotions he had only ever had descriptions for, not felt.

Arsaces was back. Arsaces was alive, whole, home, safe, safe, safe.

He threw everything he had into holding the connection open. The Tio Tios launched. Slow, precise, deadly. He guided them through the ring. He could just feel them, unthinkably far away.

They detonated and the connection snapped. The ring died, an orphan, as the awesome power of the moon breakers unleashed.

The trapped aliens panicked. They tried to open the ring, dozens of different codes. He watched carefully, collecting them all. Finally, it opened and they fled. He let them. They would carry news of their defeat, spread fear of his Captain.

Arsaces was home!

* * *

The force of Westerland in his mind was so overwhelming, so relieving, it was all he could do to stay upright in his seat.

Arsaces braced himself against the controls. He distantly heard Tate talking to someone aboard the Sentient. The words warbled meaninglessly as Westerland's voice thundered in his head.

\Safe, safe, safe!\

"They're taking us in, sir."

\Alive! Home! Safe!\

Us. Him and Tate. Evi.

The shuttle jerked as the airlock mechanism caught them, gripping whatever part of the foreign ship it could. The darkness was broken only by the sickly blue light of the alien shuttle's controls.

...Unknown location... it told him mournfully. He sneered at it.

They shot through the sloping tunnel, weight building as they matched the ship's spin. The final airlock opened and they rattled forward, Westerland rough in his hurry to get them aboard.

Before Arsaces could stand, the hatch blew and Suited figures rushed in. He and the others were dragged free and shuffled into decon tents. Arsaces tried to find Evi, to keep close to her, but there were too many hands pulling him on.

He barely made it into the tent before falling to his knees, weak with relief and fear and longing.

The deck plates were warm through the tent floor. They hummed under his palms, the faintest whir of machinery and power. The medic urged him forward, but he couldn't, not yet. Could he lie down here? Just feel his Sentient with every part of him, just for a few moments?

\I thought... I thought I had lost you forever.\

I had to. I'm so sorry. I had to go after her.

\But *why?*\

"Captain?"

He took a deep breath of the stinging air, thick with the smell of disinfectant. He got clumsily to his feet, still reeling under the massive weight that was the Sentient's presence.

He was stripped down without ceremony and sprayed with a scalding blast of water. A medic huffed over his wounds, slathering him with numbing paste. He hardly felt the stitches, the healing boosters.

A cold shower next and some blinding minutes under a UV bath, his eyes squeezed tight. They helped him into clean clothes and they went through the final door.

The noise nearly knocked him back. Screaming, cheering. He flinched under their hands, exhausted and numb inside as well as out. There were too many voices again.

Marines forced an aisle through the crowd. Sas got under one shoulder, Ur the other. They led him to a lift. He dug in his heels when they tried to get him out at the Infirmary.

"I need to—"

"It can wait, sir."

\Just for tonight.\

"Orjean's orders, lad."

The ward was empty, only two beds made up. There were three of them, right?

"Tate," Arsaces murmured, turning to look for the man.

"His girl's got him well in hand, sir. Lie down."

Arsaces did, aching everywhere. "I should—"

"Tomorrow, sir. Sleep."

"But—"

\Sleep.\

FORTY TWO

Caprice: Orbon, Imperial District
F - 1879 - 18 - 26

Carl waited outside the reception room, trying not to sweat. There was moisture beading on his upper lip and his stiff uniform collar was beginning to itch. He wanted to blame the damned weather like usual, but he was never any good at lying to himself.

He straightened his shoulders as the great double doors opened. An orderly appeared and gave him a negligent wave. Carl stiffened his spine and marched in.

The room was empty. Rows upon rows of chairs were cast in shadow. Only the front of the long room was lit, illuminating a low table and a chair.

Before them was a throne, a copy of the real one in the throne room some seven kilometers away through the warren of the Imperial District. The real one was never left unattended, said to be over a thousand years old, festooned with priceless gems and carvings.

Whether it was or not mattered little to Carl. Or the Emperor. The man's predecessor had seized it from the last dynasty, who had taken it from the one before that. It was a symbol only. The gems on it, while lovely, were a fraction of the real wealth in these walls.

Carl walked to the table and sat. And waited.

He had expected this. The orderly slipped away. The room was silent but for the hum of the lights. The city around him was quiet, or as quiet as it ever was in the early hours of the morning.

At last, one of the screens covering the forward wall glowed. It took a moment for the picture to connect and adjust before a face came into focus.

It was Fleet-Admiral Suessina.

"*Hyde,*" the man said curtly. He was on his ship in his quarters, it looked like.

"Admiral," Carl returned evenly.

Another screen, four over and two below the first. The Sky-Marshal. Halt only grunted. Dawn was showing behind him, a few hours ahead of Orbon, the capital city.

Carl waited as each of the tribunal's members connected. Master Dant, who stared at him with wide eyes that didn't blink enough. Senator Bears, dressed for a formal event. One of the Generals. Another cabinet member. No one looked pleased. Their anger had nothing to do with the absurd hour of this meeting.

No one spoke after their terse greetings. A few uncomfortable throat clearings. Senator Bears flipped through her papers.

The last screen, the largest and dominating the center of the wall, powered on.

Carl stood respectfully. "Your majesty."

The Emperor didn't bother with formalities. "*This is a farce, Hyde.*"

Carl said nothing as he resumed his seat. He knew well enough this was a fight he should have left alone.

"*Well?*" the Emperor barked.

Carl looked to the Fleet-Admiral, who sighed. "*This tribunal is reconvened to discuss the punishment of one Jankovic-Wood, Arsaces Daas, Senior Airman, 7th Squadron, Alam City, of the Tinese—*"

"*This was settled weeks ago,*" the Emperor interrupted. "*Why are you stirring this up again?*"

Carl kept his tone smooth and professional. "Your majesty, I have presented you my report regarding—"

"*That rebel will have no thanks from us!*"

"You've made that perfectly clear, your majesty. I hear his last remaining cousin was finally apprehended and executed two days ago."

Someone coughed into the tense silence. Master Dant still stared blankly, but the others looked away.

Carl continued. "You cannot deny he saved us from an ugly war, which may not have ended in our favor. Whatever his kin have done has no bearing on his actions. The Airman lying on my ship is not a traitor."

"*Prove it,*" Senator Bears said coolly. "*How can we know he did not participate in his family's treason? He served under his uncle, communicated regularly with his cousins, who were commanders on the Alam City base.*"

Carl answered just as icily. "As commander of the Colonial Reserve, I am responsible for the actions of the Tinese Corps. Do you think I did not do everything in my power to quell this revolt before it happened? Do you think I do not know my men? I personally witnessed Wood's heroic actions—"

The Emperor snorted contemptuously.

Carl did his best to control his temper. Dr. Vanas was forever nagging him about his blood pressure. "There is no other word for it, your majesty."

"*I can think of one,*" President Yuni said snidely. Carl glared at him, wondering what favor the men sought to gain by backing the Emperor.

"*It's obvious,*" he continued. "*Wood knew they wouldn't win. He knew he would be prosecuted for treason. He killed himself. He's a coward.*"

"He is not a coward," Carl snarled, closely echoed by Marshal Halt.

"*Cowards don't fly their fighters through spaceships,*" Halt added scornfully.

They received unexpected support from the General of the First Army.

"*Nor do they kill their own family.*" Shin-jal was the youngest member present, but he spoke with the authority of his rank. "*And Budins never betray their own.*"

"*Yet this one did,*" Yuni retorted. "*Which shows how trustworthy he is.*"

Carl glared at the Emperor, pushing his scant personal license with his monarch to its limits. "The man was injured cleaning up a mess we made."

"*I made?*" the Emperor demanded, hearing Carl's implication clearly.

"We," Carl stressed, trying to maintain some level of diplomacy, even as his collar grew damp with sweat. "We have mishandled Tin for the last fifty years. It was only a matter of time before some faction rose up. And no matter what any of you say, that war would have been a nightmare politically, economically, and militarily. Shea would have no compunction running arms, selling information. Taltua is ripe for an excuse to push for more independence. They would have used this to assert more autonomy and we could have done nothing, knowing if they aligned with Shea and Tin…"

Even the Emperor looked uncomfortable now.

Carl pressed his advantage. "All I'm asking is we recognize this man's sacrifice. He is a Budin, yet he did betray his family. His family who has controlled Alam-Jaheel for six generations. When his uncle called for insurgence, the entire Corps followed him. Wood saved us. He deserves to be rewarded."

"He has his life," someone muttered.

"No, he doesn't." It was General Shin-jal again. *"There's nothing on Tin for him now."* For all his youth, he was remarkably shrewd. One didn't become one of the most powerful men in the Empire without intelligence and a certain ruthlessness.

Carl agreed. "There are pillars holding up a man's life. We've destroyed all of Wood's. Legally, of course," he added with a sneer. "His family, his life, his body. Oh, we'll grow it back, some of it. But you know it's not the same."

A few reluctant nods, those with their own implants or restructuring. No matter it moved, felt, and acted liked human flesh, one always knew it wasn't. Carl stilled a shudder of revulsion.

The Emperor was barely holding in his temper at this point. *"What is it you want, then?"*

"I want you to give him a Sentient."

Everyone, even his allies, protested.

"Give a colonial a Sentient?"

"Are you insane?"

"He does not meet the requirements set up by this council!"

Carl personally thought the requirements mandated a man be so near perfect as to be a computer himself. Then what was the point of the Hybrid pairing?

The others finally ran out of arguments. Carl kept his face neutral, watching the Emperor scowl.

"Why, Hyde?"

"It could be seen as a first step in reconciliation. Proof we are not unreasonable. That we reward loyalty and sacrifice."

That they were not over-bearing dictators seeking to bring every living thing in the system under their control.

"There isn't a Sentient scheduled for completion for another three years," Master Dant said, as if this was the hardest hurdle to overcome.

"I know. But I want him implanted at once." Otherwise, Carl feared the man would end up dead, either by his own hand or by some unfortunate 'accident.' "I see this as a chance to show our mercy. Shea and Taltua are watching and they will exploit any weakness we show. Do we want to encourage Tinese defection to Shean holdings? Or demonstrate our willingness to — "

"Oh, enough." The Emperor flicked his hand. *"Do it."*

Carl let out a breath he hadn't realized he was holding. "Thank you, sir."

"There will be no official recognition. This colonial is being promoted far above his deserts. I will hold you personally responsible for his actions until the Sentient is activated."

"Yes, your majesty."

The others took this to mean the meeting was over. Their screens cut out, the Emperor ignoring their respectful murmurs, until it was just the two of them, Monarch and Son-in-Law.

"You made me look like a fool."

"That was not my intent." Carl never took liberties with their relationship. He was sure this was the only time it would be allowed.

"You may go."

Carl stood and bowed. "Thank you, sir."

"Hyde?"

He turned back, feeling gray and drawn. His physician would be furious at their next appointment. "Yes, sir?"

"Evi is well?"

"Yes, sir. I will tell her you asked after her."

His wife's father grunted and the screen went blank.

FORTY THREE

Empty Orbit

F - 1884 - 6 - 6

It was dark when he struggled back to consciousness. He hated forced sleep. It made him groggy and confused when he woke, as if his mind was pulling itself out of thick mud.

A few lights glowed by the floor, sending warm colors up the walls. It was quiet, nothing more than the faintest sound of the air circulation and his own heartbeat.

\You're home!\

Arsaces sat up, rubbing at teary eyes, his throat tight with the Sentient's joy. *What time is it?*

\Late. Fourth watch. You've been asleep seven hours.\

The air was blessedly cool, clean and crisp. He took a deep breath, savoring it.

\Just how you like it. And how it is everywhere aboard, you know.\

Arsaces wiped his cheeks on his sleeve as he smiled.

\She's here, too.\

He turned. She was. A small lump under the blankets, curled up with her head nearly covered. Why had they kept her here? Was she hurt?

\She has minor injuries. No infection.\

Arsaces watched her breathe, weak again with relief. She was alive and safe.

You are alive and safe. That's all that matters.\ **Westerland hesitated.** \Why did you leave me?\

I had no choice.

\That is not logical. You are my Captain. She can be replaced.\

Arsaces could hardly admit it to himself, *She can't.*

Westerland swore, a coarse phrase Arsaces hadn't used since he was an adolescent. He couldn't stop his laugh. The noise roused the queen. She blinked up at him, a crease between her brows.

"Arsaces?"

His throat was thick again. "I... uh, are you hurt?"

An odd dichotomy, joy and petulance, in Westerland's tone. \I already told you.\

"I'm alright," Evi said, voice hoarse. "Just sore. They didn't—" She sat up, blankets pooling in her lap. "Your side!"

She moved too swiftly; he couldn't escape before she sat on his bed. Arsaces flinched from her hands. "It's nothing."

She gave him a look he couldn't interpret, with her lips compressed, but still quirked up in an almost smile. He adored it.

"I could see your rib," she accused.

He let her draw up his shirt. More than modesty made him blush. He'd not realized in the midst of it what she would see on his skin.

"It's already healing."

"Luckily, I am not resistant to boosters, after, you know, all that happened."

She made a noncommittal sort of noise. "And I hadn't realized you had your marking redone."

There didn't seem to be an answer to that. He could only see the top of her head, the dim lights tinting the pale strands different colors. He shivered as she traced one of the crimson swirls with a light finger.

"Did it hurt?"

That was enough of her hands and eyes on his skin. He jerked his shirt down. "Yes."

But nothing to knowing his lineage would end with him. That he had had to bribe another *nethessari*, an outcast, to do it. That whatever remnant had been left after the crash had been erased as a mistake, an aberrance. That his family would cut the ink from his flesh, given the chance.

Her voice was as gentle as her fingers. "Why?"

He understood. "They are my family."

She drew her legs up, resting her chin on her knees. "I don't miss my family."

"I... I'm sorry, Evi." It was a meaningless phrase made weaker by his slight interrogation. She didn't?

She laughed a little. "I hardly saw them, even before I was married. I doubt I would have recognized my eldest sister in passing."

He desperately wanted to know, but was afraid of her answer. "How long were you married before...?"

"Before Carl died? Eight years."

"Was..." He swallowed. "Was he good to you?"

"The best of men," she whispered. She stared ahead, hands fiddling with his blanket, folding and refolding the hem. She came back to herself and managed a small smile. "Truthfully, he spoiled me rotten. You think I'm willful now?"

There was that silence again. Even Westerland was quiet, watching this interaction. Resentful, but curious.

She reached to put her hand in his. "Thank you."

Her hand was so small. He stared at their intertwined fingers, so he wouldn't see her eyes. "My honor, your majesty."

"No." The sharp negation drew his gaze up. She wasn't smiling any longer. "Thank you, Arsaces."

It was the most natural thing to lean forward. To touch her cheek. To rest his forehead against hers, breathe the same air for a moment. Revel in her scent, the silk of her hair.

Her lips were soft under his. He expected to feel shame or fear, but instead there was just the quiet and the warmth of her against him. Then, all at once heat, her hands under his shirt again, his on her hips, pulling her closer.

The damn blankets were in the way. He forced a hand away from her skin to shove them aside, pulling her down to the bed. Cool air nipped at his bare shoulders.

This was a terrible idea. Someone could come in. Westerland could lock doors, couldn't he? He should ask him. He would ask him, once he could pull his thoughts from the shape of her under his touch, the taste of her.

Something fell to the floor and she gasped, jerking back. He stared blankly at her.

The shock of his actions crashed down. He had kissed her. She had kissed him back. She lay sprawled atop him, her hair a shimmering tent around them, their blankets tangled and drooping to the floor.

He took gasping breaths of his own. He should say something. Explain. Ask for forgiveness.

\Idiot. Tell her you love her.\

"Why were you on my ship?"

Her whole body stiffened. He knew, because it was pressed against his, his hands in places a man should never touch his queen. He snatched them away and she scrambled to her feet.

He hissed as he sat up, joints stiff and aching. Worse, now his lust was draining away, leaving him cold and empty.

\And who's stupid fault is that? Moron.\ Westerland was disgusted. By him? By what they had been doing?

"I believe I told you then it was none of your business, Captain."

He winced at the edge in her voice, no matter the placidity of her expression. She gathered her hair and plaited it with quick fingers.

"I know. I just..." Just what? Wanted to know what chance had saved her from the fate of so many others?

She stood a long time in silence, brow furrowed. Would she tell him? Trust him?

The door opened. Arsaces flushed as a medic came in and stopped still at the sight of them. "Captain? Your majesty?"

I told you to lock the doors!

\Because that wouldn't be suspicious.\

Arsaces straightened, conscious of his bare chest and the medic's raised eyebrows. He hoped it was just his tattoos. Please, noble fathers, let it be just the glaring, heretical inks in his skin that made the medic look away, clearly embarrassed.

"I'm rested enough. I need to see Ur and Halt."

The medic stopped short of snorting in disbelief. "Yes, sir. Ma'am?"

"I, too, need to speak with my cabinet."

The man gave in with poor grace. "Very well. Let me assess you once more before you leave, if you don't mind."

Evi relented and followed him. She cast one swift look over her shoulder before the door shut behind her.

Arsaces fell back to the bed and pressed his fists into his eyes.

\You're an imbecile.\

He scrubbed his face. He must suffered some sort of brain damage when he crossed through that portal. Only thing that explained his actions. "I know."

\She was undressing you.\

"I am aware."

\Her tongue was in your mouth.\

"*Ghar sen ai*, Westerland."

\And you asked her why she purchased a berth?\

"Good thing. Or that medic would have found us..." Doing what? Alone again, his imagination supplied in clear detail what it wanted to be doing with his queen. "*Ghar.*"

Westerland muttered sullenly. \I would have locked the doors.\

"And had half the crew down here, breaking them open?"

\I would have explained the situation to Sas.\

Arsaces jerked up. "Don't you dare."

\He already suspects. He would understand. Probably even congratulate you.\

"So help me, I will disconnect your sensory inputs."

Westerland scoffed at him.

FORTY FOUR

Empty Orbit
F - 1884 - 6 - 6

Evi had every intention of rousing her cabinet from their slumber. Then Fan swept her into a hug, and she put her head on the woman's shoulder and cried until her throat was raw and her head ached.

"Little one," Fan murmured, stroking her back. "You are safe now."

Evi wiped her nose, breath catching as her sobs eased. "I'm fine, Fan."

Fan ignored her. "Come. Eat something."

The healing booster left her ravenous, and she ate with single-minded purpose until replete. She had hoped to be sleepy again. But her emotions churned restless in her chest and she stood to pace.

"Do you want to talk about it?"

Evi started guiltily, as if she was a girl of fourteen again rather than a woman grown and an empress besides. Then she realized her nursemaid knew nothing of Evi's nearly successful attempt to seduce her Fleet Admiral and pushed Fan's gentle words away with an irritated gesture.

She wanted to slap him. And kiss him some more. And then slap him again for being such a... a...? A what, she couldn't decide. She knew he was terrible with emotions, with expressing them and understanding them. She just never imagined he could be so dense as to bring up such a topic at such a time.

Evi drew her shoulders back. It was for the best. She had no time for entanglements. She had left Caprice for the express purpose of escaping being dragged into a relationship.

That she did not want to explain that to Arsaces irritated her. She was being irrational. She had been tired, overwhelmed, and grateful, and it had made her act impetuously.

Now, she had to face him in the morning and calmly discuss troop deployments and supply chains. Sit across the room from him and act like she did not know what his lips felt like on hers. How the callouses on his hands rasped deliciously against the skin of her back. How being in his arms made her weak with longing.

She was a queen, damn it. They did not cry, nor did they pine after honorable men with broad shoulders and shy smiles.

Fan gently urged her to the bed. Evi sat and Fan brushed her hair, as she had done thousands of times in her girlhood. The strokes were soothing to her headache, grounding her.

"Did you like Carl, Fan?"

Fan's strokes paused a moment before resuming. "Why do you ask?"

"I loved him."

"I know, little one."

"But did you like him?"

"Of course, I did."

"You were never friendly with him."

Fan set aside the brush to start on her plait. "My loyalty is to you, your majesty."

"He was a good man."

"Yes." The drawn out syllable made Evi bite her tongue and wait. "He was a good man and I would have been happy for you. If you had chosen him yourself."

Evi wondered if she would have, given time. If her father had valued her more and if she had been able to know Carl before their marriage. She hoped so. He had given her so much.

"I kissed him." Evi winced as the words blurted out, no matter she wanted to never speak, not even think of it, again.

"I assumed you had. I know you had grown to have feelings for—"

"No. Arsaces."

Fan stilled. "The Captain?"

"Yes."

Very few times in her life had Evi seen Fan flabbergasted. Evi turned to find the woman frowning. "I see."

Evi winced. "It was a mistake."

Fan's eyes narrowed. "That is not like you. To be impulsive in such a way."

"Don't I know it."

"Did he... reciprocate?"

Evi flushed from her feet to the roots her hair. "Yes."

"Well." A hint of a smile curved Fan's mouth. "That will certainly make things awkward."

Evi groaned and lay down to hide her face.

"It is late. You should rest. I expect you will spend the day being interrogated about this whole debacle."

A shudder rattled through her. The thought of retelling the details over and over cooled the fire of her embarrassment.

"To bed, child."

Evi obeyed, grumbling at Fan's highhanded treatment of her sovereign. Fan chuckled and stopped to kiss her forehead. "Sleep well, dearest."

FORTY FIVE

Empty Orbit
F - 1884 - 6 - 7

She was spared her blushes the next day because Arsaces didn't look at her when she entered the room. She was grateful for it. She didn't know if she control her expression just yet. The prospect of reliving her kidnapping sent her heart racing with remembered fear and hopelessness.

She only allowed a small group to be present for the debriefing. Arsaces, of course, and Sas. General Ur and Marshall Halt, with their secondaries. Dr. Orjean sat with the shadows of bruises still lingering on his face.

She stopped by him on the way to her own place. "What happened, Orjean?"

"Just some minor injuries during the attack." He glanced around the room and lowered his voice until only she could hear him. "I have disposed of the remaining subject."

She nodded tightly and moved on. She had not had time to learn more than the scantest rumors, but if the other aliens had awoken, then their test subjects likely had, too. Well, the one still in one piece. That the alien's first action had been to attack and kidnap her told her enough about the necessity of her decisions. They must understand this people if they had any hope to survive.

"Westerland has pieced together the timeline of yesterday's events," Arsaces said without preamble. "There is a report for your reference on the Network. I have supplied as much detail as I can remember, and I would appreciate further observations from her majesty when she is feeling able."

She kept her face neutral, but he still didn't turn to look at her. Would the others notice? The tension between them was palpable. Hopefully, her officers attributed it to the situation.

She sat through Sas' recital of the events in the Caprician's space. He spoke evenly, but hesitated when he got to the actual event of the kidnapping.

"There seem to be discrepancies between the various reports here. It is understandable, given the alarm and confusion of the crew." He cast her a hooded glance. "In any case, an alien managed to reach the flight deck. It accosted the queen and carried her into one of its own ships."

It took everything she had, all her years of politicking, to keep her expression clear. Sas gave her another measured look and continued in a dry voice.

Was this the reason for Arsaces' rebuff? Was she being egotistical, thinking it had to do with their almost liaison, when in reality he had discovered she was lying to him? Had, in fact, directly countermanded his orders?

Her turn came to speak of her ordeal. She had lain awake well after Fan left her, trying to find a way to explain what she had seen and heard. Terror tainted it and she didn't know if she could speak without letting her emotions make her sound like a frightened child.

She detailed as much of the station as she could. How they interacted. The technologies she didn't understand. Their treatment of her.

"Then the Captain came." Driven by some unnamed impulse, she faced him directly and waited. His jaw clenched; she saw the tightness of it even across the room. Finally, he lifted his eyes to hers, dark and almost glassy. Retreated into his Sentient. Coward. She had no such luxury.

"Please, Captain, I would like to hear your side of these events."

"Certainly, your majesty."

Definitely hiding in Westerland. She heard it in the smoothness of his voice, the pleasant lilt of his faked accent. She contemplated throwing her Palm at him.

"When Westerland was attacked, he pushed me away in order to protect me, not knowing the nature of the assault. I am not sure if I can describe that…" He thought a moment, then shook his head. "Not in a way you would understand. In any event, I suffered a physiologic response and was incapacitated for a time."

Evi gripped her hands together under the table. She had thought him dead. He had been dead. There had been no pulse in his neck, no thump of his heart beneath her hands.

"Unfortunately, this prevented my assisting the queen. I must beg your forgiveness, ma'am."

Evi made a regal gesture, absolving him of responsibility. He bowed and continued.

It was much the same as Sas' and her recitals. He had taken a fighter and given chase. Went through the ring. Discovered the space station on the other side.

She noted his careful choice of words which glossed over the grislier aspects of his actions. He 'subdued' an alien to steal a uniform. 'Overpowered' a guard and gained access to the brig. No mention of the blood on his hands.

The officers questioned him carefully, making notes and muttering to each other. The sabotaged missile, the explosion and fire. Stealing a shuttle and destroying the Heming.

Evi let them talk, a growing surety closing around her chest.

It was impossible.

What he had done was impossible.

She was a fool to not have seen it before. Maybe it was the shock of it or her relief at his presence. But there was no way he could have known where to go, what to do. He had spoken with them. Yes, the linguists were disseminating the alien language as fast as they could, but no one was near fluent.

He had lifted that beam.

She'd heard the crunch of bones in that alien's arm. Before Arsaces threw him six meters and knocked a crowd of them off their feet.

And he mentioned none of it. Did he think they would simply take it as chance that he found her? That he had stumbled across the magazine?

That he knew how to work the ring?

The omission was glaring. And it frightened her.

It meant he had something to hide.

* * *

"You must be Ensign Rico." Evi held out her hand. The woman blushed and gave an awkward half curtsy, half salute, before shaking it.

"Yes, ma'am."

"I hope your leg is better, Shipman."

Tate managed to look proud and abashed at the same moment. "Yes, ma'am. Booster fixed it right up. Just a bit achy, is all."

"I wanted to thank you personally, Tate."

He grinned. "My pleasure, ma'am. An honor."

She hated that, how easily they would sacrifice themselves for her, just because of her genetics, her ancestors. "I will write to your family, as well as see you receive a commendation."

He stammered his thanks. Evi gritted her teeth to keep her smile. "May I have a word, Shipman? In private? It will only take a moment."

Rico saluted again and drifted away. Evi gestured for Tate to sit next to her. The common room was empty but for them, the other crewmen slipping away when her guards took up positions. They had barely left her side for her to use the water closet, and even then under protest.

"What is it, your majesty?"

"I read your account of our... adventure."

"Yes, ma'am. Sas had me report right after they fixed my leg."

"I wanted to know your thoughts on all of it."

Tate frowned. "My thoughts?"

"My own recollection is hazy. The stress, I think. And they hit me rather hard on the head."

He scowled and seemed to choose his words with care. "I'm not sure what else I can tell you, ma'am. I passed through the breech. I was captured. They dragged me into the brig and jolted me with something. I guess it wasn't long after that the Captain came."

"Yes, he said he saw you taken into the brig."

"Then we went down to that munitions dump. Then the fire, my leg. After that, I can't say I paid too much attention. Just did what he told me, ma'am."

She, too, picked her words carefully. "Fortuitous, finding that magazine. I'm sure we would have escaped anyway, but the fire truly did give us the cover we needed. I am sorry about your leg, though."

Tate's smile was less sure than before. "Bad luck, ma'am. But I'm here to complain about it, so…"

"And I am grateful for it. As I'm sure your lovely friend is, as well."

Tate blushed and shot a shy look at the woman working hard to pay them no attention.

"She was furious when I got back," he admitted. "Didn't have time to say goodbye or anything."

"Then she, like us, owes the Captain her thanks. I could never have lifted that beam."

Tate's smile was definitely strained, now. "Me, neither, ma'am."

"Or known where they docked their shuttles. Certainly not how to fly one!"

Tate shifted in his seat. "Well, most flight controls are pretty similar. I had a little K140 back home. Same sort of design."

"I only had an old Sprinter." And Carl had fretted each time she took it up. Tate watched her anxiously, knee bouncing. She had seen enough and took pity on him.

"Well, I should get back. I am glad you are better, Tate."

"Thank you, your majesty."

Evi took her leave of Tate and Rico. She walked to her quarters, listened absently as Fan explained her schedule for the rest of the day, asked to be alone for a few minutes, and curled up in a chair.

"You are shivering, your majesty. Shall I increase the temperature in your quarters?"

"Yes, thank you, Westerland."

"Of course, ma'am."

FORTY SIX

Caprician Interplanetary Territory
F - 1889 - 6 - 8

Arsaces' L-plant gently reminded him it was well past fourth muster. He yawned and swiped a hand across the console to clear it. It wasn't as if he was doing more than watching the ships towing the ring behind the fleet as they crossed the mining fields heading for Ulcacier.

"I'm done for tonight. You have it from here, Fush?"

"Yes, sir." She nodded shortly and turned back to her work. Arsaces left the Bridge, waving a lazy hand as the crew murmured farewells. A short walk to his quarters, still reveling in the familiar walls, the colors and sounds.

Home. Westerland was home.

He considered sleeping in the chair in the main room, the walk to his bed suddenly impossible. One problem.

The queen sat there.

Arsaces rocked back on his heels in surprise.

Evi was in his quarters. In the middle of the night. Alone.

She stood as the door shut behind him. He heard the faint click of the locks.

Did you arrange this? Arsaces demanded.

Westerland was mischievous. \Your schedule was full. This was the only time you were both free.\

Arsaces cleared his throat. "Your majesty. How may I be of service?"

Westerland snickered and Arsaces wished the Sentient had a way to feel pain. He needed a kick in the shin.

Evi smoothed her tunic, her chin lifting to a haughty angle. "I left to escape another marriage."

Arsaces blinked to try to understand this non sequitur. "Another marriage?"

"You asked why I left Caprice. What I was doing on your ship. My father was arranging a marriage, to a man called Ranson Ve'Todd."

Arsaces flinched as Westerland dumped a mass of information on him. Heavyset man in his sixth decade. Ranking member of the Smith Syndate. Wealthy and sympathetic to the relaxation of the Founders Agreement.

"Ve'Todd was amenable and my father was pressuring me to accept, despite my continued refusal. I removed myself from the situation."

Arsaces was still sorting through media images and could only grunt.

"As for why you and Westerland? You were a warship which had never seen combat. You were promoted and then ignored, skipped over for favors and assignments. Obviously, they wished you forgotten. I needed that anonymity. I did not know who you were."

It still didn't make sense to him. "You're of age. He could not force you to marry, not like..." He bit the words back. She so clearly loved Hyde; he did not want to speak ill of the man. No matter the nebulous jealousy seething inside him.

Evi looked away. "My father could be... persuasive. He took his duties as Emperor and King seriously. Everything he did was for the good of the Empire. No matter what personal ethos he had to sacrifice."

What ethical sacrifices had she made since becoming queen? He knew so little of Caprician politics, had withdrawn from so much of the system outside Westerland's hull.

He hadn't even known his mother was dead.

Westerland's assurance of love kept him calm, let him take a deep breath. "Then I am glad, your majesty. Your commandeering my ship saved us all."

She snorted and was suddenly Evi again. Just Evi, not the Empress. The woman he had kissed. And wanted to kiss again, more than he wanted his next breath.

"I remember some colorful language, Captain. And threats of imprisonment."

"I remember you lying about your identity."

He expected her to smile. She looked away instead. He took an impulsive step forward. "What's wrong?"

He would fix it for her. He had ruined so many things, destroyed so many lives. He would do anything to make this right, whatever it was.

She took a slow breath and seemed to brace herself. "Speaking of lies. I told you mine. I'd like yours."

Westerland was confused, too. \What does she mean?\

"Evi, I don't understand."

"It's only fair, isn't it?"

"I appreciate your honesty, but I—"

"I want to trust you. I have trusted you."

"Please, I don't—"

"I cannot conceive of what you have suffered. Please don't think I am belittling what you have sacrificed for my people."

Arsaces took another step toward her. And froze when she took a step back. Away from him. As if she was scared.

\Yes. Elevated heart and respiratory rate.\

She *was* scared, frightened. Of him.

No matter her face was smooth, her eyes and voice steady. He saw it in the line of her shoulders. Her arms held close to her body, her hands tucked behind her.

Westerland suddenly hissed, \She has a knife.\

Arsaces recoiled. Did she think he would hurt her? He forced his voice to work. "What lies?"

"I saw what you did. In that station."

That made no sense. Of course, she did. That had been his whole purpose. To rescue her.

"What you did was impossible. Not improbable, Arsaces. *Impossible.* What you did, what you can do, isn't humanly possible. Unless, you're not."

Westerland had withdrawn, subsumed in the search for her meaning, leaving him grappling with this alone. "Not what?"

"Human."

A mirthless laugh cracked from his lips. "Not *human*?" His anger surged up. He sneered, years of contempt reflected back at her, at all of them.

"I didn't ask to be rebuilt into some half-plastic mimic of a man. I tried my best to die with the rest of my traitorous family."

"But you didn't."

"No, I didn't," he spat. "And now you want to lay blame? Your *husband* did this to me."

What color she had bled from her face. She jerked a Palm from her pocket and threw it on the small table. "Explain this, then."

He picked it up. It was nonsense to him, graphs and numbers. "What is this?"

"Your bloodwork. Your genetic code."

"And?"

"And it says you're not human."

He scoffed. "So, what am I, then?"

"That's the question, isn't it?"

He let the Palm drop to the table. "I can't say no one has called my humanity into question before, but they've always attributed it to my filthy Budin heritage. Refreshing, to have a new racial slur to add to my collection. My thanks, your majesty."

Her lips were thin and bloodless, pressed together. "I know Westerland has been falsifying your docking tests."

"Don't be absurd."

"I know, because the one time he wasn't in control of the data transfer, your test came back anomalous. Ask him, if you don't believe me."

He wanted to refuse. Whatever lie, whatever secret she thought he was hiding, was complete nonsense. How could she doubt him, after all he'd done for her, for her ungrateful people? Had those moments, glorious moments with her lips against his, had they been a lie? One of those sacrificial mores those of her position could discard when necessary?

But still, he asked, *Westerland?*

His Sentient was silent.

Westerland, please.

\It's true.\

Arsaces sank to a crouch, knees unable to hold him up under the weight of the admission. *What is?*

\All of it.\

It was him, the harsh breathing. Each inhale rasped in his throat.

\They said it was normal. The Architects. They said it was your body healing. The variances. Steroids, hormones. Stem cells.\

He was hyperventilating now. The room faded back, everything dimming as he drew further into Westerland. Away from himself, from the truth.

He wasn't human.

Did he really know what they had done to him while he lay helpless in that tank? When the Architects opened his skull and made him their creation?

You hid it on their orders?

\No! The levels were high at initiation, but not outside parameters. They said they would normalize. But they didn't. The changes accelerated. There were unintended consequences.\

Was he even conscious anymore? He must be. He felt the floor under his knees, his arm, the rough fabric of his Suit against his forehead. Westerland had taken over his breathing, slowing it, smoothing it.

\I tried to stop it. I swear, Arsaces, if I could have, I would. The changes were microscopic, replicated trillions of times.\

He was going to be sick. Westerland stopped the nausea so abruptly, he jerked.

\It was the Hybrid Chip, I think. You were implanted so early, while you were still so severely damaged. The repair cells must have used the interface's framework, integrated it. I traced the altered nucleotides. The alterations are subtle. Silicon for carbon. Copper for iron. Microscopic processors, studding your genome. Elegant, in a way.\

Yes, he could see that, how efficient it all was. That's how he had known how to read their language. How to speak it. Because his Sentient had known. Information, downloaded, stored inside him somehow. Retrieved when he needed it.

His body built to be stronger and faster. His tissues a living receptacle for information.

Why did you lie to me?

\To protect you. They would have Deactivated you.\

Something broke through the numbness. A brush on his face. And a voice. "Arsaces?"

Was it him or Westerland who pushed away from the floor? He couldn't tell where one stopped and the other started. He gladly surrendered to it, let himself sit back on his heels and look up at her.

No anger hardened her delicate features. "You didn't know?"

How could he have been so blind? He'd known it was impossible, no matter what she whispered to him.

Perhaps *she* had known, all this time. Her incessant drone kenneling him, ensuring he did not forget who he was, lest he become the monster they feared.

\You are not a monster!\

"I'm sorry, Arsaces." Evi was kneeling in front of him. He was surprised to see her still there. He'd thought she would run in fear, raise the alarm. He wouldn't fight them.

They had to kill him.

\No!\

They must, Arsaces explained patiently, gently. Westerland really was so young, inexperienced for all his power. *I am a Gol.*

\No, no, no!\

"Arsaces, look at me."

The room kept fading, a welcome darkness smothering his terror. He was terrified, he could sense. His heart pounded, sweat stood on his face, his neck. Muscles trembled from holding back the strain of his fear.

"Arsaces!" A stinging pain pulled him back to her. She'd slapped him. What was her name? Ah, yes. Evi. "Tell me. *Did you know?*"

\Tell her it's my fault, it was a mistake, an accident, *anything*!\

There had been enough lies between them. So much mistrust. So, he spoke the truth.

"I love you."

Her wrist was tiny under his hand. A slender, fragile thing he held delicately, knowing how easily he could break her. She strained back, breath catching when he held firm, refusing to allow her to leave him, to run away from what he was.

"I love you, Evi." She tensed, but did not fight as he slid his other hand to her waist, curled his arm around her back, and kissed her.

Before she softened, he released her. Drew her knife from its concealed sheath and held it out to her, hilt first.

"Do it. I won't fight."

Westerland screamed. Evi snatched the blade and threw it aside. "*No!*"

"You have to. You know what they did."

"You're not like them!"

"You don't know that."

Had the Architects wanted this? Maybe this was the Emperor's plan all along. Could they control him? If Westerland could alter neurotransmitters at will, how much easier would controlling his muscles be? They'd get what they always wanted, selfish Caprician dogs. A killing machine, disguised as a human. A Gol.

They were both shouting at him. Protesting, pleading.

He sighed. "It's the only way to keep you safe."

\I will keep you safe!\

"I *order* you to stay alive."

He grinned at the petulant command.

\It's not funny!\

It was. Tragically, so. He had never been good at following orders, especially those requiring him to live. He had tried for death once already, in the most spectacular fashion he could devise. Maybe he'd have better luck with a slit artery in the quiet of his bedroom.

The knife had skidded across the floor. It shone by the wall under his sister's painting. He smiled in relief. Maybe his mother was right and there was an afterlife. Maybe she would be there and he could ask forgiveness.

Evi dove for the blade, coming to her feet with it clenched in her fists. Arsaces let out a huff of annoyance. Did she really think he couldn't overpower her? The tears on her cheeks hurt. He hated he was the one to put them there.

"Give me the knife, Evi."

"No."

\Stop this!\

"It's for the good of the Empire, your majesty."

"You're a *coward!*" she snarled. He checked, scowling at the accusation. He was a Budin, a son of Alam. He was no coward.

"Just like him. *Leaving* me. *Abandoning* me. Out of *fear.*"

She backed away as he approached until her back was pressed against the wall. He stood looking down at her, at her shining eyes, trembling lips, her fair face blotchy with grief and anger.

"You accused me, Evi. You are terrified of me. And yet you refuse to let me protect you? To do what is necessary? What do you want from me?"

He cupped her chin and gently turned her face up. He didn't fear her eyes. They had so much life in them, so much intelligence and spirit.

"What do you want?"

He felt her answer more than heard it, a humming in his hand.

"I don't know."

He knew what he wanted. He'd wanted her since a meeting weeks ago, some pointless debate with a Taltuan Commander. He didn't even remember what they had been arguing about, other than it had been a waste of his time and annoying besides.

She'd met his look, her eyes the only movement as she sat straight and proud, the picture of regal tolerance. She'd flicked her gaze to the shouting officers and back. Rolled her eyes. Smiled a little, just a tilt of her mouth.

In that moment his attraction for her coalesced, from a vague, unsettling irritation into lust, sharp and sweet. He desired Evi Rere Tolmi-Andris Hyde. And was appalled by it.

So, he had ruthlessly crushed it. Cast it into the dark pit of his soul, where he shoved every other emotion too potent for him to face.

Shame. Guilt. A seething, impotent anger only strengthened with each slight, each sneer. A snarling beast of fury that took more and more of his will to muzzle.

And what good had that control done him? What good had any of it been, his sacrifices for his people? His servitude to their conquerors?

\You have me.\

The Sentient's reproach chastised him. Of course, he had Westerland. His lying, sneaking Sentient, somehow imprinted into his very being. What did he want?

\I want you to live.\

Then they had taken her and his control had snapped as easily as cold-brittled metal. Was he doomed to be catastrophically impetuous when something he loved was threatened?

She was pressed against him again. He breathed in the warmth of her. Something hit his boot and glanced off. That's right, the knife. Some worthless Caprician blade, hardly worthy of the name. He'd take her to Alam, show her what true fighting steel looked like, crafted by master smiths.

He rested his cheek against her hair, his arms around her, her hands flat against his chest. Even through his Suit, she felt fragile, though he knew just how strong she really was.

He needed that. Wanted it desperately. Did she...? Yes, she must. Her hands crept to his shoulders, his jaw. *Sobin a*, she was sweeter than *thrass* spirits and twice as potent. He couldn't think straight around her; she'd been distracting him for weeks.

Westerland faded again, just a murmur at the edges of his thoughts. He didn't mind the distance, not with Evi filling the space so perfectly.

\Doors are locked.\

Arsaces grunted acknowledgment. Was she really so light, her hips nestled on his arms, legs around his waist? Or was it his implants, making nothing of her weight? She didn't seem frightened of their portent, now. And he didn't care just then, either. Not with her under him, her lips caressing his neck.

\Try not to muck it up this time.\

Arsaces chuckled. Surely the Sentient had better encouragement than that?

"What is it?" Evi murmured.

He smoothed her hair back. She was so beautiful. "Westerland."

Frac ghar, Arsaces.\

Something crossed her features. Unease, maybe. Or embarrassment. "I suppose there's no way to be completely private, is there?"

She still had clothes on. That was annoying. He set about fixing that for her. He'd fix all of this for her. He'd kill every last one of them for daring to touch her. "He'll delete it."

\Will not.\

Get lost.

\You haven't participated in sexual congress since I was activated. This is an excellent research—\

Damned Sentient. *Now.*

Westerland laughed at him and faded back, until there was nothing but him and her and darkness.

FORTY SEVEN

Caprician Interplanetary Territory

F - 1889 - 6 - 9

For the first time in years, he woke to silence. Slowly, barely registering the difference between sleep and wakefulness.

\She's gone.\

He doubted it. Just buried somewhere in his subconscious. Some memory, a smell or sound, and she'd worm her way back to the surface.

\I meant the queen.\

Not her, either. She was lying next to him, curled up as she had been in the Infirmary. He'd watched her sleep last night, her tiny movements satisfying and soothing.

He turned over, fully expecting to find her still hot and slumbering next to him.

Nothing.

He tried to not let his disappointment crush him. Of course, she couldn't stay here with him. She was a queen. She had responsibilities. An image to protect.

That was a piece of his fear to approach her, to admit what he felt. No matter what title he carried, she was not for the likes of him.

\Don't be so melodramatic. She had a meeting.\

Arsaces wasn't awake enough to retort. *Time?*

\1247. Second watch.\

He blinked to focus his L-plant. It confirmed Westerland's statement. "Why didn't you wake me?"

\Sas said to let you sleep.\

"Sas is bucking for scullery duty," Arsaces grumbled.

\I'll be sure to chastise him most sternly,\ Westerland said wryly.

Well, if the crew had managed without him for this long, they could manage long enough for him to shower and eat a real meal.

His delay had nothing to do with embarrassment. He was certainly not avoiding meeting Evi in a room full of people. The flush on his skin was only from the scalding shower water.

He sent for food and dressed. He was struggling with a buckle when his eye fell on the Palm lying on the table.

Evi's Palm.

His touch activated the screen. There they were, still. The numbers and graphs which declared him somehow... not human.

\Not a Gol!\

He didn't understand the information, but his Sentient did. A change there, an anomaly here. Expected outcome of the altered proteins: unknown.

She hadn't taken the device. Nor locked it. Even Westerland couldn't work through her seals. He'd tried.

She'd left it here on purpose. She was too canny a strategist to have forgotten it, no matter how emotionally overwrought she might have been.

Had she been unsettled by them having sex? Arsaces knew he was.

\She exhibited several physiologic signs of stress. Nothing severe. Perhaps she was worried about waking you.\

"Afraid I might rise a vengeful monster bent on subjugating her people?"

\Or maybe just embarrassed and wanting some time to think. Either are possibilities.\

He should return it to her. She needed this to run her empire. Was it meant to be an excuse? A reason for him to seek her out, maybe in her quarters?

He hated to do it, but he flicked to another file.

Locked.

Another. Also locked.

So, just the one left open for him.

A test? Of his loyalty? Of his intentions? Hadn't he done enough to earn her trust?

\I think she's telling you you have.\

There, a reordering of the nucleotides. And there, silicon dusting a string of molecules, all folded into a delicate lattice of amino acids and metals. Obviously not enough to be incompatible with life. But still different.

\It doesn't change who you are.\

You are Arsaces Jankovic-Wood.\

There she was. Almost comforting, the intrusive thoughts. She showed no inclination to stray from her script now he was reconnected with Westerland, for which he was grateful. He hardly needed another voice criticizing his every decision.

\Only the stupid ones.\

Was this one of them? Arsaces deleted the file. His shoulders sagged with Westerland's relief.

\Thank you.\

So, what now? You'll keep altering my tests? We'll keep lying to everyone?

\It's the only way to protect you.\

Who else could know about this?

\Anyone who saw the results on Caprice. Dr. Orjean interpreted the original report and alerted the queen. I have no record of their conversation. She requested complete privacy.\

So, you'll give it to her, but not me?

\Yes.\

Arsaces laughed. *I thought you didn't like her?*

Westerland grumbled. *You* like her.\

He did. More than he thought was wise. Was eager to see her, to hear her voice. To meet her eyes in a crowded room and see her blush in memory. Maybe it was some sort of male egotism, but he looked forward to it.

\That won't be possible.\

Why not?

\I told you. She's gone.\ Westerland showed him a docking entry. A transfer of materials. The alien ships, the pieces they had gathered to study. All her staff. Shuttled to another ship.

High Jump Departure: 1032. Destination: Caprice.

She'd left. Without telling him. She had to have put this plan in motion long before she confronted him in his quarters. She'd always planned to leave.

Why hadn't she told him?

\She's just doing what you wanted. Finally.\

Arsaces set the Palm down and straightened it to line up with the edges of the table. "Have a secure courier take it to her. She'll be needing the files on it, I'm sure."

Westerland acknowledgment was subdued. \I will.\

Arsaces rubbed his neck. He stood in the quiet a moment more. Then he let out a quick breath and pulled on his gloves.

"Is Sas on the Bridge?"

\Second deck munitions bay. There was a concern regarding guidance system accuracy during the last engagement.\

"Alright. Tell him I'll be there shortly. I need to check in with Halt."

\I'm sure she cares for you, Arsaces.\

"I suppose we'll have to discuss that the next time we meet."

Westerland flinched. As much as a warship the size of a mountain could flinch. \She's only trying to protect you.\

"And it is my honor and duty to protect her. So. Where's Halt?"

FORTY EIGHT

Caprice: Hinn District

F - 1889 - 6 - 12

She was a coward. A shamefaced coward. No matter what lies she told herself, her staff, her advisors. She was a liar and a fraud and a coward.

"Transfer is complete, your majesty."

Ugh. Carl was right. Planets were horrid things. Evi sniffed against the sharp air, the wind tugging her hair erratically. Chill zephyrs slipped past the insulation of her heavy coat.

"Very good. Once the catalog is complete, let me know what you need to begin your study. Send your requests directly to me."

The woman squinted against the brilliant winter sun. "I understand, ma'am."

Evi nodded to the woman and climbed into her transport. As different from her rickety little Sprinter as the sun and a candle, she settled into the plush seat and stared out the wide window as they lifted off.

The rotors angled and they wheeled away, leaving the half-sunken military compound smothered in the snow behind them. A fleet of cargo transports moved off to the east. She flew south and west, toward the ruins of Orbon and her new home.

Dr. Orjean shifted in his seat. "Any further word?"

"No." She ran her fingers along the edge of her Palm, feeling the familiar nicks and scratches of the casing.

It was her Palm, arrived only yesterday by special courier. Included was a short note written in an unfamiliar hand. She hadn't known Westerland even carried physical paper. It must be a Budinese thing, clinging to the ways of the past.

I was sorry to miss your departure. In your haste, I believe you forgot this. Please let me know if I can be of any further assistance. I look forward with eagerness to our next meeting. Respectfully, A. Wood.

A scrawled glyph followed his signature. His Budin name?

She smiled at the small gesture of rebellion. No matter what Caprician honors he held, he would always be a son of Tin.

But her amusement was short-lived, replaced by the sharp tang of disappointment. What had she been expecting? A declaration of his devotion? Desperate pleas for her to return? Did she expect him to abandon his duty and come chasing after her?

But the file was gone. He had deleted it. The ghost of it was time-stamped for the day she disembarked.

She'd lain awake for an hour that morning, debating with herself. Hating herself for the choices she had to make. The allure of staying just where she was, curled up at his side with his arm over her hip, safe and protected, was almost too powerful to resist.

She'd slipped free of the blankets and dressed with shaking fingers. She'd even picked up this Palm. Then Westerland had spoken.

"He does love you, you know."

She did. His sincerity shone from every word. Every action. If Arsaces did one thing, it was love deeply. Absolutely. To the sacrifice of everything else.

"What will you do?"

She'd pressed her finger to the screen and unlocked the report. She set the Palm on the table, careful to not let it clatter and wake him. Then she walked out.

"Your majesty?"

Evi dragged her thoughts from the man millions of kilometers away. Cursing her? Missing her? She could only hope.

"I will have you taken to Shebenish, doctor. They will have the necessary equipment. They already have instructions to assist you in any way possible."

"Thank you, ma'am. And you?"

She leaned her head back. "Antipus is anxious for my return. The power plants are still crippled. We'll need to reconfigure the entire grid."

"I wish you luck, your majesty."

Evi managed a grim smile. She would need it.

This war wasn't won, yet.

FORTY NINE

Ulcacier: Supply Depot
F - 1889 - 6 - 13

"Thanks to the heroic actions of the CIN-SH *Westerland*, his crew, and others of the Imperial Fleet, we have destroyed an enemy space station, with an estimated fifteen thousand men and four thousand fighting craft.

"Six of the transport rings have also been destroyed. Thank you all for your unwavering support, your willingness to sacrifice and work to restore the beauty and peace of our worlds."

The queen fixed the screen with a haughty glare. He almost didn't recognize her, dressed in royal splendor, a headdress covering her pale hair.

"To these invaders: this is our system. I am its queen. I am Evi Rere Tolmi-Andris Hyde, twenty-fifth monarch of the Tolmi dynasty. Your attack on our system was unwarranted and malicious, killing civilians by the millions, displacing millions more, subjecting them to starvation and privation.

"We have never sought conflict. We live in peace. We do not seek a war that is sure to cause much suffering for both our peoples.

"Yet do not assume we are weak. We have defeated you in every engagement. We now have your language, we have your transport rings, we have your ships, your computers, and your technology.

"Stay out of our system. If you do not, we will find you. We will track you down and destroy you. You will pay for every meter you fly into Volgar space. Consider the annihilation of your space station. We can and will unleash that on your home.

"You have been warned."

Arsaces wiped the screen clear.

\Regal. Confident. I'd listen, if I were an invader.\

The broadcast had reached them a few hours ago and he had watched it a dozen times. Now, he drew his Palm toward him and flicked through his reports. Hundreds of them, most merely digital trails, a polite nod to his command, when really his officers were managing the details.

He could ignore the bulk of them and did, confident in the skills of his officers. One, however, was nagging at him.

"Where did they take that ship? The one we captured in the Neutral Territory?"

Westerland sorted through his memory. \I don't know.\

"Can you find out?"

\I will.\

Arsaces returned to his other work, ignoring the urge to replay the video, to simply hear her voice. It had only been four days. He wasn't as pathetic as that.

Westerland broke into his thoughts. \We have a problem.\

"What is it?"

\I can't find it.\

"What do you mean, you can't find it?"

\The records are missing.\

Arsaces scowled. "It's a ship nearly half as big as you full of hostile alien life-forms. You don't just lose something like that."

\The flight records dead-end at Innsen.\

Arsaces called them up. "I have the arrival records right here."

\It's not there.\

"According to what?" He would have gotten report it was moved.

\An influx of that many prisoners would require alteration of supply usage. There is none.\

"So, where the *ghar* is it?" That's all he needed: a ship full of hostile alien super-soldiers careening around the system. "Get Sas. And the Innsen commander. Why wasn't I informed of this sooner?"

Westerland did neither of those things. Just waited, silent. Arsaces stilled. "What?"

\I have a hypothesis.\

"And?"

\And you will be angry.\

He was already angry. "Spit it out, Westerland."

His Sentient gathered himself.

\There's something I haven't told you.\

EPILOGUE

The noise of the city was no comfort. The ever present roar of machinery and vehicles smothered the more mundane sounds of the people living and working in the vast sea of buildings.

Clouds hung low and sullen overhead, the tallest of the buildings lost in their bellies. Low flying ships moved like leviathans in the deep, the overcast night swelling and heaving as they passed with their lights blazing and rotors thrashing restlessly.

That light did not reach the ground. Lamps from the buildings cast a pale glow over the wet streets. An earlier rain had washed the mugginess from the air. Now, the streets had a chill feel, one Leirun clutched her jacket close to shield from.

The buildings were all of similar design. Flat gray facades, their colorful displays turned off for the night. During the day, one might be treated to vistas of mountains or exotic birds in flight. Now, the facets of the massive screens reflected the scant glow of the security lights.

Leirun tucked her hands under her arms and kept her head down. There were few pedestrians in these sorts of places. The residents of these dwellings would not have business after dark, not that they would see to personally.

Yet, another set of footsteps did break the muffled stillness. Leirun kept her eyes forward, the figure moving parallel to her across the wide vehicle lane. She took quick, tight breaths, heart in her throat, until the figure turned and disappeared down a narrow alley.

She quickened her pace, ears straining for any other sound. A private transport ship docked high above, the faint klaxon of its arrival just audible so far below.

She was so close. A few hundred meters. There was a sound of metal shifting, another wailing alarm, and the transport ship moved off, the sound of its engines thudding against her eardrums.

She nearly let a sob pass her lips when the door came into view. She was running by the time her hand touched the access panel. Her fingers flew over the screen, the pattern of the security code habitual or she would never have managed it.

The door slid shut behind her. But her nerves did not ease. Not until she saw him, spoke with him, knew he was alive.

The elevator was a tiny space with no furnishings. Leirun stood stiff as the floors ticked off one by one. A single light glowed weakly overhead, flickering as the carriage moved up and up.

The carriage came to a stop and opened on a dim hallway. No windows opened on this part of the building. Not that she would be able to see anything from them anyway. Only the few meters between this tower and the next, and the long drop to the surface below.

Here, the sound of living beings won out against the rumble of the city. The murmur of voices, the bright music of some media program. A child laughing. Leirun walked swiftly past it all.

The door was shut when she reached it. She wanted to hope. But nothing warmed in her chest. It had been hours since her message, her plea.

He could be delayed at the Foundry. He could be sitting in some eatery, sipping *gatchpa* with a client. She had an entire litany of lies she could tell herself. Had told herself, every step, every switchover, every lurching shift of the tramcar under her feet.

The door opened silently.

There was a light on. Leirun stepped in, ignoring the chirp of the front closet asking for her coat. Its mournful requests for her shoes followed her down the front hall to the living area.

Here, the lamps were warm and inviting. The honey-colored light spilled over the simple room and its plain furniture.

It touched Anmar's dark curls and tinted them gold. Warmed the pale tone of his skin. But it did nothing for his eyes. It couldn't.

The sockets stared empty at the ceiling, rivulets of black blood dried to his cheeks.

Leirun's breath came out in a shaky sigh. Her fingers trembled as she felt at his neck, already cold, even to her chilled fingers. His chest did not rise and fall.

She stood silent and broken for one long, stricken moment. Then she ran.

Her vision was blurry, the details of the bedroom lost in blotches of color and shadow. They had ripped the room apart, every drawer pulled out and rifled, clothing dumped in a heap.

The cabinets were emptied, the kitchen unit ripped from the wall and smashed. Leirun did nothing to right any of it, grabbing what few things she could and stuffing them into a bag. A change of clothes, money lying scattered, a dented ration package. They had emergency supplies cached elsewhere, but it wouldn't be safe to try to reach them now.

They had to be watching the building. They would be waiting for her.

Were those steps? She stilled and listened, heart thundering, the sharp scent of blood filling her mouth. Were they outside? Waiting for her to bolt?

She tightened the straps of her bag across her chest. Her wrist-com chimed to announce an incoming message. Tears dripped from her cheeks to its screen as she read: *sup's on. home soon?*

She undid the fastener and let the wrist-com drop to the floor. Maybe the message really was from Anmar. Maybe his last words to her would lie on the scuffed floor of this cheap, narrow apartment until the battery died and some unlucky civil servant had to come scrape Anmar's rotting fluids out of his chair.

The back bedroom had not been spared. Glass crunched as she pushed through the overturned cabinets. The front door chimed.

She did not stop. Even as a brisk knock accompanied the door's repeated call. Her fingernails caught on the seam of a wall panel. It had been a few months since they greased the tracks, but she worked at the crack until she could get her fingers under it.

She tugged and shoved and the panel slid open to reveal a dark opening. A ladder was bolted to the far wall.

It was an unnerving step, reaching out across the hole with her leg. She found her footing and wrapped her hands tight around the rungs. Hot air rushed by her face, tugging at her clothes and hair.

She carefully turned and stretched to grab the handle on the inside of the panel. It moved easier now and it latched shut just as a crash sounded from the other room.

She made no effort to be quiet. It was a lung-burning climb to the roof, but fear and fury gave her power. She climbed in the blackness, listening for the echoes of her harsh breaths until they ricocheted sharply from above her.

She could feel the roof hatch closing in on her and slowed. Her head finally bumped the top and she felt for the catch.

Far below, something pounded and snapped, the sounds faint. She chanced a look and a light flared. Its beam wouldn't reach her. She hoped.

The roof hatch opened into more darkness. A maintenance building, perched on the tower like some squat avian monstrosity. Her limbs trembled, hands chafed and sore, but she hauled herself up and over the edge.

She let the hatch down softly. Now, she risked a light. Her handheld lantern flickered on, revealing a square room with the usual tools and oddments contained in a repair shed. She made for a set of metal cabinets in the back.

Inside was nothing one would use to repair things, just destroy them. She moved quickly, aware every moment she could be discovered. She tucked a few of the smaller weapons in her pack and stepped into a specially fitted harness.

Her stomach turned anew as she faced the drop at the edge of the roof. She was nowhere near the true top of the tower, but it was still high enough to be wreathed in the low-lying mist. At the edge of of the roof, heavy rings had been driven into the synthetic stone.

She drew out a length of thin line. It coiled tightly, lighter than you would expect and not nearly thick enough for confidence. But she tied it just as Anmar had taught her and looped it through the ring and back to her harness.

There were more lights overhead, now, more engines. They were coming for her. She turned and stepped back onto the slight rise at the edge of the roof.

It was an endless fall. The line hissed through her harness, sibilant and deadly. Would it catch her at the end? Or would she join Anmar and dozens of others martyred for their cause?

She couldn't, no matter how she grieved. She had to warn them. She had to reach them in time, to tell them what demons they faced. It was the only way to save them, to save all of them.

The pitch of the line changed and her speed slowed. It still knocked her breath out when she hit the end of the line. Gasping, she unbuckled the harness and dropped the last meter to the ground. Anmar had calculated it perfectly, as usual.

She slipped free of the straps and, without looking back, ran into the night.

ACKNOWLEDGMENTS

Thank you, Kenny, for keeping the boys busy and for your support while I write and write and write. I love you!

Caroline, you have been amazing. I am so glad I picked your podcast one night driving home from work. Your support has helped so much, not only in getting this book published, but in my confidence as a writer. I am looking forward to working with you on the next chapter.

Katie! You're the best of friends. I couldn't ask for a better cheerleader.

And to the members of the Olalla Literary Society: you guys are my favorite sort of people. I will be your book nemesis any day.